CW00552998

Prai
Jenny

"Jenny Hale writes touching, bea............ ..... .... .... .....
**Bestselling Author RaeAnne Thayne**

"I can always count on Jenny Hale to sweep me away with her heart-warming romantic tales."—**Denise Hunter, Bestselling Author** on *Butterfly Sisters*

One of "19 Dreamy Summer Romances to Whisk you Away" in ***Oprah Magazine*** on *The Summer House*

One of "24 Dreamy Books about Romance" in ***Oprah Daily*** on *The Summer House*

Included in "Christmas Novels to Start Reading Now" in ***Southern Living Magazine*** on *The Christmas Letters*

"Touching, fun-filled, and redolent with salt air and the fragrance of summer, this seaside tale is a perfect volume for most romance collections."—***Library Journal*** on *The Summer House*

"Hale's impeccably executed contemporary romance is the perfect gift for readers who love sweetly romantic love stories imbued with all the warmth and joy of the holiday season."—***Booklist*** on *Christmas Wishes and Mistletoe Kisses*

"A great summer beach read."—***PopSugar*** on *Summer at Firefly Beach*

"This sweet small-town romance will leave readers feeling warm all the way through."—***Publisher's Weekly*** on *It Started with Christmas*

## BOOKS BY JENNY HALE

# Meet Me
## at
# Christmas

## JENNY HALE
*USA TODAY* BESTSELLING AUTHOR

HARPETH ROAD
PRESS

Nashville

HARPETH ROAD

Published by Harpeth Road Press (USA)
P.O. Box 158184
Nashville, TN 37215

Paperback: 979-8-9877115-7-6
eBook: 979-8-9877115-6-9

MEET ME AT CHRISTMAS:
A Sparklingly Festive Holiday Love Story

This is a work of fiction. Names, characters, places, and incidents are the product of the author's imagination or were used fictitiously, and any resemblance to actual persons, living or dead, business establishments, events, or locales is entirely coincidental.
First printing: October 2023

# Chapter One

Eleven hours ago, Stella Fisher was on the other side of the Atlantic.

The day before, after a long day of research at London's St. Thomas' Hospital, she'd hurried into the old market building in Covent Garden, weaving through the Christmas crowds. Under the festive bunting of British flags, she dipped into a coffee shop for a decaf latte to combat the cold December temperatures. Then with the hot beverage in hand, her boots clacking along the cobblestones, she rushed past the massive Christmas tree in the square, barely glancing at it as she headed for the station.

Her laptop bag slung across her body, she stole sips from her latte as she swept through the corridors and down the escalator of the underground to grab the Tube back to the edge of the city. She was ready to get home to relax and warm up, unaware that the next morning she'd be on a crowded flight out of the country.

When she'd finally arrived at 27 Finchley Road, the serene little flat where she'd been staying, she'd dropped her things just inside the door. She set her half-empty cup on the kitchen table that she'd also been using as a desk because it overlooked a charming back garden. Then she went over to the window, taking in the frosty hedges that sparkled under the fading light of an unusually clear winter sky and the curved flowerbeds that were sure to have blossoms in the spring. Unlike her cramped New York apartment, this flat gave Stella an indescribable feeling of comfort after her long hours in the busy city.

She sank down into the velvety sofa. With a groan, she unzipped her boots and wriggled her sore toes. Her feet had not acclimated to London life as well as the rest of her. They couldn't quite get used to the manic pace, sprinting around all day.

Being by herself was oddly quiet following the daily bustle, and it always took her some time to get used to it, in whichever city she'd been in over the last eight years. At first, the silence had bothered her, but gradually it had become a vital part of her day, giving her space and time to work through her thoughts.

That night, however, she didn't have much time to rest before her mother, Anna Fisher, called from Leiper's Fork, Tennessee, asking her to come home.

Now Stella was sprinting again, but this time down the sprawling, shiny floors of Atlanta's airport, trying to manage the ridiculously short gap between flights for her connection to Nashville, the final leg of her journey. Having spent two hours at Heathrow, and nine and half hours in the air, she was too tired and starving to notice her surroundings, and in too much of a hurry to pause. She had to get to the gate first and then see if she had time to grab a bite to eat. Her carry-ons dangled from her aching shoulder like two boulders as she pushed through the colossal holiday crowds, gripping her boarding pass.

She was making good progress, maneuvering skillfully around groups of people while checking her phone. The texts that had piled up during her flight were now pinging one after another since she'd regained cell service. One was from her mother, asking when she should pick her up, and another was from her sister, Lily, that simply said, "Hey."

She texted her mother her arrival time, adding that she was headed toward her connection and would see her in a few hours. Her next two texts were to her sister, but both said they were undeliverable. She sighed. Airport Wi-Fi… Just as she thought she might have enough time to grab a magazine and a muffin at the terminal shop—*whack*—she was on the floor, covered in burning coffee.

"Oh, my gosh, I'm so sorry," a woman said as she picked up a dripping paper cup and helped Stella to her feet. "I was searching for my hand lotion inside my bag and not looking where I was going. Are you okay?"

"I'm fine," Stella said, checking her boarding pass to make sure it was still legible. She tugged at her saturated shirt, the coffee seeping all the way through to her skin and making her smell of caramel. "I was paying attention to my phone and not looking either. It could easily have been my fault too."

"I'll get us some napkins," the woman said, shaking her head in bewilderment. But then she stopped short, bending down. "Oh, you almost lost this." She picked up a silver necklace with a blue stone pendant and held it out in her fist. "That would've been just terrible." She took Stella's hand and thrust the necklace into it.

"This isn't—" Stella tried to tell the woman the necklace wasn't hers, but the woman was already running from shop to shop, asking for napkins. Stella looked around frantically to see if anyone seemed to have lost a necklace, but everyone was striding past her at a clip, not a soul looking as if they'd misplaced something.

Then the flight information display rolled over with an update, and she realized she only had fifteen minutes to catch her flight. Seeing the freezing drizzle glittering on the planes out the window, she knew she could be stuck there for the night if she didn't get to her gate in time. With zero minutes to spare and not wanting to abandon the necklace for fear it would get swept into the trash, she shoved it into her pocket and dashed off.

When she finally skidded to a stop at her destination, she was the final passenger to board.

"Ah, you only *just* made it," the perky flight attendant said, her red lips curling into a smile. Then she announced the final call into the handset intercom receiver as she reached out for Stella's boarding pass.

Sticky and out of breath, Stella handed the stained paper to the woman who scanned it and gave it back to her. Then she rushed down the passenger bridge, onto the plane, and toward her seat. She wedged her bags in the nearest overhead bin with available space and squeezed herself between an elderly woman with an overpowering scent of roses and powder, and a teenager who was already slouched in his seat, hoodie over his eyes, earbuds in.

The plane started to taxi down the runway, and the crew began their pre-flight safety demonstration. Stella settled in, leaned her head back, and closed her eyes. Soon the engines whirred to full speed, pressure pushing her torso against the seat, and rousing her back to consciousness. The plane lifted into the heavens, and with a shift to the right, she caught the view out the window over the teenager's shoulder. Atlanta shrank to a patch of green beneath them.

When she arrived in Nashville, famished, weak, and a little squeamish from the sour caramel smell of her shirt she'd endured for the last few hours, she followed the herd of passengers to the concourse and popped into one of the airport souvenir shops to buy a T-shirt with swirling red letters on the front that said "Music City." She went into the bathroom and changed, stopping at her reflection in the mirror. The sight took her back to her youth when she'd lived in jeans and T-shirts. With a punch of nostalgia, she pulled the hem together and tied it in a knot the way she had when she was a girl, so it didn't get in the way when she was at her potter's wheel creating her latest masterpiece. Pop had found the old contraption in the attic of their 1820s farmhouse when they moved in, and he'd restored it with her. For Christmas that year, he'd gotten her a small kiln that they kept in the shed out back. She'd lost count of how many bowls and vases she'd made over the years.

Stella had always loved figuring out how things worked. Her curiosity started with simple mechanics, but as she got older, her interest shifted to how the human body operated. And when she got into college at Stanford, she zeroed in on neuroscience, spending eight years in their joint MD/PhD program.

School had come easily for her. She'd breezed through her high school classes, taking college-level courses in her senior year. With her stellar academic record and advanced credits in high school, she'd completed four years of undergrad in three, gone on to medical school, and then her one-year internship. After a while, however, she began to question whether or not she *enjoyed* the rigor of the program. At first, it had been exciting to see how far a small-town girl could go, but the further she went, the less she felt it was for her.

As she contemplated another three years of residency training, she heard about a job as lead researcher for *Brain Borders Magazine* from a fellow student. The lure of international travel tickling a long-held desire to visit faraway places, and exhausted from so many years of academics, on a whim she applied and in less than six months found herself traveling to Brussels on her first assignment. It had been one of the best decisions of her life.

She hadn't worn a T-shirt in years, but it felt oddly natural. As if she'd stepped back into a different side of herself that she hadn't allowed to come through in a long time. Assessing her appearance in the mirror, she couldn't help but notice how her face had grown older. Wiser? Definitely.

Stella rolled up her soiled blouse. When she leaned down to slip it into her bag, something poked the crease of her leg through her pocket. She stood up and retrieved the necklace. For the first time, she stopped to take a good look at it and gasped.

Stella peered around to be sure no one had noticed what she was holding. She scrutinized the delicate, blue-stoned pendant surrounded by diamonds that was glimmering in her hand. She clasped its silver chain and held it up, the stone swinging back and forth. The setting was almost antique… She flipped it over and tried to read the tiny inscription etched into the back of the pendant, but she couldn't quite make it out.

Deciding she'd better take good care of it in case it was worth something, she double-checked the clasp to see if it worked. When it seemed to be fine, she slipped on the necklace for safekeeping. She fumbled with it behind her neck until it was secure and then peered at herself in the mirror, the shiny pendant dotting her breastbone, juxtaposed with the new T-shirt. She ran her fingers over the stones, wondering where it had come from. Then she slipped it under her shirt. When she got home, she'd have to call the airport in Atlanta to see if anyone had reported it missing.

Her eyes stung from the time change and the long-haul flight, and her stomach rumbled. She left the bathroom to grab a bite to eat before retrieving her checked bag and meeting her mother.

# Chapter Two

Stella gripped her red Christmas mug in both hands to warm her fingers and leaned against the window frame of her childhood bedroom. The colored Christmas lights blinked merrily along the backyard fence in the dusk of evening. They'd been hung lower this season, with her mother taking on all the holiday duties after Pop died in January.

Ever the family man, her father had worked tirelessly to restore their farmhouse throughout her childhood, never taking vacations or spending his money on extras; he'd given every moment to his family. She'd asked him once if he ever wanted to leave their little town and see the world. He'd told her, *"My family is my world."*

"So you were in London this time, right?" her mother asked absentmindedly as she came in and out of Stella's peripheral vision, straightening the blankets on the bed and fluffing the pillows. The atmosphere in her bedroom was starkly different from the places she'd held a coffee yesterday, her mother having been twitchy since the minute she met Stella at the airport.

"Yep." Stella pulled her gaze from the window to face her mother.

"What were you working on?"

"I was writing an article about the effects of diet on long-term brain health." She didn't dare divulge that all eyes at work were on her for the coveted President's Award given by the one-and-only Steven Rotrosen, pioneer in brain research and president of *Brain Borders Magazine*. She had enough pressure without adding her mom's hopefulness on top. Mama had been let down enough with Pop dying last year and both her daughters barely visiting. But if Stella could pull it off, she stood to get a major promotion.

Her mother stopped, wrinkling her nose. "Oof. I don't know how you write that stuff."

Stella smiled. "The subjects can bore me to tears too, sometimes."

Even so, thirteen years after leaving this town, she was swimming in work for the magazine. So much so that she didn't really have time to return to her hometown for an extended stay, but here she was. She'd had to make it happen; she and her little sister, Lily, were all her mother had.

But she still needed to get the last bit of her work finished. The offices were shutting down to only essential personnel for the holidays, and her articles were due to her editor right before Christmas. She had to get them done if she wanted to be considered for the promotion. The London medical team had taken a bit longer to pull together their research than she'd have liked, so the magazine had pushed her deadline back as far as they could.

Originally, she'd planned to stay in London up until the holiday and finish both articles, but now she had to start over midway through. When her mother called and asked her to come home early, it had taken a bit of finagling, but Stella had shifted her writing plans. After a few discussions with her editor, she managed to get approval to do her secondary article on traumatic brain injuries at Vanderbilt in Nashville, which was only about a forty-minute drive from Leiper's Fork.

"I also don't know how you can stomach all that travel," her mother said as she continued fussing around the room. "All that back and forth between time zones—Europe to New York and then back again… It has to be hard on your system."

"I manage," Stella said. "And I enjoy it."

As lead researcher and traveling writer for the magazine, she was used to moving around. She'd been to four cities in the last sixty days. The pace of the life fueled her, and she thrived in new environments. She'd also found that it was easier to push the sadness out of her mind when she wasn't near home—sadness for the unfinished moments with her father and other painful memories no one understood but her—which was why she'd buried herself in her coursework, run to the ends of the earth, and only come back for short visits over the years.

She glanced at the simple white satin gown in her closet and then closed the doors, the memory of it too much to bear. Here in the home where she'd spent her entire childhood, she would be forced to face her past head on, but she'd start with her mother's obvious distress.

Stella went back to the view of the starless sky. A droplet of wet snow slid down the outside of the window as if the house were still crying for the absence of its owner, almost a year later. The space was so empty without Pop's jovial laughter and quick wit.

She set her mug on the dresser and fiddled with the gold hairbrush set her grandmother gave her when she was ten. "Have you been able to get a hold of Lily?"

Lily had been working in Chattanooga, a couple hours' drive away, so Stella was surprised she'd made it home before her sister.

Her mother took in a tight breath. "That's something I wanted to talk to you about."

Stella's hands stilled, and she turned her attention to her mother.

"I don't think she's coming home for Christmas this year."

This was the first Christmas without Pop. After hearing her mother's obvious need for support over the phone, Stella had assumed Lily would come right away too.

"She's in Costa Rica. And I think she got married."

Stella's eyes widened. "You can't be serious." A swell of guilt took hold at the thought of her baby sister getting married without her—even though she'd done the same...

"I'm as serious as can be." Her mother's focus dropped to an indiscriminate spot on the bed before she resumed straightening a blanket that was already in place.

Stella, Lily, and Pop had been inseparable when the sisters were small; the little girls were like his shadow. They ran errands together, played baseball in the park, and went to football games. He'd even taught them both how to tune up the engine in the old farm truck, although Stella was the only one who'd actually participated on that occasion. Lily was just there, handing them tools and chatting away.

They'd always dreamed of having their weddings on the steps of the old farmhouse, one wearing white while the other stood by her side. "*I'll spare no expense*," Pop had said when they'd climbed onto his lap at the ages of ten and eight with their bouncing blonde curls and wide brown eyes and told him their plans. They'd agreed that the minute one of them decided to get married, they'd have a big party on the porch at the farmhouse. It would be incredible with the lush green grass against rolling hills and the old oak trees.

Stella was the first to ruin that dream. By the time she was nearly eighteen, the memory of her pact with Lily had settled to the bottom of her life like a lone feather. In a rush of spontaneity clouded by young love, she and her first and only sweetheart, Henry, had gotten married with just the two of them and the officiant, Waylon Evans, an old bootlegger-turned-pastor of the country church down the road, at Jackson Falls, the massive waterfall a few minutes from town. She'd spent all her money on that white satin dress that hung in the closet.

If she closed her eyes, she could still see the tiny hesitation in her father's smile when she came home to tell him she'd gotten hitched. She'd never expected him to remember her childish wishes when she certainly hadn't. Despite the fact that her wedding day wasn't what he'd expected, he loved that she was settling down early and staying in their little town, just as he had with her mother. Now she felt the loss of that opportunity for her father. She hadn't given him the chance to walk her down the aisle. And for different reasons he hadn't had the chance with Lily either.

Over the years she'd been gone, Stella hadn't had to face why her young marriage hadn't worked, and she didn't want to think about it now. If only she could've told her father everything when he was alive. She'd always imagined she'd get far enough in life that at some magical point the guilt and shame wouldn't hurt so badly, and then she could sit him down and explain. She had no idea she'd never get the chance.

Stella swallowed the lump in her throat, forcing herself back into the conversation. "I didn't even know Lily was dating anyone." She pulled her cell phone from her pocket and opened the screen to get to her sister's number.

"You can't call her. It goes straight to voicemail. I've tried."

Stella remembered the two undeliverable texts in the airport, and she knew from living abroad that messaging from country to country could sometimes be a problem. She'd learned about other apps that could work, but doubted if Lily knew anything about them. And if her sister hadn't changed her billing plan, it could also be very expensive, which, coupled with spotty service in a remote location, could be the culprit for the undelivered texts.

"Have you spoken to her at all?"

Stella's mother shook her head, distress clear in her frown lines. "She left a quick message to say she loved me but couldn't talk then, that she'd had to go to Costa Rica, and she got married. Then the line cut out."

Stella chewed her lip, baffled. "The snow looks like it's starting to stick a little," she said, changing the subject.

"Yes," her mother said, the heaviness of the situation remaining.

Stella's eyes still burned as a result of the jarring time change from her flight across the Atlantic, and she squeezed them shut before taking in the view. A lone maple leaf on the tree next to her window finally let go of its barren branch. It floated down to the ground, shimmering in the wetness of the precipitation under the blinking Christmas lights.

She turned away. The pantry was nearly empty when she'd arrived this afternoon—only coffee and a few odd cans of soup—and she wondered how her mother had been managing. She'd barely had time to get her bags in the house before the storm rolled in. Now the snow had started coming down at a rate unprecedented for this area, and they were sure to be unable to drive down the hilly main roads safely if they didn't get out soon. They needed to get food if they wanted to eat tonight.

"We should probably get to the store before the roads are covered in ice."

Mama peered past her out the window. "Yes, we probably should." With the storm, Lily's and Pop's absences, and the holiday, her mom's worry was palpable. "My car's low on gas after picking you up. And it looks icy out there already. Think it's still safe enough to go?"

"I think so. We can just pop over to the market," she said, referring to the small gas station that doubled as a country store. It sat between two pastures around a five-minute drive from their house. "Then we can get real groceries tomorrow."

"What if it dumps more snow overnight like they say it might?" her mother asked, an edge to her voice Stella had never heard before. "How will we clear the drive?"

"I doubt it will. It never snows that much here. But if it does, I'll think of something." She racked her brain for anyone she knew within a five-mile radius who could help them shovel a drive. It wasn't many people, given the sizes of the plots in the countryside. All her friends had gone off to college when she had and then moved on to other states, but their families were probably around—she was almost certain.

"What about Casey's parents? Are they still on Maple? They might lend a hand tomorrow if we need it."

"Yeah, but they'd have to get down Southall, and the river's gonna be too high with the rain we've had. If the road isn't flooded, I bet it's already a sheet of ice."

"We could call Marty," she suggested, remembering the old farmer down the street.

"His back's been bothering him, so Penny's been driving him around, and *she* won't want to come out in this mess." Her mother shook her head. "In my first year of retirement, I should've planned better and asked around, given the extra time on my hands, but with the decorating for Christmas I tried to do outside, I've felt like I'm under water."

Stella chewed on the inside of her lip, thinking. The only other person she could think of, she didn't dare say. He wasn't there anyway. "Okay." Stella grabbed her boots from the corner of her room. "Let's go before this snow storm gets any worse. I'll drive."

"Are you sure it's safe to go out in this?" Her mother tugged on her arm.

Stella pulled on her boots and fished her old set of car keys out of the drawer next to her bed. "It's barely dusting the roads, Mama. But if we don't go now, it could get worse. Does my car have more gas than yours?"

"Yeah." With a new mixture of fear and forced strength in her eyes, her mother straightened her shoulders and opened the bedroom door. "All right."

When Stella got outside to start the old Mazda she'd driven in high school, it was still resting in its spot in the driveway where Stella had parked it thirteen years ago, before she left for good. Mama told her she and her father had taken it out a few times, but just as they'd always done over the years, they returned it to the same place.

It was cold when they finally climbed in, and Stella turned on the windshield wipers, sleet sliding back and forth in transparent half-moons on the glass. She clicked on her headlights, illuminating the icy showers that were coming down at a slant.

"We're just running over to the market," she said in response to Mama's obvious tension. "They'll have the basics."

Mama fastened her seatbelt and clasped her hands in her lap. Stella put the car in gear and slowly pressed the gas, the tires protesting against the slick layer of ice underneath them. After a few more growls of the engine, the wheels broke free and the car began to bump down the long, winding drive leading to the road.

"See? We're fine." The radio was still on from whomever last drove the car, and a quiet hum of Christmas carols surrounded them as Stella drove.

The car fishtailed just slightly on the frozen road when she turned onto it. Stella gripped the steering wheel, her eyes glued to the pavement in front of her. With the snow now covering the ground in a thin layer, she focused on the small dip on either side of the road, careful to keep the car between the lines. "We Wish You a Merry Christmas" tinkled in the background.

"This was a bad idea," Mama said under her breath. "It's coming down so fast and it's covering black ice."

"I can do it. We'll be ok." Stella channeled Pop's calming voice from when he'd taught her how to drive in his old Ford pickup during a rainstorm.

*"Driving's not about controlling the vehicle. It's about becoming one with it. Hug the curves slowly, then let her go on the straightaway, and when she gets too excited, lightly pump the brake. Don't startle her. Easy does it…"*

Her foot instinctively shifted to the brake while the car glided along the slick road. With a steadying breath, she pumped the pedal and then slowly pressed the gas to pull them around the next bend. Pride filled her as she maintained control. Only two more turns and they'd be there. Easy.

"Look out!" Mama cried.

Stella's attention flew to the edge of the road and she sucked in a breath as a deer loped across their path in front of her. Without thinking, she jammed both feet on the brake to avoid hitting it. The animal gracefully darted into the nearby woods unharmed, but she barely had time to feel relief before the car slid off the road and landed with a thump in the ditch.

Christmas carols still playing, the headlights now two unmoving beams of yellow against the falling snow, Stella and Mama sat silently, their chests rising and falling from the near collision.

With shaking hands, Stella put the car in reverse and pressed the gas. The wheels spun wildly in place against the wet, muddy terrain.

Pop's voice whispered: "*Don't panic*." She shifted back into drive and tried to go forward. The car lurched a smidge but didn't go anywhere.

"We're stuck?" Mama asked, lines of apprehension showing on her face even in the darkness.

Stella gazed at the steering wheel, focusing on her breathing to calm her after such a start. Then she tried again to free them, but to no avail. Her temples began to pound, and she reached over and grabbed her cell phone. "I'll get us a tow truck. Someone is sure to be in the area with all this going on." She clicked open an app on her phone, but it wouldn't load properly.

"What's wrong?"

Stella tapped the screen. "The service is spotty." She didn't dare mention that she only had about ten percent battery, and her phone charger was back at the house. However, she was nearly certain they would be walking down this ditch to the market in a few minutes.

The Christmas music too jovial for the moment, the two of them stared out at the mixture of falling snow and ice, probably both thinking the same thing: what were they going to do? Pop would've had an answer. Getting through winter, and life, without him was a new reality they would both have to get used to.

Exhaustion from all the travel and her emotions started to overwhelm her, and Stella suddenly wanted to be back in her flat in London. Yet she had to keep going for Mama somehow. She tapped the screen of her phone again, trying unsuccessfully to get cell service. Reception wasn't good out there on a regular day, and this little storm certainly wasn't helping.

Mama put her face in her hands and started to cry.

"It's okay," Stella soothed her.

"*Just get through this one moment,*" Pop always said when she was having a rough time.

Stella blinked away her own tears, missing her father terribly but heeding his advice. "We're warm, we're safe, and we're... fine."

Mama rubbed her face and cleared her throat, evidently also trying to get herself together.

Just then, like some sort of miracle, the blinding headlights of a truck rounded the curve heading toward them. "Oh, oh! Someone's coming!" Stella honked her horn and blinked her own headlights as she shielded her eyes from the brightness of the oncoming vehicle.

To her absolute relief, the truck slowed down and came to a stop beside them. Through the spots in her vision, a man in a tattered ball cap, jeans, and a thick leather coat with a woolly collar got out and marched over to them, his boots crunching against the icy road.

Stella rolled down her window. "Oh, thank you for checking on us. I'm so hap—"

She stopped in her tracks when the man leaned down into the car. She'd know those blue eyes anywhere. The breath suddenly drained from her lungs, and she lost the thought that had been on her lips.

*Henry.*

When their eyes met, his gaze was distant, the adorable lips that used to smile at her set in a straight line, unleashing a dagger's stab to her heart, even after all these years. The hair peeking out from under his ball cap seemed to have fewer golden strands than it had when she'd seen him last, and his skin was more weathered, his boyish good looks replaced with a ruggedly handsome appearance. The boy she'd known her entire life, the one person she'd given herself to entirely, was now a man, making her suddenly question all the years she hadn't spent with him. It felt as though time had slipped away from her, never to return.

His all-too-familiar spicy, cedar scent slithered through the air as if it were finding her, driving home the fact that they were face-to-face.

She dug a fingernail into the thigh of her jeans to be sure this wasn't a dream—or rather a nightmare she'd surface from with a wild gasp.

He grabbed the handle and flung open the door, shaking his head. "Y'all get in the truck," he said, his voice so low she almost hadn't heard it over the wind. Then he marched off through the falling snow and climbed into the driver's side of his vehicle.

"There's something I didn't tell you about Henry," Mama said in a near whisper while Stella rolled up the window and turned off the engine.

"That he's back home?" Her blood ran through her veins like the ice outside. She exited and looked back at the car, wondering if waiting for another ride might be a better option than getting in a truck with Henry Dutton.

## Chapter Three

Stella clutched her purse in her lap after she squeezed in beside Mama on the long bench seat of Henry's old Chevy farm truck. She took in shallow breaths to avoid the truck's familiar aroma of pine and soil that plunged her back into the long days they'd spent together in the fields of wildflowers on his family's dairy farm.

Out of the corner of her eye, she tried to view him from the other side of Mama. She could make out the laugh lines around his square jaw and the slight squint at the corners of his eyes, but the darkness taking over the sky made it difficult to see the entirety of his expression. She looked away when the memory of his laughter slipped into her mind, punching her right in the gut. She'd always loved his laugh… She had enough to deal with without having to face him too.

"Where y'all headed in the middle of an ice storm?" he nearly growled at them.

Mama leaned forward slightly and offered a feeble smile as she replied, "We were trying to get to the market for groceries."

With an irritated inhale, he made a U-turn right in the middle of the deserted road, the ice no match for his large tires, and headed toward the Leiper's Fork Market, leaving their car to disappear behind them. He didn't say a word the whole way until he pulled into the empty parking lot next to the gas pumps.

"I'll wait," he finally said as they got out.

Mama shut the truck door behind them, and the cold slithered around Stella's neck.

"He lives with only his sister now," Mama said into Stella's ear on their way into the store.

Aware that Henry's eyes were still on them from the truck, she didn't react until they were safely inside. "Where's Janelle?" she asked, remembering how lovely his mother had been.

Janelle Dutton was a single mom to Henry and his sister, Mary Jo. Their father had left when Henry was a baby and Janelle had moved back home to run the family farm that she'd eventually inherited from her parents. They had goats, horses, and all the tasks required of a working dairy farm, yet never once had she seemed frazzled. She was always happily baking things and whistling as she tidied up around the house, the farm tasks seeming to have been magically completed. While she did have a farm crew to help, Janelle had always been up before the sun, taking care of the farm so she could devote time during the day to her kids. Between truck runs to the local shops, she'd spent hours with them, running through sprinklers on the front lawn, riding horses, or playing flashlight tag once the sun went down.

Family had been everything to Henry, and growing up without his father, he'd vowed to be the best dad for his kids. He'd wanted a house full of them, and when he and Stella married he couldn't wait to get their little dream started.

"She passed away a few months ago. You've been so busy I hadn't had a chance to tell you. I didn't want to do it over text."

The news hit Stella like a wrecking ball, knocking the life right out of her. She turned her head to view the truck's two headlights, the engine running, Henry still staring straight ahead at them. While they hadn't been in touch, and there was no need for him to be, a tiny ache filled her chest that he hadn't at least reached out to tell her. Janelle had been their cheerleader growing up—she'd been to all of Stella's school events. Stella had even made her a clay flowerpot that she'd proudly kept on the mantle in their house. Stella would've liked to pay her respects.

Mama waved hello to the store owner, grabbed a basket, then took Stella's arm and led her down the canned food aisle. "I heard he hasn't been the same since he came home from the army."

"Really?" She didn't want to think about it. After she'd left, she hadn't been in touch with him again. Mama had told her he'd joined the army only a few months later. At one point, she heard he'd been sent to provide support to Iraqi Security Forces. He hadn't been able to come back for Pop's funeral when Mama asked him to.

"He just got back into town, apparently. The army sent him home." Mama grabbed two cans of chicken noodle soup and set them in the basket.

"Why?" Stella palmed a loaf of bread and dropped it in, stealing another glance at the truck.

"I don't know. Mary Jo told me the other day when I ran into her at the pharmacy that he'd moved back into the cabin on their property. She was picking up some medicine for him. She said he'd had an accident and he's not himself these days, but she didn't have time to fill me in on much more than that."

Stella's words escaped her. Henry had been so full of life when they were growing up that she couldn't imagine him any differently. Always laughing and playing silly pranks on her just so he could lean around and kiss her at the end. He was never in a bad mood. Had her leaving changed him? Trying not to let the guilt overwhelm her, she focused on getting the rest of the groceries they'd need. But as she shopped for flour, butter, eggs, and milk, walking the aisles of the market, her mind drifted back to a different time, and she couldn't get the memory of when everything changed out of her mind.

✻

"I want an annulment," she said while they stood under the shade of the old oak tree in the middle of her favorite field of yellow wildflowers on Henry's farm. She held out the small diamond and gold band set that Henry had placed on her finger less than a year prior, his face so blurred by her tears that she saw only glimpses of the pain on his young face.

"If this is because I can't find a job, I'll do it, Stella. Just give me time."

Their first year of marriage had been rough, with her working as a waitress at the local diner and Henry trying to find a job that paid more than hers. She'd graduated valedictorian, and everyone had asked what colleges she'd applied to, assuming she'd be the first one out of that little town. While she had applied to some, her heart had been with Henry and she'd decided to stay there, with him.

"It has nothing to do with that," she said. "I wasn't eighteen yet, and I don't even know if Waylon is ordained, so the marriage isn't valid." She wiped her tears, clearing her eyes.

"We're old enough to know what we want," he said, the agony in his face more than she could bear.

Her chest ached with the sight of his pain. "We're too young." That was what she'd told him. There was more to it, but she spared him the rest of it because she knew he'd only want to work through it, and he deserved more than what she could offer him.

"If this is about giving you a house," he pleaded, clearly trying to find her motive, "I can make it happen." He stepped up to her with intention, his gaze full of strength. "I've just gotta work to get what I need and then we'll restore an old farmhouse like we said—whatever kind you want."

"It's not the house either—you know I don't care about that." She turned away, his pleading eyes nearly making her falter.

She could still remember the frustration showing in his biceps as he ran his fingers through his hair, spinning around aimlessly, trying to manage after being blindsided by the one person who'd promised never to let him down. Fighting the urge to put her arms around him, knowing it was for the best if she didn't, she'd taken his hand and pressed the rings into his wide palm.

"I can't," she said, her voice breaking.

He took her arm, turning her around gently, and those blue eyes bored into her. "Don't do this."

She'd never seen him so vulnerable. Unable to handle how much she was hurting him, she turned away and left him there under the tree. "I'll walk home."

She didn't look back because if she had, she'd have changed her mind, and this life wasn't what either of them needed. She'd barely escaped it, and he had no idea what lay ahead of them. Even though she wanted to crumble to the ground in anguish, she put one foot in front of the other, one step at a time, until she made it to her childhood home. Then she went into her bedroom, collapsed onto her bed, and cried herself to sleep. The next day she left for California before she even knew if she'd gotten into Stanford. That way, she couldn't change her mind.

❄

Still in shock from sliding in the ditch and seeing Henry again, Stella stood at the checkout counter with Mama while she paid for the groceries. She considered inviting Henry in once they got home, maybe try to set things straight, but with the storm, it probably wasn't a good idea. This wasn't how she'd wanted to see him again—she hadn't even thought he'd be in Tennessee. He had every right to still be angry with her, even though she hoped thirteen years apart would've softened it a little.

"Stella, can you take this?" her mother said, holding out one of the bags and pulling Stella from her thoughts.

Stella took it and carried it against her chest, then after her mother opened the door, she climbed back into the truck. Before she knew it, she was in the middle, pressed against Henry's side, her mother pulling herself up into the truck and shutting out the frigid air. Stella swallowed as her arm touched his leather coat. He turned toward her, their eyes meeting, but he wasn't allowing any thoughts he may have to show. All she wanted to see was a flicker of that affection he'd felt for her, but she knew she'd never get it, and even if she did, it would only make things more difficult. In his mind, she'd hurt him too badly to deserve it anyway. Even after thirteen years, that was pretty clear.

"Where do you live?" he asked.

"I'm staying with Mama," she replied.

"What street?"

What was he talking about? He knew good and well where to take her. He was just being obstinate now. But she couldn't blame him for treating her like a stranger. She hadn't handled things like she should have, even though she was too young back then to know how.

"The one we've always lived on: the magnificent Willow Lane."

Years ago, whenever his friends would ask where he was going after school that day, he'd grab hold of Stella's waist and say, *"The only house on the magnificent Willow Lane, home of the most wonderful woman in the world."* Then he'd pull her in for a kiss, making all his friends roll their eyes. She'd used his words now, hoping to lighten the situation, to let him know that she still remembered their fond moments together, but she didn't receive any indication that he cared to remember.

He searched her face and then his jaw clenched. Saying nothing, he put the truck into gear and drove them home.

"If we get much more ice, I'd wait to call a tow truck until after they come through to salt the roads," he said through his teeth when they got out in the driveway in front of Mama's house.

Stella nodded. "Thank you for taking care of us." She offered him another small smile that he didn't return, breaking her heart again. A heaviness fell over her as she followed Mama into the house and set the bag she'd been carrying on the table. Then she went to the window just in time to catch a glimpse of the Chevy pulling onto the snow-covered road, Henry's red taillights vanishing into the darkness. "He's definitely different, isn't he?" she said, turning back to Mama, still trying to get herself together.

"Seems that way." Mama grabbed the bags of food and took them to the kitchen to unpack.

Stella followed, digging into one and pulling out the baking powder and a container of salt, placing them in the spice cabinet, her mind entirely on Henry. Little snippets of happier times that she'd long buried hit her left and right, and while she tried to push them out of her memory, one moment in particular took hold. The task of putting away groceries faded easily as she slipped into the past.

"You can't escape me, Stella Marie!" Henry had called from behind her one day, chasing her down the snowy lane after she'd clocked him in the side with a snowball. It had been one of the few winters their part of Tennessee had gotten enough snow to collect on surfaces.

Pushing her muscles to the brink through all her heavy clothes, the icy wind at her face, she gasped, trying to overcome his giant strides.

She was unsuccessful, and he grabbed her around the waist. "Gotcha!"

When she struggled to wriggle free, he scooped her up and they fell together onto the snow-covered ground. Seemingly unfazed by the cold temperatures, he drank her in with those adoring sapphire eyes of his.

"I love you," he said out of nowhere. Then his freezing lips had met hers…

"Good thing we have food now," Mama said, pulling Stella from the memory.

Glad to abandon their conversation and her thoughts about Henry, Stella added, "Yes. With no four-wheel drive on these icy hills and one car in the ditch, we're at the mercy of the salt trucks."

Mama gave her a tight smile. "Well, it'll give us time to get the house in order. We have a lot of Christmas decorating still to do." She waved a hand at the empty Fraser fir tree in the corner. "I figured we could start in here."

"That sounds like a plan." Decorating would hopefully get both their minds off heavier things for a little while.

Mama clicked on the Christmas music. "Help me get the boxes out of the attic."

Stella followed her mother to the hallway between the living room and the bedrooms until they reached the small rope-pull hanging from the ceiling.

"Your dad made me promise I'd keep going for him, so I worked on getting the lights up outside before the storm and buying the tree down at the lot, but that was all I could do." Her mother's eyes glistened. "The rest I figured we could do together now that you're here."

Stella grabbed her shoulder, squeezing it to release the pain, as if her stress had settled there.

"I just can't get myself excited for the holiday—not without him."

"It's going to be different," Stella said, the ache of loss forming in her chest.

"Yes," Mama said quietly. She stood there facing Stella in the hallway, her tired eyes filling with tears. Then she tugged on the rope, and the old hinges groaned as the door lowered open above them. Mama reached up to grab the bottom rung of the pull-down ladder, letting out a little grunt. "Your pop always used to do this part—climbing into the dusty attic for us." She swiped a tear off her cheek.

Stella turned away, unable to manage herself. She cleared her throat. "I'll go up," she offered. Already things were too quiet without him, and with Lily nowhere in sight, she wasn't sure how to handle it. She didn't even want to think about what Christmas Day would be like. She'd keep waiting for him to come through the front door with more firewood or something. But right now, she had to focus on her mom. "You stay here, and I'll hand you boxes."

"You sure?"

"Yeah." Stella put her foot on the lowest rung of the ladder and tested its sturdiness, trying not to let her grief show for Mama's sake.

Mama stepped back, and Stella climbed to the top. She hoisted herself into the rafters and clicked on the bulb overhead, illuminating the freezing, musty space. Her heart squeezed. Mama's Christmas bins were stacked neatly to the side of the opening the way Pop had always left them. She made a mental note as to how he'd arranged them so she could put it all back the way he would've liked.

Christmas had always been full of joy when he was around. He'd put Christmas carols on the radio and even simple things like what they were doing now became part of the festive atmosphere. Stella put her hand on one of the bins and closed her eyes, wishing she could hear the whisper of his humming along with the holiday music playing downstairs, but she was met with only the whistling of the wind through the vent. She opened her eyes, the absence of Pop and their fractured little family weighing heavily on her. What was Lily thinking, leaving them like this? At the very least, she would know how hard it would be for their mother.

"Do you see them?" Mama called from below.

"Yep." She reached over and pulled the bin off the top of the stack, steadying it in her grip and then leaning down through the opening. "Here's the first one."

Mama stepped up a few rungs and took it from her as dust fluttered through the air. She sneezed, nearly dropping the bin.

"Bless you," Stella said, the sound of Pop saying the same thing floating through her mind, their two voices in unison. She looked around the attic as if she'd see him. For that one instant, it felt as if he were there with her. *I miss you, Pop.*

"Thank you," Mama said, still collecting herself. "Okay, I'm ready. Send down the next box."

Stella grabbed a bin of ornaments and handed it to her mother. She passed her a few more boxes until there was a stack on the hallway floor. "That's it," she called, clapping the dust off her hands. She climbed down and folded the ladder back into the ceiling. "We should turn up the Christmas music." Maybe the sound would drown out her thoughts about Pop.

A flicker of recognition passed over Mama's face, and Stella knew she was thinking the house was too quiet without Pop and Lily too. "Yes, we should." With a hefty breath, she picked up a couple bins. "Let's carry these into the living room."

Stella lifted the largest of the containers—the one Pop would've gotten—and carried it into the room for Mama. Then she went back down the hallway to get the others. Her breath caught when she noticed a larger handprint in the dust on the edge of the lid. She stretched out her fingers and laid her hand on the print, the size of it swallowing hers. As she stared at it, wondering if it had been last year when Pop made that print, Mama turned up the radio. *Silent Night* sailed through the downstairs.

The timing made her smile. If Pop could have arranged that little moment to tell them all things were calm and bright, she was sure he would have. She peered around at the empty hallway, wondering if Pop *was* actually there with them, and the moment felt a little lighter somehow.

Through the doorway to her bedroom, she had a view of the Christmas decorations on the fence. "I'll have to help her with the lights on the tree," she whispered, just in case Pop could hear.

"Could you help me with these lights?" her mother called.

Stella smiled.

*"You'll have to help her with a lot."* The thought came almost as if Pop was standing there beside her.

"On my way." She grabbed the last few boxes and headed down the hallway.

When she got to the living room, Mama had pulled a chair over to the tree so they could reach the top. Stella set down the boxes and climbed onto it, reaching for Mama to hand her the strand of lights. Her mother's thoughts were clear on her face, her struggle with the holiday evident in the frown lines around her lips.

"It might sound crazy, but I feel like Pop is here with us," Stella said, hoping the idea would console her mother, even a little, the way thinking of Pop had helped her.

"I feel him sometimes," Mama said, surprising her. She held up the lights for Stella.

"You do?"

Mama nodded. "Occasionally in the dark of night, I can almost swear I sense him beside me, his arms around me…" Her eyes glistened in the twinkling lights. "I freeze in that spot and don't move, hoping I can stay awake until dawn so I don't lose the feeling of it, but I always drift off." Mama went over and sifted through a box of ornaments, her sniffles audible.

Stella started wrapping the lights around the tree, the branches soft under her fingers. She'd only experienced love like her mother and father's once. With Henry. They'd planned out their future, and there was a time when she couldn't imagine life without him. Recalling it now caused her to slip back into another memory.

"We have to have a huge farmhouse—bigger than this one," Henry had said, spreading his muscular arms wide while the two of them rocked on the porch swing of her parent's home.

Stella was reclined on her back with her knees up, resting her head on his thigh as she gazed up at him. "Why so big?"

"Because I want so many kids that we can't chase them all down." He tickled her sides, making the swing wiggle as she flinched, squealing.

She pulled herself up into his arms and kissed his lips before resuming her position. Those blue eyes on her, he ran a finger down her cheek. "I want a house full of little boys and girls who look just like us." His eyes widened. "We can make our own baseball team."

Stella shook her head, laughing while he pushed the large bench swing back and forth, lulling her.

She'd been so young back then that it had never occurred to her that she might not get another chance to feel love like that again. And, if she were being honest, she hadn't considered what it felt like to be without it for quite some time. The insane hours she kept traveling and working doing a good job of keeping her thoughts at bay. The distance in Henry's face tonight flashed in the front of her consciousness, making it hard to breathe. She couldn't wait to dive into work tomorrow and get her mind off it.

"Speaking of your dad," Mama said, coming back over and holding the strand of lights out so it wouldn't get tangled. "He always planned the Leiper's Fork Christmas parade." That look of worry settled on her mother's face once more.

Stella had fond memories of the parade. No matter what was going on in their lives, everything stopped the day of the parade. They gathered—the whole family—along with all their friends and neighbors, the scent of fire-roasted caramel corn in the air and the tinkle of jingle bells mixing with the chatter of the crowd. It didn't get much better than that.

"The town committee asked if I wanted to plan it this year or if we'd like to find a replacement. I should've passed it along, but I promised your dad I'd keep everything going." Her bottom lip wobbled. "I told them I'd plan it." She fiddled with the lights on her end. "I also told them everything was going well, but every time I've tried to work on it,

I just couldn't. I put in for the parade to be the day before Christmas Eve this year to give me the most amount of time and now that's less than two weeks away." She shook her head. "It just doesn't seem right not to have him there."

The reality of the situation set in slowly. Pop worked almost all year on the parade, coming up with ideas, organizing the floats and the school bands, the farmers, the vendors…

"Wait. You mean you haven't planned *anything* yet? Pop usually started official participant registration in October. Has that been posted?"

"Yes." She reached for Stella's hand. "I need to organize it all, though. You used to work on it with him, so you know what to do, right?"

The parade had been *their thing*. Lily had never been interested, but Stella was the organizer of the two of them and had always bonded with Pop over the Christmas parade. The two of them stacked flyers, scheduled events, booked bands…

"Will you help me plan it?" her mother asked.

She had a deadline looming for the article she'd been researching in London, and she hadn't even begun the second. She still needed to get permission from all her sources and back up her facts with credible publications, and there was an email she was waiting for that she needed to follow up on or she wouldn't have the most recent research… There was no way she could take on something as monumental as the Christmas parade.

But she wavered the minute she saw her mother's anxious expression.

*"You'll have to help her with a lot."* Pop's voice came through once more.

With resolve, Stella squeezed Mama's hand. "Of course I'll help you."

## Chapter Four

The next morning, Stella tried to call Lily again, but the phone went straight to voicemail.

"Hey," she said, momentarily at a loss for words. What should she say to her little sister who'd run off and changed her life without even bothering to tell Stella? "I'd love to know what's going on. Call me." But the dull silence made her wonder if the line was even connected.

She blew air through her lips as she clicked off her phone and tossed it on the bed. Then she padded down the hallway and into the kitchen wearing the long sweatshirt and fuzzy socks she'd thrown on last night, the jet lag having caught up with her. She'd passed out in bed in a matter of seconds.

The tree they'd decorated gleamed in the open space between where she stood and the living room.

"Morning," Mama said from the table, the news on the small television in the corner. "I made pancakes and coffee if you want some." Her mother's tone didn't match the offer; she held a balled tissue in her hand. With a sniffle, she got up and tossed it into the trashcan then poured herself a cup of coffee. From the lip print on the mug, it looked like it wasn't her first of the day.

Stella yawned and made her own cup of Joe, topping it off with sugar and cream, her mind flitting back to her sister. She should be with her family right now, she thought. Even if Lily had to face being there without Pop, she should do it, because the rest of her little family needed her. And who was this mystery guy she'd eloped with? Had she only just met him? Why all the secrecy? Wouldn't she want him to meet her family? Even though Stella had done something similarly impulsive, it didn't make handling Lily's choices any easier. If anything, it only made it harder.

The romance of the situation did sound like Lily; she'd always been the dreamer of the two of them, seeing life through rose-colored glasses. While growing up, when Stella had her nose in one of her textbooks, often Lily would sit next to her, chatting on and on about her friends at school or her latest hobby.

The only time Stella had ever felt carefree was when she was with Henry. In those moments of laughter, when she'd gotten lost in his eyes, she would get a sense of how her sister viewed the world. When Stella was with Henry, it was as if everything she'd done in life had led to that time. Nothing mattered—not school, not college, not her choice of career. She found joy at home, with him.

Now at the age of thirty-one, she sometimes wished she could go back and do things differently, although she wasn't sure it would've changed anything.

"The weatherman said the storm came in quicker than they'd expected." Mama's elbows were on the table as she lifted her coffee mug to her lips, focused on the TV, unaware of Stella's contemplations. "Looks like most of it's out of here already."

"That's good news." Stella walked over to the table and sat next to Mama. She leaned away from her to get a glimpse of the frosty yard through the window. "How do the roads look?"

"They're not great, but give 'em a few hours of sunshine and they should get better. We should probably call a tow truck to retrieve your car this afternoon."

Henry's face floated into Stella's mind, and she rubbed her eyes to make it stop.

Mama's gaze turned to her, lingering.

"I'm still getting over the jet lag," she said to cover it up.

"Mm." Mama seemed preoccupied, her attention returning to the news where cleanup efforts were going on around town to clear fallen trees that had succumbed to the heavy ice. She looked exhausted.

"You okay?" Stella asked.

Mama's lip quivered. "I miss your pop." She reached over and grabbed another tissue as a tear fell down her cheek.

"Me too," Stella said, putting her arm around her mother.

They sat together under the quiet hum of the newscast, both fighting tears. Stella looked over at the chair where Pop had sat every evening. If she closed her eyes, she could see him eating dinner while wearing a paper hat she'd made for him in grade school one year. He'd worn it that entire week.

Mama shifted, touching the pendant around Stella's neck. "What's that?"

Stella had forgotten she was wearing it. "Oh, it's the strangest story," she said, clearing her throat. She lifted it from the collar of her sweatshirt so Mama could see it and filled her mother in on her collision with a caramel latte and how she'd ended up with it. "I should probably call the airport today to see if anyone has reported it missing."

Mama leaned in to inspect the stones. "You definitely should. Those diamonds look real." She squinted. "And that looks like a... sapphire? It's a bit light to be one, though."

"I'm not sure what it is," Stella replied, peering down at it.

"It's hard to say. I'm no expert."

Glad for the distraction from other matters on her mind, she offered, "Maybe we could try to look it up. We might find a picture of the stone—it's an unusual shade of blue, a frosty color."

"Yes. Let's see if we can figure it out. While you get your computer, I'll heat up the pancakes for us."

Stella abandoned her coffee and got up from the table. "That sounds amazing. I'm starving," she said over her shoulder as she headed down the hallway.

When she returned, Mama had plated her two fluffy pancakes with a pad of butter melting on top of each one, the entire surface drizzled in a thin glaze of warm maple syrup. Stella set her laptop on the table and opened the search engine, then typed "light blue gemstones." After cutting herself a bite of pancake, Stella scooted the plate out of the way and leaned in to view the results. Her screen was filled with images of blue stones in various shades.

Mama tapped the screen. "It looks like a blue diamond, doesn't it?"

Stella examined the stone around her neck once more. "It does." She typed "blue diamonds" into the search bar to pull up more photos.

Mama clicked off the news and turned her focus to the computer screen. "Look," she said, stopping Stella before she scrolled. "That says, 'Blue diamonds have been around since the 1600s.' I've never heard of a blue diamond before. How interesting."

"That *is* interesting, isn't it?"

"I wonder when they found the first one," Mama said before sipping her coffee.

Curious, Stella typed "oldest blue diamond." When the search results came up, an article caught her eye. "It looks like the first one ever found was in India." She took a sip of her coffee while looking through the various posts. "I never knew there were so many kinds." She clicked on "images" and perused more photos. Then she stopped, recognizing one and comparing it to the stone she was wearing. "That looks exactly like this one, doesn't it? 'The Christmas Diamond'…"

"It does." Mama set down her coffee mug, leaning in closer. "What does it say?"

As she dug into her pancakes again, Stella pulled up the article and began to read. "'The Christmas Diamond is a rare blue jewel that was originally commissioned in 1764 by a wealthy British nobleman while traveling in Barbados. It was thought to have originally been a gift for the bride of one of England's lords but, at the last minute, he changed his mind and got her a different gift.'

"'The locals of the town in Barbados where it was mined believed that the blue jewel could hold the energy of the divine, and that if it wasn't given and received in love, the jewel would cast punishment on anyone in its wake.'"

"What a curious legend. Read some more."

Stella continued. "'The diamond was later purchased in 1768 as a holiday gift for wealthy aristocrat Mrs. Agnes Hastings from her husband's father. He bought the diamond for his son's new wife as a congratulatory gesture, since his son William was about to become a father himself. It was rumored that Agnes wasn't in love with her husband, and instead was romantically involved with the town blacksmith, whom she'd always loved, but he was not of an acceptable class.'"

Mama gasped. "Oh, my." She leaned forward on her elbows, her eyes wide.

Stella grinned, reading on. "'Three days after receiving the gift, while wearing it, Agnes delivered a stillborn child.'" The seriousness of the subject matter caused Stella to stop, the words blurring in front of her. Any lightheartedness she'd had about the story vanished. A child had died. The pancakes set like a brick in her stomach. "How terrible," she whispered.

Mama sobered. "Do you think it was her destiny because she didn't love her husband? Or maybe the baby wasn't her husband's..." She clapped a hand over her mouth.

Stella shook her head, unsure, looking back down at the necklace. Suddenly, it felt heavy, and she had the urge to take it off.

"Keep going," her mother said.

Forcing her gaze back to the computer, she returned to the article. "'Mrs. Hastings delivered three more stillborns after that—all while wearing the diamond. Shrouded in grief and convinced the Christmas Diamond was cursed, she ripped the necklace off and placed it in her jewelry box. The next year, she had a son. Agnes and William went on to have three more children.'"

"That's an incredible story." Mama reached over and pinched the pendant around Stella's neck, scrutinizing it. "It sure does look like the one in the photo, doesn't it?"

Now that Stella was no longer under the spell of the legend, her rational side kicked in. "If this really was the same necklace, I doubt very seriously it would have been on the floor of the Atlanta airport. An antique like that would be secured."

"I agree. But you should still call the airport. It definitely belongs to someone, and I'm sure they're missing it."

"I'll call right now," Stella said. She took off the necklace and set it on the table between them. The blue stone shimmered in the gray light filtering in from the window. It definitely looked too harmless to be bad luck. Maybe she'd actually have *good* luck and find the owner.

❄

While her mother called a tow truck to get the car out of the ditch, Stella sat on her childhood bedroom floor and added more to her piece on long-term brain health, implementing the studies she'd worked on while in London. She'd spent the last couple of hours writing after sending emails to all her sources and double-checking a few final details with St. Thomas' in London.

Her mind, however, had been on the necklace that was sitting on her dresser. To whom did it belong? Was it an elderly lady, someone's mom, a young girl? Did it have sentimental meaning and the owner was missing it? The person she'd spoken to at the airport hadn't had any inquiries, but he'd taken down her information in case something came in. It belonged to someone, and it had a story. She decided she wouldn't wear it again.

The ringing of her cell phone drew her attention right away. Seeing her sister's number, she answered quickly. "Lily?"

"Hi! I can't talk long because I lose connection, but—" The rest of her words were garbled.

Stella cut her off. "I can't hear you." She pressed the phone harder against her ear as if that would help.

"I'm not—" The words fell apart again through the line.

"You're not what, Lily?"

"…Love you!"

The phone went dead.

Stella tried to call her right back, but it went to voicemail. Disappointed, she set the phone on the carpet beside her and stared at it. This was absolutely not what their father would've wanted for their first Christmas without him.

*Are you here, Pop? Do you have any idea what Lily's doing?*

No response.

She didn't have time to figure out why her sister had decided to completely abandon them at Christmas. She had to check if the roads were clear yet, then get the ice off her mother's car so she could make the drive to Vanderbilt Hospital. She needed to work on her final article and try to win the President's Award.

# Chapter Five

Later that afternoon, Stella had an appointment with her new contact at the hospital. Even with the salt trucks, it had taken an hour and a half on the icy roads to make the normally forty-minute drive to Vanderbilt Hospital in Nashville. After parking and then finding the correct department, Stella was cutting it close. She hurried to the office of Dr. Abigail Astley, her point of contact, and walked in.

"I'm glad you were able to get here. The streets are absolute madness," Dr. Astley said.

"Thank goodness for the warmer temperatures that came in today," Stella said, unwrapping her scarf. "And thank you for allowing me to do this." She held out her hand.

Dr. Astley shook it. "Of course. I jumped at the chance to have a feature in *Brain Borders*." She offered one excited bounce of her eyebrows. "I read your piece on cognitive dissonance. It was relevant for the patient you'll see today." She set a file on her desk next to a miniature Christmas-tree card holder.

"Patient—as in one?" Stella had been hoping for more options.

Dr. Astley gestured to the empty chair. "Have a seat."

Stella complied.

"We explained what you were doing to five of our patients who we felt fit your criteria, but only had one of them consent to observation."

Stella's visit had been last minute, and with the holiday approaching one patient was better than nothing. She'd have to take it, but she wasn't sure if she could get enough data from one person.

The doctor pulled an iPad from a stack of papers and swiped. "I just need a few signatures from you stating that you'll keep all personal information confidential."

Stella took the device, ticked the various boxes, added her signature, and handed it back.

Dr. Astley placed the iPad on her desk. "The session has already started, but let me brief you before you go in." She went around to her side of the desk and pulled up a screen on her computer. "Our patient is recovering from a traumatic brain injury that he received about two months ago."

Stella pulled out her laptop, balancing it on her thighs.

The doctor clicked a few keys and an image appeared on the screen. "As part of a government partnership, the medical team from Fort Campbell, Kentucky, is working with us to provide care for the subject. He experienced an injury to the hippocampal formation and is now receiving therapy with us for impairment of intellectual function, after his discharge from the army for irrational behavior."

"What kind of irrational behavior?"

"Anger, some signs of depression, lack of concern for the consequences of his actions. It's as if he doesn't care at all what happens to him, which puts him and his fellow soldiers at risk." Dr. Astley brought up another screen of test results. "But, apart from that, we're perplexed by this unusual case because his recall skills don't fit the usual pattern."

"What do you mean?" Stella asked.

"Well, as I'm sure you know, memory is more complex than just short-term and long-term, but we can generally categorize memory *loss* into one of those two areas. With this patient, the symptoms present almost as if he experienced a particularly distressing event and has blocked it out. He's unable to access the memory of an entire portion of his life. He remembers some things, like how to drive a car, but we think that's because he was probably sixteen when he learned. His more recent memory is nearly nonexistent."

Stella typed madly to get the facts down. "Traumatic brain injury affects short-term memory usually, right?"

"Yes. And we're hoping it can be improved with treatment, but stress is slowing progress, and the subject has dealt with an incredible amount. As I mentioned, your earlier article interested me because the subject experiences conflicting information about things he has done in his life that directly oppose his values." She glanced at the clock on the wall. "I've got to run, so I'll let you handle that investigation first-hand and then we can chat after you meet the patient."

"Sure," Stella said, finishing up her notes.

"Do you have any questions before I take you to meet him?"

Stella shut her laptop. "Not at the moment, thank you."

Dr. Astley clasped her hands together. "All right. They're in therapy room 344."

Stella stood, tucked her laptop under her arm, and turned to leave.

"Miss Fisher." The doctor stopped her. "The patient is a bit combative during therapy. I wanted to warn you so you aren't alarmed. He's aware of it and we're working with him. He's also aware that you're going to be observing today."

"Okay," Stella said, preparing herself. She'd been through similar situations before in her line of work, and since she was only there as a writer, she could usually hang back and take notes unnoticed.

They walked down the hallway toward the therapy wing, past rows of stockings labeled with names of staff in silver puff-paint. An elderly man pushed a walker, his belly grazing the handles. He locked eyes with Stella, his cheeks lifting. "What a delight to see your smile today." He passed them slowly going in the other direction.

"That's Mr. Ferguson," Dr. Astley said. "He's eighty-seven. Can you believe it?"

"He doesn't look it." Stella peered over her shoulder to get a second glimpse of the old man. The youthful light in his eyes stayed with her even after he'd gone.

"That's because, despite all his struggles, he's the kindest soul you'll ever meet. Kindness keeps us young."

"I can tell."

"Your door will be the third one on the left. They know you're coming."

"Thank you."

They parted, and Stella made her way to the room. As she neared, she could hear the patient's muffled barking at the therapist.

"This isn't helpful!" he roared.

Combative, indeed.

"How is this supposed to help me?" the voice boomed once more.

It also sounded familiar. Stella sharpened her hearing to get a better handle on the voice, but she was met with only silence.

When she reached the room, she knocked on the door. The holiday wreath hanging from a plastic hook shimmied as she let herself in. "Hello?"

The minute she was in the room and in view of the patient, her gaze met his, and she froze. She'd know those blue eyes in any crowd, eyes that once enveloped her with love, but now stared back at her with an emptiness that made her shiver. *Henry.* All the breath left her lungs. Suddenly, his behavior in the ice storm came back to her—the harsh reception, him asking where she lived… Her laptop and handbag clattered to the floor, the contents of her bag spilling all over the white tile.

She broke eye contact. "Oh, my goodness." The words came out in winded shock as she scrambled to pick up her computer and checked to make sure it still worked. The screen lit up, to her relief, and she closed it once more.

The therapist, a pleasant-looking woman with mousy hair in an updo, walked over. "I'll help you," she said and began picking up the contents of Stella's bag.

Stella hardly noticed. She'd already looked back over at Henry, unable to believe what was happening. She was supposed to be an observer, not involved in the therapy in any way.

A flicker of interest showed on his face, and he said, "I took you home last night."

Not breaking eye contact, she slowly reached down and picked up her handbag, still trying to process this revelation.

He stood and walked toward her, bent over, and snatched up her lip gloss and wallet and handed them to her.

Their years together vanished right in front of her. "Henry?"

Upon hearing his name, he stiffened, and then walked back to a sofa on the other side of a muted green rug and took a seat. Leaning on his thighs, he balled his hands into fists, his knuckles turning white.

"Do you and Henry know each other?" the therapist asked as she picked up a few last items from Stella's handbag that had rolled across the room.

She handed them over, and Stella shoved them into her bag, her mind filled with questions. If she said "yes," it would certainly be a conflict of interest, and she wouldn't be able to work on the case. But Henry was the only person who'd consented. Also if she admitted that she knew him, she wouldn't be able to write her second article, and a possible promotion depended on it. That promotion was hers to lose, she'd been told, and she was just about to lose it.

"Uh," she said, still rattled. She locked eyes with Henry and offered him a pleading stare. "No. Dr. Astley gave me his name."

"You don't have to talk as if I'm not capable of answering," Henry snapped from the sofa, quickening her pulse.

*Please, Henry. Don't tell her.*

"We're sorry, Henry," the therapist said. "You're right. Perhaps you'd like to have a direct conversation with…" She peered over at Stella.

"Stella. Stella Fisher." She stared at him to get his reaction and to her surprise and utter relief, a flash of a look of solidarity crossed his face.

"Stella," he said slowly before his brows pulled together, his face crumpling. Then he studied her as if he were mentally taking stock of every one of her facial attributes. "Nice to… meet you."

Light-headed, she forced herself to take in small, steady breaths. Carrying her computer and bag, she walked over to an empty chair at the back of the room.

She considered the fact that last night he'd had no knowledge of their breakup, which was a relief. His short-tempered drive to her house was due to whatever this was, not because he was still angry with her. She felt lighter knowing his resentment wasn't directed at her, but the fact that he'd been horribly injured and had no memory of their good times together made her feel like she'd lost something wonderful.

The therapist stepped closer to Stella. "My name is Sarah Weixel. I'm a military clinical psychologist serving at Fort Campbell. I'm here as part of the military-civilian trauma team training. Because Henry lives closer to Vanderbilt, we decided to treat him here so we could also have—and learn from—the expertise of Dr. Astley's team. We see him every day to start, and then we'll reassess his plan once we've made some progress."

Stella opened her laptop and typed a few notes about the partnership.

"Today we're working on reducing negative thought patterns," Ms. Weixel said, her shoes clacking against the floor as she neared Henry. "I was asking Henry to tell me three positive things that have happened today."

"It's a waste of time," he growled.

Stella typed a note to herself: *Combative. Not receptive to suggestions.*

"What makes you feel the time is wasted?" Ms. Weixel asked.

Henry rolled his eyes but didn't answer.

The woman slipped her hands into the pockets of her pressed trousers. "Let's see if we can find one pleasant thing about today?"

Henry stared into space, his adorable lips set in a frustrated pout.

Stella quietly typed below the initial description Dr. Astley had given her: *Subject is obstinate, distressed. Seems to have shut down.* When she looked up, he was staring at the laptop, evidently curious about what she was typing.

"Not going to participate today?" the therapist asked him.

He exhaled audibly. "Nothing good has happened today." His gaze fluttered to Stella's face, and the interest in his eyes made her question his statement.

"Ok. Let's see… Did you set an alarm to get up this morning?"

He turned his attention back to the therapist. "Yeah, why?"

"Did you oversleep?"

"No."

"Then you can say that a positive for today was that you woke up on time. And you got where you needed to go."

Henry shook his head. "That's not a positive."

"Oh?" Ms. Weixel leaned against the counter lining the side of the room, the skin on her forehead creasing. "Why not?"

"We all have to get up. It's expected that I won't sleep in. If I do, it's unfortunate, but if I don't, it's just part of the day."

Stella added another note: *Unwilling to participate in therapy sessions.*

"It's fair to decide that getting up on time isn't necessarily positive or negative for you, so perhaps we can move on to another example," Ms. Weixel said.

As Stella typed, Henry ran his fingers through his hair. The defeat in his expression took her back to the memory of the day she left him, and she had to look down at her keyboard to avoid the pain of it overwhelming her.

"I'm done." He stood.

"We still have a few more minutes," the therapist said.

"I don't care. I'm finished for the day. My positive is that I'm leaving." He strode past Stella and walked out the door.

She typed: *Therapy session was a total failure. Try again tomorrow.*

Stella packed up her laptop in a daze, still stunned that Henry was the patient she'd been assigned to.

"I'm sorry you didn't get much today," Ms. Weixel said.

"It's okay," she lied. Then she gathered her things as quickly as she could and rushed out of the hospital, unsure if this project was going to work at all.

# Chapter Six

On the way home, needing a minute to herself, Stella stopped at the coffee shop on the edge of town. It was a little walk-up booth with outdoor seating, and in summer, the tables were full of people, but today, with gray skies and snowy grounds, the place was empty. She parked her car and got out, her winter attire doing nothing to ward off the cold temperature, but she was so lost in thought that she didn't really mind.

She ordered a latte, noticing the red Christmas baubles hanging in the trees around the booth. Once she had her coffee, she surveyed the wet benches.

"Stella?"

She turned around to find Mary Jo standing opposite her. Only five years her senior, Henry's sister looked a lot older. The years had certainly taken their toll, but she still seemed to possess the rugged vibrance she'd had in her youth. Her dark curls were piled into a messy ponytail that could almost pass as a new beauty trend, but her worn, mud-stained boots and tattered dirty jeans from her daily farm work said otherwise.

"It's good to see you," Mary Jo said with a hesitancy Stella understood. They had once been close, but when Stella left her brother in ruins, she'd abandoned Mary Jo as well.

Stella went over to her. "You too." Her coffee steamed into the air between them as she leaned in for a hug. "I'm so sorry to hear about your mom."

Grief flooded Mary Jo's expression as if it had been hiding under the surface the whole time, waiting for its welcome. "Thank you."

"I didn't know, or I would've come back."

"I was so overcome that it didn't occur to me to reach out. We kept it to just me and Henry and a few locals."

"I've seen Henry," Stella said, the weight in her words letting Mary Jo know she was aware of Henry's struggles. "How did he handle the funeral? Did he… remember?"

Mary Jo's chest filled with air. "Thank God he was still himself when that happened. Since the accident, it's just his recollection of her later years that's spotty. He remembers most of his life with Mama."

"So the accident was after…?"

Mary Jo nodded. "Yeah. He's been very different since. His memory loss has made him angry. I've never seen that side of him before. "

"I know, me neither," she agreed. Stella had certainly seen him frustrated and defeated at times, but never angry. That wasn't who he was. Henry had always been patient and kind. But she knew that damage to the brain could cause changes in behavior, including managing anger.

"Want to get a coffee and we can talk in the car?" Stella asked.

"Yeah, that would be nice."

"I'll get it warm for us."

While Mary Jo made her way to the coffee-shop window, Stella slid into the car and started the engine, cranking up the heat. With a shiver, she took a sip of her latte, the creamy, sugary sweetness not improving her mood. She had hoped to sit alone and let it warm her while she tried to clear her mind, but it didn't look like she would get that chance. Anyway, it would be good to catch up with Mary Jo. She hadn't realized how much she'd missed her.

As she watched her waiting for her coffee, the leftover snow and the dull glow of the sky against the holiday decorations in the daytime had her mind searching for happier times, and she drew upon a memory of the two of them.

"I made you something for the wedding today," Mary Jo had said just before Stella jumped into Henry's truck. Her long, dark curls bounced against her back as she pulled Stella across the field of wildflowers toward the main house.

Running with Mary Jo, Stella was unable to stifle the absolute joy of marrying Henry. It was spontaneous and exciting. The rest of her life had been highly focused, planned out just so in order to manage the huge academic load she carried. Henry had been the more impulsive of the two of them, the one who always pushed her out of her comfort zone and showed her how fun life could be. It was as if he were the opposite piece to her personality puzzle, and when they were matched up, they fit perfectly. She knew that without him, she'd never feel whole.

"Wait here," Mary Jo said.

Henry's sister left Stella on the wide front porch of the farmhouse, the screen door clapping shut behind her. Stella's long, sandy hair and simple white dress billowed in the summer breeze as she stood on the gray-painted boards of the porch that had been under her feet so many times that it felt like home. She'd always wanted to live in that farmhouse. If she closed her eyes, she could imagine her and Henry there with their kids and extended family—all of them together.

Mary Jo returned with a bound bouquet of wildflowers. She handed the purple-and-yellow bunch to Stella. "You can't get married without a bouquet."

Stella peered down at the grouping of flowers—bluebells, blazing star, buttercups, and chicory—tied with a wide strip of white satin to match her dress. She ran her fingers through the big loopy bow and put the flowers to her nose, inhaling the smell of her childhood.

"That ribbon is actually my mama's scarf that she wears to church," Mary Jo said. "She doesn't know I took it." Mary Jo clapped an excited hand over her mouth.

"Thank you," Stella said, hugging the bouquet and realizing then that soon Mary Jo would be her sister. The older girl had always been like a big sister to Stella, and she couldn't have asked for a better send-off.

"When are you and Henry gonna tell Mama?"

They hadn't told either of their parents, both of them worried they'd be talked out of it, given their young ages, but Stella knew it was right. She didn't need anyone telling her otherwise. "I promise we'll tell everyone as soon as we get back."

Mary Jo nodded, her eyes sparkling. "Go! Start your forever!" She gave Stella a playful nudge just as the horn on Henry's old Chevy honked in three little beeps.

"When I come back, we'll officially be family," Stella said, her heart wanting to burst. She leaned over and gave her soon-to-be sister a kiss on the cheek. Then, with all her dreams ahead of her, she ran off toward the love of her life.

❄

Stella emerged from her memory to find Mary Jo on the passenger side, shifting her cup to her other hand and opening the door.

She slid inside and shut them in. "Good grief, it's freezing."

"I know. Good thing we've got coffee," Stella said, keenly aware that was the last of the pleasantries they had to share and it was time for the conversation to move to more difficult topics. She took a long drink of the warm liquid to center herself.

"I missed you," Mary Jo said, jumping right in. "It's been awful living in that big farmhouse all by myself. It's so good to have you back."

Without warning, tears sprang to Stella's eyes. Not because she'd missed Mary Jo, but because she hadn't allowed herself to until this moment. "I'm sorry." The words came out on a breath that felt as if she'd been holding it for the last thirteen years.

"You left without even a goodbye."

Stella fiddled with her coffee lid absentmindedly, the pain of that day feeling like a fresh wound. "I just couldn't, Mary Jo."

"You two were so in love and perfect. And you just left us all. What happened?"

Divulging her secret now would only open up the past, and Stella wasn't ready to do that. "I just wanted something different," she said instead, knowing the response was flimsy at best.

Mary Jo understood both Stella and Henry too well to believe the excuse, but if she suspected it, she didn't say anything.

"My brother was a total mess after you left. He didn't sleep. He barely ate. He didn't want to see anyone."

Another tear escaped down Stella's cheek.

"Then one day he showed up on the porch and told me and Mama he was joining the army."

Stella wiped away her tear, the wounds she'd caused almost too much to bear. Henry wasn't competitive; he didn't have an aggressive bone in his body. "Why did he go into the army? That doesn't seem like him."

"He doesn't know the answer himself. Henry has been battling how in the world he ended up doing a job that required him and others to be in harm's way. He knows how honorable it is, but it's made him anxious and frustrated. Handling that level of danger just isn't in his nature."

Stella recalled what Dr. Astley had mentioned about Stella's previous article: *"Your earlier article interested me because the subject experiences conflicting information about things he has done in his life that directly oppose his values."*

Mary Jo continued. "I told him that I'd asked the same thing when he'd enlisted and he'd said at the time that he didn't have a direction. He needed to test himself to find his true limits. He wanted to be a part of something bigger than himself. But I think the issue was his decision to enlist was never about what he actually wanted. I have to wonder if it was to *lose* himself in the crowd, to put himself through something so rigorous that he didn't have time to tear himself apart over you."

Stella's chest ached. She'd run off and done the same thing by jumping into her college years and then traveling. In college, she stayed out with friends or had her nose in a book until the last possible minute so that when her head hit the pillow, she was out. It kept her mind busy so she didn't have to think about Henry.

"I didn't want to hurt him," she said, her voice barely audible. "I didn't mean to hurt anyone."

Mary Jo brightened a little. "The greatest thing about life is that we can start again whenever we want to. I think about that all the time…"

"Are *you* thinking of starting something over?"

Mary Jo chewed on her lip, seeming to wrestle with the question. "I hate living in that farmhouse all by myself. I need family around, and Henry doesn't really feel much like family anymore."

Stella's heart broke for her friend. Silence settled between them.

As if they both knew they couldn't get any further today, Mary Jo looked at her watch. "I've got to run so I can get back and plan feeding schedules for the animals." She opened the door. "Come and see me sometime?"

"Okay."

Mary Jo shut the door and jogged to her truck at the edge of the lot.

Her words rolled around in Stella's mind, and she considered if starting over was really that easy. She put her car in gear and headed home.

❄

"I got the car towed," Mama said when Stella arrived home. In the light of day, her mother's age showed in her face, the stress from losing Pop undeniable. "They'll bring it by in the next hour or so."

"That's good." Stella rubbed the pinch in her shoulder and dropped her handbag and laptop case on the floor.

All the way home, the fact raced through her mind that, given Henry's hostility, progress was going to be slow. He needed time before he would show marked growth, and she didn't have that kind of time for her article. This Henry was different from the boy she'd known, but one thing was the same: he was stubborn. Henry was a fixer. He always took control of things when they needed to be mended. And now he was out of control, powerless and clearly frustrated by it.

Mama, who'd been tidying the blanket that she kept on the arm of the sofa, stopped mid-fold, and put her hand on her hip. "You look like you've had a tough day."

"To say the least." Stella slumped on the sofa in front of the fire. Mama held out the blanket and she accepted it, covering herself and closing her eyes.

"Wanna talk about it over a cup of hot cocoa? I have marshmallows." Mama excitedly wiggled her fingers the way Pop used to.

The action caught them both by surprise and they took a second to catch their breath.

"That sounds wonderful," Stella said with a smile, trying to channel Pop's way of seeing the best in everything. Realizing she was sitting on the sofa where her father used to plop down next to her, and reluctant to be on it alone, she threw the blanket off her legs, folded it, and followed Mama into the kitchen. "I'll help you."

"So tell me about work—what happened?" Mama filled the kettle with water and set it on the stove. Then she pulled down two of the clay mugs Stella had made in high school.

"Well, for starters, I only have one patient to use as a case study for my next article, and he's not terribly open to therapy." She rubbed her aching eyes.

"Oh dear."

"And there's something else that makes it even more... unusual." She opened the drawer and retrieved two spoons, then handed them to her mother. "The patient is Henry."

Mama whirled to face her, wide-eyed. "Henry?"

"Yeah... He was in an accident in the army and doesn't remember parts of the last fourteen or so years. He doesn't remember things like... being married."

Mama's mouth dropped open, her surprise evident. She had been there to dry Stella's tears when she'd come home after leaving Henry all those years ago. Mama understood the choice Stella had made that day. Having fallen in love and married Stella's father at a young age, her mother had transitioned from childhood right into married life, and by the time she was twenty-three she had two toddlers running around. And while Stella had never once seen a shred of regret from her mother, when Stella told her she was leaving Leiper's Fork, there was a sparkle in Mama's eyes that revealed to Stella that a part of her mother had always wondered what might be out there in the wild world.

Her mother didn't fully understand then why Stella had chosen to go, but it had been clear that she'd supported it, even though she'd wondered openly about how Henry would manage. Now, it was evident that she had connected the fact that if Henry didn't remember his recent past, he didn't know what he'd lost either.

The kettle whistled on the stove. Mama took it off and poured water into the mugs, then handed one to Stella. "What happened to him?"

Stella chewed her lip, trying to squelch the idea that this was all her fault. "I'm not sure. I only know there was an accident. They didn't give me details about the lead-up; it isn't part of my job to know specifics of how the injury happened, but rather how they plan to fix it."

"Henry didn't give you any more details?"

Wrapping her hands around the chunky mug, she replied, "He wasn't really giving anyone anything. Today made his attitude last night seem like a walk in the park."

"I know he must be scared," Mama said, putting her hand over her heart. "What doesn't he remember?"

"I ran into Mary Jo and she told me that his memory of his later years is spotty at best."

Mama shook her head. "That poor boy. He's been through so much."

Her comment only served to make Stella feel worse. "I've learned a lot about life in my time away," she said as she stirred the chocolate mixture in her mug. "I don't regret leaving entirely, because I've had a lot of great experiences that have changed me as a person. I do regret, however, having to let go of what I had with Henry. I try not to think about it, but it does enter my mind."

"Do you miss him?" Mama asked.

Stella didn't want to recall those early, lonely nights she'd spent when she'd first arrived at Stanford, crying into her pillow, the ache without him almost too much to bear.

"Yes."

But now, even if she wanted to try to explain, that version of Henry was gone. And just as it had happened with the rest of her family, she hadn't paid close enough attention until the damage was nearly beyond repair.

She and Mama settled into their cups of cocoa, moving on to lighter topics like Mama's plan to buy a new comforter set to cheer up her bedroom. They chatted into the evening, Stella actively pushing the stress from her mind and settling into the conversation. The Christmas tree and the crackling fire gave Stella a little burst of festiveness, and both she and Mama decided that it would probably be a good idea to work on the parade.

"You seem to have most of the regular entrants registered for the parade and you have a grand marshal—someone named Jackson Cole," Stella said with her laptop on her knees, her legs folded under her on the sofa. Her eyes were heavy, the jet lag still hanging on. She really needed to be thinking about how to pull her second article together in a matter of weeks. And she had to finalize the one from St. Thomas' before sending it in for edits, which meant pressing the doctor in London to send her the final study she was waiting for. Plus, she still hadn't spoken fully to Lily, and she'd like to track her down and try to convince her to come home.

Mama set another mug of hot cocoa on the table in front of her and sat next to Stella, holding her cup as if it were a security blanket. As she took in Mama's weary face, Stella knew she needed to get this worry off her mother's plate first, before she tackled anything else.

Pop's voice floated into her mind. *"Everything will work out."*

A rush of fondness for her father fell over her. "You always say that," she'd challenged him once when she was about seventeen. "How do you know it will?"

"Because it has less to do with reality and more to do with how you perceive it."

"I don't follow."

"When you get to be my age, you realize that everything really does work out exactly how it's supposed to. The bumps and bruises heal, the tests in school come and go, and your uncertainties eventually fall away. One day you'll look back and realize that the tiny blip that kept you up through the night all those years ago has been consumed by the years that have buried it. So you do your best in the moment and know that everything will end up the way it was meant to be."

But he hadn't been referring to all the big things, the things that weighed on her mind. Those wouldn't work out, would they?

"Okay," she said to Mama, picking up her mug and returning to the task at hand. She blew the steam from the top of the chocolaty liquid. "Let's take a look at who's entered so we can send out confirmation emails and build the lineup."

"I'm so happy you're here," Mama said, a crack of emotion in her voice. Planning the parade had always been one of Pop's favorite jobs, and even sitting next to Stella while she handled it seemed to be difficult for her mom.

"I wish Lily could be with us," said Stella.

"Me too," Mama said.

Stella set down her hot chocolate and pulled out her phone. No missed calls. At the end of the day, she couldn't be as upset with her sister as she'd like. Stella had run off herself. The burden of her choices again fell over her. She could feel her father's hand on her wrist even now when she thought about the day she'd come home after leaving Henry. Having heard her sobs, Pop had come into her room and sat down next to her on the bed.

"I never imagined you and Henry would split up," he'd said as he patted her arm.

"I need to get out and see the world." She wiped away an angry tear.

Pop brushed a golden curl from her face. "Dreams are like the sails of a ship. You have to run full speed to blow life into them, and then, before you know it, whoosh! You're sailing and all the hard decisions you made will be worth the work."

But now, looking back, were they always?

"I'm sorry I missed so many holidays," she said to her mother.

Mama set her mug on the table. "You didn't miss them."

"I didn't come long enough to really spend time with you and Pop." The fire crackled and popped between them while remorse took hold of Stella.

"But you were working."

"That's a poor excuse for not spending time with family."

"No, it's not." She took Stella's hand. "As a parent, all I've ever wanted was for you kids to feel successful and inspired as adults. Your dad's job and mine was to give you the foundation to do that, and then we let you go."

"But at the end of the day, a job doesn't love us back. The people in our lives do. We shouldn't waste an extra minute on anything but family." She was saying the words, but her father's voice was speaking them into her mind as if he were driving home the truth for her.

*I hear you*, she thought. *If only Lily could too*. But, then again, maybe Lily was busy building the foundation for her own family, something Stella had failed at.

# Chapter Seven

Stella made her way to Vanderbilt Hospital to begin her second session with Henry. The morning sun peeked through the gray clouds, shining a beam of white light onto the dashboard, but it did nothing to diminish her anxiety about seeing him again. The drive felt quick, her contemplations rolling around in her head the whole way there, eating up any opportunity to consider the length of the journey. Unsure if she wanted to continue with the research, given the unique situation, she'd pondered alternatives for her second article, but she reminded herself that with the holiday, other opportunities were nonexistent.

On arrival, she rushed through the automatic sliding doors, stopped at the main desk to get her visitor's badge, and headed for the therapy wing to check in with Dr. Astley, something she'd been instructed to do each day before therapy sessions.

"How was yesterday?" the doctor asked from behind her desk.

While Stella considered how to answer, the doctor's gaze remained on her computer as she continued.

"Ms. Weixel said the patient gave you a bit of a start." She pulled off her reading glasses and peered over her computer with a sympathetic squint.

"Yes." He was definitely a surprise. Stella shrugged off her thick winter coat and draped it over her arm. "I used to... know him," she admitted. "Do you feel comfortable with that?"

The doctor came around the desk and then leaned against it. "I'm not sure if that's a conflict of interest or not. It's your article, so it's your call."

Stella considered whether the doctor was giving her an out, and she was very close to taking it. But leaving wasn't an option. Not if she wanted that promotion. "Given that he doesn't remember me as an adult, and he's totally different now from the person I knew, I think it's fine."

Dr. Astley nodded. "Good. Well, I'll let you head on back then."

Slightly more jittery than she should be, Stella left the office and walked down to the therapy room for their hour-long session, relieved that she didn't hear any shouting this time. When she entered, Henry was the only one in the room. He was on the sofa, his lips set in a straight line as he stared out the window. She peered past him to see the tips of grass beginning to show through the melted snow and ice. He didn't greet her, and her heart ached just a little.

"It's hard to believe the storm that knocked me in the ditch is now just slush on the roads," she said as she got situated.

Henry didn't answer, nor did he glance her way.

"Thank you for saving us the other night," she said anyway.

He finally looked her up and down with that scowl that seemed to belong to this version of him, but there was a slight softness in his assessment that reminded her the old Henry was still in there somewhere.

She looked away and opened her laptop.

"I have no idea what you're going to get from sitting in on this. It's a total crock," he said.

"Glad we're all here," Ms. Weixel interrupted, swishing into the room. "How are we today?"

Henry stared at the therapist, silent.

"We're safe and healthy—that's good," Ms. Weixel said.

Henry exhaled and Stella typed: *Gonna be a fun morning.*

"Okay." Ms. Weixel walked over to the counter and picked up the office iPad. "Yesterday you mentioned your frustration with this situation. I think it might be helpful if we delve into emotional regulation today."

The therapist sat in the chair opposite the sofa and then filled in some information on the tablet, while Stella typed *Emotional Regulation* as a header on her document. Henry's gaze moved from the therapist to her, their typing seeming to irritate him.

Ms. Weixel looked at up. "I understand that this is frustrating, Henry. But your reality is that you're safe, out of harm's way, and with people you can trust."

At the word *trust*, Stella held her breath, her cheeks flaming with heat. If he could remember, he might not agree with that statement. She bit her lip, their final moment under the oak tree floating back into her memory. He turned his attention to her, curiosity in his stare. She looked back down at her laptop.

"It's important that we begin to challenge those initial feelings of anger," Ms. Weixel continued. "Let's see if we can attempt to reframe your perspective."

Henry rolled his gaze from Stella to Ms. Weixel.

"How do you feel right now?"

He looked back over at Stella, his eyebrows pulling together in confusion, not responding to the therapist's question.

"Can you label your current emotion?" Ms. Weixel pushed on.

Stella silently urged him to answer.

"Lost," he finally said without looking away from Stella.

Her heart breaking for him, she almost forgot she was taking notes. Quickly, she typed his response, considering how bewildered he'd been the day she left him. Feeling lost probably wasn't much of a change from then, although that was for a different reason. At the young age of eighteen, she'd imagined they would both move on, get over the breakup, and one day, when they were in their mid-forties, maybe they could laugh about it. What she hadn't planned for was the hole it left in her heart and the way she'd compared everyone she'd dated since to him.

"Good answer. That's a very honest response." Ms. Weixel clasped her hands together. "Can you elaborate?"

"Sometimes I feel like the military fits me and sometimes I don't."

"What part of it fits you?" the therapist asked.

"The thrill of the hunt. But other than that, I'm... confused. A job in the military is such an honorable thing; it isn't something to take lightly. But I have this strange feeling that I just jumped into it without realizing what it entailed. I can't put my finger on what the feeling is exactly. But it's as if I don't understand myself or my motives."

"Okay," Ms. Weixel said, "well, rather than going straight into the things that confuse you, let's focus on the things about your personality that you are sure of. When do you feel the calmest?"

Henry glanced at Stella again, and she wondered if her being there might be impeding his recovery, but then he answered.

"Sometimes I drive along the dirt road by our farm. On sunny days, I roll down the windows and punch the gas. That seems like me... whoever I am these days."

Stella dipped her head behind her laptop, pretending to type as an unexpected prick of tears surprised her. She recalled a long-ago day when she'd leaned against his tailgate and he'd brushed a curl out of her face before leaning in and pressing his lips to hers.

❋

"Yeeew!" Henry's friend Tobias yelled from the open passenger window of another truck as it sped past, distracting them.

"Hang on one second." Henry took Stella's hand and brought her over to the open door. "Hop in!"

She climbed up and scooted to the passenger side.

Henry jumped into the driver's seat. He grabbed her by the waist, nibbling her neck, making her laugh. "Tobias owes me twenty bucks and I know where he's going. It's on the way home anyway."

While Stella fumbled for her seat belt, Henry took off, following the truck out of town, both gaining speed as they hit the dirt road.

"You ain't gettin' away that fast!" Henry yelled out the window.

Stella could see Tobias's wide smile in his rearview mirror as they closed in on him.

"All this over twenty dollars?" she asked with a giggle. Her hair blew out the open window, the wind rippling her sundress.

"It was a good game of pool."

She reached over and put her hand on the gold stubble of his face. "You don't need those twenty bucks," she said. "You've got all you need right here."

Those sapphire eyes landed on her. Tobias's truck pulled away, leaving a cloud of dust between the two vehicles as Henry's decelerated to a stop.

"You're right," he said before pulling her in for another kiss. "I hope the two of us drive this road together until we're so old we can't even see it anymore." Then he hit the gas again, making her yelp in surprise. "I can see it now, though!"

She laughed again, pawing for the door handle to steady herself.

They bumped down the lane kicking up dust behind them, the buttercups sliding past on both sides in a yellow blur as they sped into the sunset.

"Do you feel any other emotions right now?" the therapist asked, cutting into Stella's memory.

"Angry," he whispered.

"Can you tell me why you feel angry? Are you able to pinpoint the catalyst for your frustration?"

"I wake up every morning and I don't remember what I like to do and what I don't. I have no friends here that I can recall because I don't know who I was still friends with as an adult, and even when I try to connect with people from my old life, they feel like complete strangers. That's frustrating."

"I can imagine."

Stella, who'd been working to get herself together, jotted down the notes, taking advantage of this moment of transparency from Henry. At least they were getting somewhere today. Even if it was utter torture to relive the wonderful days before she'd ruined everything.

"I'd like you to try to compartmentalize the side of you that you don't remember. Let's focus on the person you are now. What do you like to do first when you wake up in the morning?"

"Eat."

A huff of laughter unexpectedly escaped Stella's lips. She pretended to cough to cover it up when both heads turned toward her. "Sorry," she said. He always liked to eat right away—as soon as his feet hit the floor. He was a bottomless pit in the morning. She dared not think about how he used to bring her breakfast in bed…

Ms. Weixel offered her a gracious smile before she turned back to Henry and continued. "What you might discover is that the things you like and do now could be the same things you did before the accident. You can find peace in the routines that come naturally for you."

Henry didn't respond, but the tightness in his jaw lessened, and Stella wondered if Ms. Weixel's suggestion had helped him. She jotted it down in her notes, thinking it would be a good strategy to research, to see if there was any further information on channeling natural routines.

The rest of the therapy session was devoted to strategies for emotional regulation, where the therapist assisted Henry in finding a quiet spot where he could go if he felt overwhelmed, labeling his emotions, sitting with those emotions, and pinpointing his triggers. Even though he was participating, a couple times he peered over at Stella and shook his head subtly to let her know he wasn't buying any of it.

When the session was over, he gathered his coat and hat, and rushed out.

"Sorry if I disturbed the session today," Stella said to the therapist.

Ms. Weixel smiled at her. "It was interesting. I noticed how he reacts to you. Your presence seems to bring his frustration down."

"Really?" Stella put on her coat and slipped her handbag onto her shoulder.

"He didn't shout once today, and he frequently does. He was also much more open than he usually is."

They walked toward the door, and Stella couldn't help but feel a glimmer of hope that maybe—somehow—Henry might be okay.

# Chapter Eight

When Stella got to the car after Henry's therapy session, she checked her phone, finding a text from an hour ago. It was a photo of Lily in a white dress, wearing a ring of flowers around her mass of blonde waves. Her arms were around a man with an olive complexion, a wide, gleaming smile and sparkling green eyes, dressed in a tuxedo. They each had confetti in their hair, which looked like a dusting of snow. The message said, "This is Mateo. I adore him."

She tried to text her sister back, asking for more details, but her message was marked undeliverable once more. With a sigh, she slipped the phone into her pocket and started the engine.

Her spirits lifted quickly when she reached the main drag in town, the small stretch of Old Hillsboro Road that she knew so well. It was lined on both sides with quaint wooden art galleries and Southern shops—all of them elegantly decorated in holiday greenery, the remnants of the storm shimmering on either side of the road as if leading her home.

For the first time, the appeal of the area hit her. Growing up there, she hadn't been able to see its worth—it was just a part of her—but now, after traveling the world, she could view it through a new lens. She slowed the car at the weedy corner where she'd always sat to eat her ice cream from the café down the road as one particular day came to mind.

"There's a skill to it," seventeen-year-old Stella told Henry as they sat there, the shade from the maple tree that covered the corner still no match for the blazing summer sun. "You have to lick it all the way around." She ran her tongue along the edge of her ice cream, catching the drips, until it had flattened in the cone. "Then you bite off the bottom and eat up to the top." She nibbled the small waffle cone from its point.

Henry did the same, but his cone broke open, sending melting ice cream down his arm. "How did you do that?" he asked as he wiped his forearm against his shirt. "I'm all sticky."

Stella popped the last of her cone into her mouth and held out her clean hands. After swallowing, she said, "Not everyone is a master ice cream eater."

Henry cut his eyes at her, a grin surfacing. "True," he said. "Let me give you a big hug to celebrate how great you are." He held out his sticky hands toward her.

Stella jumped up, squealing as she ran down the sidewalk. "Get away!"

"Why? I'm just celebrating your skill!" He chased and pawed at her while she dodged him.

A car came up behind her, forcing her mind from the memory. Stella pressed the gas, and Leiper's Fork gave way to the countryside. She was approaching the pop-up Christmas tree farm, decked out with its signature red trailer, booths of games and holiday wares, and the swirling sign that simply read: *Christmas*.

The business had gotten its singular name because the town didn't decorate for Christmas until the lot was up, so it wasn't *Christmas* until then. Making the first visit on the day it opened every year had been a tradition for her family. Then, when she'd gotten older, she and Henry went together, but they still made sure to meet her family there.

One of the booths offered chocolate-covered candy canes of every size and shape. She and Henry used to get a different kind each year. Another vendor brought an array of fudge in unusual flavors, like buttered popcorn and caramel latte, and served it warm with a tall glass of milk. She saw the Holiday Hoops stall from the road, and the memory of the feel of Henry's strong hands holding hers washed over her.

Their last Christmas together, she'd come home to the guest cabin behind his mom's farmhouse after her shift at the diner and found a piece of paper taped to the door that read: *Meet me at Christmas*. After untying her apron, she hung it on the banister of the porch and got back in the car, heading to the tree lot. Her feet were sore from working, her shoulders tired, but there was no way she'd miss spending time with Henry.

"We can definitely win if we do the red hoop," Henry had said with a devious glint in his eyes when she found him at the Holiday Hoops booth. He reached over and took a wide red Hula-Hoop from the hook on the side of the stall.

Stella eyed it suspiciously. "So we both have to keep it going together?"

"Easy." He handed a dollar to the attendant and "Rockin' Around the Christmas Tree" poured from the speakers. Henry stepped closer to Stella and slipped the hoop around them. Then he pressed their bodies together. "When I say 'go,' hula to the right." After a kiss on her lips that tasted of peppermint, he said, "Go!"

They began to move their hips together, their thick coats cumbersome, and when she started to giggle, he grabbed her hands, looking into her eyes with that grin on his face, doing most of the work to keep the hoop spinning at their waists.

"Keep going," he said as the timer clicked away in digital numbers. "We just have to get to ten and we win." He caressed her cold fingers with his, their hips going in circles.

She'd worked an entire shift, but she barely noticed her fatigue when Henry's attention was on her. With one smile, he could wipe away all the long hours. The clock clicked seven, eight, nine...

"Ten!" the attendant called out.

The hoop fell to the ground.

"Which bear would you like?" Henry waved at the array of stuffed animals, all clad in various Christmas outfits.

Stella attempted to study her options, but Henry distracted her, wrapping his arms around her and stealing kisses, his cold lips making her shiver.

The hoops that day had been one of her favorite memories, one of the last of happy times before the weather turned warm and everything changed.

She drove past rows of dark-green trees with strings of lights above them, and she slowed again to really take it in. It had been another interesting day with Henry, and she wanted nothing more than to enjoy the sights of Christmas to get her mind off the article, Henry, and her family worries.

*"Christmas is what family's all about. It's the season of happiness."* Her dad's voice seemed to be finding her quite a bit since she'd been home. She hoped she wasn't letting him down. With Lily out of the country and Stella working so much, she wasn't doing a very good job of bringing their family together. Maybe being happy was just too difficult for her, given what had happened here.

When she passed the last row of trees, she nearly came to a stop in the middle of the street. Henry's truck was parked in the lot, and he was walking the aisle, looking the trees up and down. She felt as if she'd gone back in time. His gait was the same, his broad frame moving in a slight swagger as he walked. For a second, she thought he might turn around and grin at her like he had all those years ago, maybe make a silly face, or run toward her with that flirty look in his eyes, but then she reminded herself that she'd lost that Henry.

Something caught his attention, and he looked up and locked eyes with her through the windshield. Then, tentatively, he raised his hand to wave hello, a gesture she'd never expected from this Henry. She eased the car to the side of the road and rolled down her window.

"Decorating?" she called to him, taking a chance at lighter banter though completely unsure how he'd respond. The least she could do was to be friendly.

He didn't answer, but after a moment of what looked like deliberation, he motioned for her to join him.

While she'd much rather climb into a warm pair of pajamas and curl up by the fire, she complied, turning into the tree lot, and putting the car in park. She got out, cinched her coat tighter against her neck to combat the cold, and trudged through the slush to where Henry was standing.

"I don't have a tree," he said without a hello as he scrutinized the one in front of him. "Mary Jo told me I should get one on the way home to spruce up my cabin, and I think it would make her happy to see me trying." He appeared completely out of sorts. His lips were downturned, his shoulders hunched near his ears. The old Henry would have adored looking for a tree.

A shot of guilt hit her in the gut. Stella knew that cabin like the back of her hand. It was where she and Henry had lived while they planned renovation ideas for the farmhouse they were going to buy and restore once they were on their feet financially. The farmhouse that never had a chance to materialize.

"You might find that it will lift *your* spirits too," she suggested softly.

He yanked his gaze from the tree, his eyes landing on her once more.

"I know the cabin pretty well. If you let me know where you and Mary Jo are planning to put the tree I could help you choose one."

"We want to put it in the bay window."

"Okay," she said, trying to slow her racing heart. "You mean those big windows in the den with the window seat?"

He stared at her, his shoulders still tense. He seemed uneasy that she knew such a personal detail about his living quarters.

"I think it *would* look nice in that spot," she agreed, biting back a swell of emotion, recalling the live Fraser fir they'd put there together. He'd insisted on a fish ornament that had made her cringe every time she looked at it. After lengthy debates, her love for him won out, and she'd hung that ridiculous thing on the tree front and center. When he saw it, he'd come up behind her, wrapped his arms around her waist and kissed her neck under her ear, making her simultaneously squeal and pull him closer.

Stella forced the thought out of her mind quickly before she made him more uncomfortable with her tears. Standing opposite him was proving more difficult by the minute. His mere presence forced her to acknowledge her actions in the life she'd run from, and even after all these years, she still wasn't ready to come to terms with it.

He started walking and she joined him, the two of them moving through the lines of trees, their breaths puffing out in front of them, the smell of pine tickling her nose. She wondered what she was doing there with him, why he'd waved her over in the first place. But then she remembered he didn't have many memories of friends or neighbors; perhaps he'd just been relieved to recognize someone he could ask. Part of her wished she could let go of all the memories they'd made, watch them fly into the air like helium balloons until they disappeared, but then she'd have to give up the good ones too, and she didn't know if she'd ever want to let those go.

Henry paced along, row after row, studying the different trees. Stella wasn't sure if this pairing was the best for her psyche. As she walked next to him, the pang of longing, of missing out on the life she might have led, took hold.

They entered another row of trees and he stopped in front of one. "This one," he said.

A Fraser fir.

She looked up at him, the old Henry somewhere in there, locked away. She wondered what it would feel like to have his arms around her again. But accessing the old him would be both a blessing and a curse. While the smiling, carefree man might return, she'd have no choice but to face the fact that she'd known him all her life—loved him—and hadn't had the decency to give him a real explanation for leaving. She couldn't have. Not back then. He would have tried to make her stay, and she loved him enough that he probably would have convinced her. It didn't matter. That Henry wasn't in front of her now. In both instances, she'd lost.

Now she was facing a brand-new future with him. Henry had been through so much in the last few years, and his struggles were unfathomable. She had to put aside their past and get to know this version of him. He needed a friend—support—as he moved through this new reality. She owed him that much.

"I'll go pay for the tree," he said, taking his wallet from his back pocket and pulling the tag from a branch.

She followed him, and as they walked together in silence, he stopped briefly by the Holiday Hoops booth. The prizes had barely changed in thirteen years, making her heart patter. The skin between his eyebrows creased as if he was confused.

"Do you remember something?" she asked.

He shook his head. "No. Why, should I?"

She glanced at a bear with a little green vest and red bowtie, wishing so many things could've gone differently.

"No reason that I know of," she lied to spare him. "What were you just thinking about?"

"Mary Jo's finishing up with the farmhands and she's gonna be tired. Do you think you could…"

He seemed unsure, and so was she, but she pushed him to finish what he wanted to say.

"Could I what?"

"Could you help me decorate it? I'd be terrible at it."

"Sure."

But truth be told, she wasn't entirely sure at all. However, given what she knew of him since he'd returned, this was the first time he'd asked anyone for anything. Plus he hadn't shouted or snapped at her, and he was buying a Christmas tree to make his sister happy, for goodness' sake. He was trying.

Stella pulled to a stop under the oak tree, behind Henry's truck, and took a deep breath before getting out of her car. The old log cabin, built in a little clearing in the woods behind the farmhouse, looked the same as the day she'd left it. The two rocking chairs on the covered porch where she and Henry had sat in the warmer months were still there, now holding remnants of snow, void of the holiday cheer she would've added. The front doormat she'd bought, weathered from the years, also remained.

Henry hopped into the back of the truck and untied the tree, then hopped down and pulled it from the bed. He reached in and grabbed hold of the trunk before hoisting it over his shoulder, half the tree dragging on the ground as he moved along the little pathway to the porch. If he were anyone else, she'd worry they'd slip, but not Henry. He'd always had an uncanny ability to stay on his feet. As a boy, he could climb a tree in a flash, his balance so steady he could make it all the way to the thin branches at the top with barely a misstep. He used to call her to join him, but she never could, only making it about halfway.

One day, when they were sixteen, he'd climbed up and stopped on a thick bottom branch while she'd clambered up beside him. They sat there, legs dangling above the ground.

"Why do you climb so high?" she'd asked while gripping the tree.

"Because I can see the whole world from up there," he'd said.

She'd looked out at her limited view, considering this. "Then why didn't you climb to the top today?"

He gazed into her eyes. "Because I can see my whole world from right here too."

That was the day he'd kissed her for the first time and their friendship had exploded into so much more.

Refocusing on the present, Stella watched the front door open and the last of the tree brushing the edges of the doorway before it disappeared inside. After taking a quick second to prepare herself, she walked up the three stairs and into the house she'd once shared with Henry.

# Chapter Nine

As her vision adjusted to the low light, she was suddenly unsteady on her feet. She closed the door, then walked to the sofa and sat down, frantically blinking away the tears springing to her eyes. Henry was fitting the fir into their old metal tree stand and hadn't noticed.

Stella took slow breaths to try to quell her emotions, but with each inhale she got a familiar noseful of cedar mixed with the scent of lavender and earth from the farm, prompting a deluge of feelings. She remembered waking up in the crisp sheets of their shared bed, the diamond ring and wedding band still new on her finger, and the morning sun streaming through the window of the bedroom. She leaned forward from the sofa to get a glimpse of that room, the foot of the bed visible through the doorway, and she felt as if the wind had been knocked out of her. She wouldn't think about that room. She couldn't.

Still unaware of her silent breakdown, Henry went into the kitchen and turned on the faucet. The tree stood strong in the center of the bay window overlooking the rolling Tennessee hills out back. She squinted, imagining it fully decorated, the way she'd done it their first Christmas, but that only caused more tears. She cleared her throat and tried to focus on something else, but everywhere she looked was another memory.

A knock at the door ripped her from her inner turmoil.

"Can you get that?" Henry called from the kitchen.

"Yeah, I'll get it," she replied, then cleared her throat, trying desperately to get herself together.

When she opened the door, Mary Jo was on the other side.

"Hey, Stella," she said, appearing confused, but then wrinkling her nose and grinning. "Where's Henry?"

"The kitchen."

"Hey, Henry!" his sister called.

Henry's deep voice floated into the entryway over the running water. "Hey. I'll be in, in a sec. I'm just trying to get the sap off my fingers."

Mary Jo turned to Stella. "I didn't know you were coming over."

Stella moved to the side as Mary Jo entered. "I didn't expect to be here."

Mary Jo stepped into the small entryway and peered through the opening to the living room. "I can't believe he actually got a tree. I saw the truck go by the house. And I recognized your car following."

"He asked me to help him decorate the tree. He never was any good at it…" Divulging her thoughts, voicing the tiny shard of a memory after so many years, made her feel vulnerable, even if it was to Mary Jo.

Mary Jo huffed out a laugh, sharing her amusement at the comment. "He could've just asked me to help once I finished with the farmhands," Mary Jo said. "Did he actually call you?"

"I was driving by Christmas and he stopped me."

Mary Jo nodded. "Right place, right time."

They moved closer to the tree, the conversation fading. There wasn't any more to say, really, and Stella wondered if it was as hard for Mary Jo to navigate this moment as it was for her. Then her eyes fell on the chair in the corner and the blood drained out of her. Her old books were still stacked on the table next to it. Had Henry never moved them? She walked over and thumbed through the top one just before he came back into the room, holding a cup of water, with a kitchen towel over his shoulder.

"Oh, hey," he said to Mary Jo.

His sister put her hands in the pockets of her jeans. "Hey."

"Anything good?" he asked, looking at Stella.

His tone was flat, that ever-present frustration lingering under the surface despite the normalcy that permeated the space. Any onlooker wouldn't think a thing about the three of them standing in this cabin together, ready to decorate a tree for the holiday, but there was so much more going on.

Stella closed the book and ran her finger over the cover. "Um… Yes. I've read this one," she said as she placed it back in its spot.

"They came with the house, or at least that's how it feels," Henry said before he crawled under the tree and filled the stand with water. "They seem a little girly for me, so I'm guessing they were left by a lady friend or something."

Stella eyed Mary Jo, swallowing hard to push the lump in her throat back down.

"Mary Jo, you don't know whose they might be?" he asked.

"I don't know," Mary Jo replied.

Stella gave her a loaded look, wondering about her motives.

"It's not really important anymore, is it? Since they must belong to someone from the past," Mary Jo said, raising her eyebrows and daring Stella for a rebuttal.

"What if the *someone* is important?" Stella asked.

Henry righted himself and set the empty water cup on the table.

"I think we all have lots of paths in life, and it's up to us to figure out who's important to us," Mary Jo replied, folding her arms. "Henry, do you need any help, or do the two of you have things under control?"

"We're good," Henry said.

"All right." She leaned over to Stella. "Come by the house and see me sometime."

"Okay."

After Mary Jo left, Henry turned to Stella. "How do you know which path to pick?"

"What?"

"Mary Jo said we have lots of paths in life, and it seemed like you agreed. How do you know which one's the right one?"

She considered his question and chose to answer with why she'd taken her own path, leaving him. "Well, for me and probably most of us, we take the path of least resistance."

"I get that," he said. "It's why I'm putting up a tree. Because it's the path of least resistance, and it makes my sister happy." He stared off as if his thoughts were consuming him, those stormy eyes full of concern. "I've got some boxes in the attic labeled 'Christmas.' I'll bring them down."

After he left the room, she sat on the edge of the sofa, taking in more deep breaths. So much had happened in the last few days. She was still herself, yet everything had changed, and she was aware of all that was lost. Was this how Henry felt?

"Hey, have you ever seen one of these before?" Henry asked when he returned.

He'd lugged in her old wooden potter's wheel. She observed the contraption about the size of a large suitcase with new eyes. Perhaps the dimensions she remembered had been skewed to encompass the magnitude of love she had for the machine. The turning platform had seemed so big when she was a girl, but now it was as if it were in miniature, resting only a few feet above the floor. The iron rods and metal bearing were discolored with age.

"I have," she replied. "You make pottery with it."

"You used to do that when you were a kid," he said. "You made plates and mugs."

"Yes, I did." She rose and walked over to him, trying to guess how long it had been since she'd stopped using it. About fourteen years ago, she decided. "This is actually mine. One of the metal bearings had come loose, and you promised to fix it." Wanting to move it to her new home at the cabin anyway, they had put it into Henry's truck and brought it here. She'd left only a few days later.

Henry ran his hand along the loose carriage. "Right here," he said. "This is what needs to be fixed."

"Yep."

"I'd forgotten it was you who made pottery."

"I used to love it."

"What made you stop?"

Phew. That was certainly a loaded question. "I just… got too busy." Busy with falling in love, busy getting married, then busy with trying to carry on despite what she was going through, pushing away her feelings for Henry.

"That's too bad." He lifted the contraption into his strong arms easily. "I'll leave it in the attic until I have a chance to look at it. Maybe I can fix it after all, and you can try your hand at it again."

She smiled, their old world colliding with their new one. "That would be nice."

"Be right back with some Christmas decorations."

"All right," Stella said.

Henry returned with a stack of boxes and set them on the floor. He pulled out a string of lights and plugged them in to test them. They lit up in bright colors just as they had the last time she'd wrapped them around a tree. While he checked each of the bulbs, it occurred to her that he was going through the motions, but the absolute joy he used to have doing this task was absent.

She wanted to tell him that they'd blared holiday music while they decorated together that last time and that he'd pulled her into the middle of the room and dipped her, nearly setting the house on fire when he knocked over one of her cinnamon candles. She eyed the dark spot still on the rug where he'd stomped out the flame before they fell on the sofa together in relief.

Henry picked up the lights and reached toward the top of the tree.

"Wait," she said.

He stopped and looked her way.

"It's Christmas." She walked over to the radio. "We shouldn't decorate the tree without some music." If anything, the sound would lift her mood and take her mind off the fact that this Christmas was very different from any other. She clicked on the radio and tuned it to the local station playing festive music on a twenty-four-hour loop.

Without a reaction, Henry tried again to reach the highest part of the tree. As he worked, Stella could feel his inability to relax, and she considered that, apart from the accident, she didn't have a clue what he might have gone through in the military. She remembered once more what Dr. Astley had said when they met: *"The subject experiences conflicting information about things he has done in his life that directly oppose his values."*

For her article on cognitive dissonance, she'd studied the effects of brain health on people who chose to do things that didn't fit their beliefs. One patient had been battling lung cancer and he had struggled so much with the diagnosis because he'd chosen to smoke even though he'd known that smoking was bad for his health. Faced with the repercussions of his actions, he had to undergo therapy to manage the intense remorse. What had Henry dealt with in his recent past that conflicted with his values?

He wound the lights along a branch at the top, the cord hanging loosely to the ground. "I'm not sure how to do this," he said over the music. His eyebrows pulled together. "Have I ever known?"

She went over to him and took the strand. "Well, if it makes you feel any better, I can confirm that you didn't know how to do it before your accident either." She offered him a consolatory grin.

"Have we done this before?"

"Yes. I helped you decorate a tree a long time ago..." Curiosity appeared in his expression, but she didn't want to answer any questions, so she moved the conversation along. "Do you mind bringing in one of the kitchen chairs so I can reach the top?"

His gaze lingered on her before he turned away and retrieved a chair. He set it next to the tree and she climbed up on it.

"The trick," she said as the music pulsed, "is to wind the lights in and out of the branches." She pushed the strand into the center, encircled one of the limbs and then wound it back out. She continued—in and out—around the tree. "Could you hold this for a second while I move the chair?"

He came up from behind, leaning around her and taking the lights, his familiar woodsy scent overwhelming her senses. She wanted to turn around and wrap her arms around his neck, but she knew better. He needed to focus on his recovery, and she should definitely not let her memories contribute to impulsive decisions. She climbed down, scooted the chair into the correct position, and then took the lights back from him.

"So..." He gathered the cord that trailed the floor. "We were... friends?"

She found it difficult to pull in a full breath of air. "Yes," she managed. She wasn't lying. For many years, they were just friends.

"There are things about the adult you that feel familiar sometimes," he said. "I can't quite pinpoint it, but every now and then, something in the way you walk or the look you give me—it's as if I can almost feel the recollection surfacing, but I can't quite reach it."

With the brightly colored strand of lights in her hands, she faced him. He looked up at her, so many questions in his eyes, then turned away.

Stella went back to stringing the tree before she did something she shouldn't and poured her heart out to him. With the music jingling, she continued, strand after strand, until the tree was covered in bright, happy lights. She moved the chair and stepped back to view her work. "How's that?"

"It's good. Thank you."

"You're welcome." She slid her hands into her pockets and admired the tree in the big bay window that used to be hers. "I should probably get home," she suggested. She'd suffocate on her buried memories if she stayed any longer.

"That feeling, it's happening right now," Henry said, his face crumpled in confusion. "There's something about you standing here by this tree that feels… natural."

It was anything but. Nothing about them as adults was normal.

His attention slowly turned to the bedroom door and then back to her, something else possibly registering. She kept her focus on his face, blinking to keep the view of the bedroom out of her peripheral vision. She wasn't sure of her expression, but whatever he saw in her eyes caused him to look back at the bedroom door once more. Her heart felt as if it would burst right from her chest; her hands began to shake. Right then the one deep memory she'd tried so hard to run from all these years assaulted her before she could rein it in.

"Remember when I said I helped you decorate a tree before? It was a lot like this one," she said, trying to keep herself together. *Continue talking about the tree.* "Perhaps that's why."

"Yeah." He nodded, but an interest deep behind his gaze made her even more nervous.

She clicked off the radio. "Well, I'll see you tomorrow at the hospital." She needed to get out of there. Her old life was swallowing her up, and if she stood across from Henry much longer, she wasn't sure she'd have the strength to maintain her composure.

"See ya," he said.

She went to the front door and let herself out, keeping her gaze straight ahead. Her heart hammered. When she got into her car, it took everything she had not to gasp for breath and sob into her shaking hands.

She'd refused to think of the memory of that horrible moment in the bedroom for so long—until she was faced with it today, the vision of it slamming into her temples. She squeezed her eyes shut to keep the mental image at bay, but it burst through anyway, as if trying to break its way out of her mind: the cramps, the menstrual cycle she wasn't sure she should be having, the negative test that had been positive only a few days before…

Sitting in her car now, she felt as if she might not survive the one secret she'd been holding for her entire adult life: she wasn't capable of having children. The doctor's voice had been eerily tranquil as she told Stella, *"You have a uterine malformation that will make carrying a child to term nearly impossible."*

She'd never told a soul except her doctor about anything—the pregnancy or the loss of it. And until today, she'd been able to keep running, to put miles between herself and all the reminders, to fill her days with new cities and people in an attempt to drown it out.

How would she ever be able to face Henry tomorrow?

❄

"Took you a while to get home from the hospital," Mama said when Stella walked in.

"I stopped by Christmas." She stripped off her winter garb and relished the warmth of inside.

"That's festive." Her mother breezed past her, patting her on the back as she headed into the kitchen.

Stella followed, still in a cloud of unease.

"What were you hoping to find?"

She had no idea what she'd been hoping to find by going to Henry's. Her mind still on what she'd just left, she could barely process her mother's question. "What?"

"At the Christmas tree farm. What were you looking for?"

"Oh. Nothing really. I just thought it would be nice to walk around," she lied, still unable to face the events of that fateful day that were pouring through her mind like a torrent.

"Well, the cold temperatures have done a number on you. You're white as a ghost! I know what will fix it: I'll make you some hot cinnamon cream tea and then we can get to work on the parade. Having you working on it with me gives me strength..."

Her mother kept talking, but Stella was still distracted and didn't hear any of it. Her eyes had landed on the diamond necklace that was stretched out on the kitchen table. It seemed to shimmer defiantly, reminding her of its curse.

Right now, the bad luck that it supposedly carried didn't seem too far-fetched. She'd had burning coffee spilled on her in its presence, returned to an almost empty family home except for her grieving mother, had barely enough to work with on Henry's case to write her second piece, and now… Now she was dealing with old skeletons in her closet.

She reached over and picked up the necklace, the delicate chain hanging from her finger, as she wondered if it hadn't been lost by someone at all. Perhaps it had been discarded on purpose. Part of her wanted to throw it out with the trash and never see it again, but the possible value of it stopped her. She set it back on the table.

"Here you go." Her mother handed her a mug of tea, the steam dancing above the creamy liquid, but all she could think about was whether she'd done the right thing by running away all those years ago.

It had seemed right at the time. She'd loved Henry so much that she'd wanted to give him the chance to have children with someone else. If he could have a happy life—the kind he'd imagined for himself—it would be worth her loss. If she'd stayed, would *she* have been happy, with the knowledge of her limitations? She wasn't so sure she could've been. But she couldn't shake the idea that Henry had never moved on, and if she *had* stayed, Henry would still be Henry.

# Chapter Ten

After a rocky night of sleep, Stella's very early morning began with a check of the online parade forms she and her mother had begun looking over the previous night. Only eight days away from the big day, they were still missing a few entrants. She looked down at the old list from a few years back she'd found in Pop's desk and ran her finger down the checkmarks she'd made, comparing this year's roster with that one. Would they have enough people? She didn't want to think about what might happen if she couldn't pull this off. It was more than coming through for the town; she owed it to Pop. This had always been his baby, and if she didn't make it happen for his memory, she'd never forgive herself.

She hadn't had breakfast, and after an hour or so, her mother was clinking dishes in the kitchen, but Stella didn't want to face her with the update on the number of participants just yet. She decided to stay in bed and focus on her next big problem. While working on the parade, she'd been going back and forth with the senior editor at *Brain Borders Magazine*, Amy Callahan, asking if there was any possible way she could expand upon the single article from St. Thomas' and scrap the second. She wanted to call Vanderbilt and tell them she didn't need the research after all or that it was, in fact, a conflict of interest, but her editor insisted that they needed two articles, since they were for different issues of the magazine.

Stella's next tactic was to ask if they could push back the deadline for the second article until after the holiday. She even mentioned that if they put it off, she'd consider doing a three-month stay in Amsterdam to document research on calcium signals in brain cells that Amy had suggested someone needed to do. But that idea was also shot down. She was skating on thin ice as it was, after reorganizing everything to come home early.

She lay on her belly on the bed and read over the final response from Amy: "*The magazine has paid your travel to Tennessee because you were writing the article. You have to write it. And I know you'll give this your best, since you're in the running for the President's Award. They love you so much over here that the whole team is asking to send you to Germany right after the holiday. Given your standing, it would be in your best interest to go…*"

She could almost imagine Amy gritting her teeth on the other end of that email, waiting for her to get this done. No matter how Stella tried to spin it, the painful truth was that she needed to get it written.

A knock on her door interrupted her lamenting.

"I thought I heard rustling in here," her mother said as she peeked her head in. "I'm trying to have breakfast, but I'm lonely." She gave Stella a little smile. "I put out the Christmas plates and made cinnamon rolls. Want to join me?"

Hungry and needing a break after lying in bed and working for the last few hours, Stella closed her laptop and headed to the kitchen with her mother. The table was set with Mama's favorite white plates with lace-pattern edges and Christmas trees painted in the centers. Next to them was a steaming tray of her famous homemade cinnamon rolls, the gooey icing cascading down the golden buttery sides and topped with powdered sugar.

Stella sat, then realized she'd chosen the seat next to where the Christmas Diamond still rested on the table. It glared at her, holding the story of the four stillborns and making her stomach sour.

"Mind if I put this away somewhere?" she asked, wondering if she hid it in a box, like Agnes Hastings had, her luck would change.

"If it happens to be real, we should probably keep it locked up in the safe anyway." Mama set a stack of napkins next to their plates.

Stella picked up the necklace, feeling as if the negativity were burning through her skin. "Good call."

She took it to the utility area at the back of the house, where Mama's washer and dryer were located, and over to the safe Pop had installed. She spun the dial back and forth with the combination until it opened and then gently placed the necklace on the velvet floor of the safe. Already feeling lighter, she shut the door, sealing it inside. She wished she could lock up all her problems in that box and focus on the cheerfulness of the holidays instead.

"What's the latest with the parade?" Mama asked when Stella returned, handing her a warm mug of tea.

Stella took a seat, dropped a spoonful of honey into the mug, and stirred, giving herself a minute to come up with a way to smooth over what she was about to say. But she came up empty, so she just spoke plainly.

"I've been going over it all morning, and I'm planning to spend some more time on it after I go to the hospital. But... We have a major issue that needs to be taken care of."

"What is it?"

"I've gone through all the entries. They're thin this year. And no one signed up to be Santa."

Mama's eyes rounded. "No one?"

She shook her head. "Must be busy at the North Pole," Stella said, trying to make light of the situation when it was yet one more thing sitting on her shoulders. It was as if her father were announcing his absence, putting an exclamation mark on it. "Who could we ask?"

"Ralph Watson is the only one who fits the bill, but he just had a knee replacement. There's no way he can do it." Mama served them each a cinnamon roll, the icing running onto the plates.

Stella sipped the warm, vanilla-flavored tea, the sweetness of the honey tickling her senses. "I'm almost certain it's too late to hire someone. Know anyone else whom we could ask as a favor?"

Mama shook her head. "Not offhand." Her mother leaned on her fists, her eyes glimmering with tears, and Stella knew she was worrying they'd failed Pop. The dance between doing nothing out of grief and doing it all for the same reason was evidently settling upon her mother.

Stella reached over and grabbed her hand. "It's okay. We'll work on finding a Santa." It wasn't Christmas without Santa Claus.

Mama nodded, a tear rolling down her cheek.

A few hours later, Stella entered the hospital tentatively. After her trip to Henry's cabin yesterday, she wasn't sure how to act. When she saw him today, part of her wanted to say hello and ask how his day was going so far, but she was supposed to be an observer. She *needed* to be an observer for his recovery *and* to get her article finished. Besides, talking to him would only open old wounds. Today, she'd dictate every single minute and then tonight she'd pour over her notes and find an angle for her story.

Stella hit the button for the elevator just as the old man with the walker toddled up next to her.

"Mr. Ferguson, right?" she asked, already feeling brighter just from being in his presence.

"That's right. And you're the lovely lady I met the other day. How lucky to get to see you twice."

She grinned despite herself. "Why is seeing me lucky?"

He shifted against the handles of his walker and squinted at her as if he could see something she couldn't. "You have a way about you that tells me there's more to you than what I see on the surface."

The reality of her struggles caused heat to rush through her cheeks. "What do you mean?"

The elevator pinged and the doors opened. Stella stepped in and put her arm across the opening to keep the doors from shutting as Mr. Ferguson entered in measured steps.

"I think you're special," he said with a grunt as he pushed his walker over the small lip between the floor and the elevator.

"Special? How so?"

The doors swished shut and she pressed the button for Henry's floor before gesturing to ask which floor he needed.

He waved her off, acknowledging that he was headed to the same floor. "I see enormous potential. More than you probably see yet."

The old man was clearly delusional. She doubted very seriously that she radiated some sort of potential only he could see.

"Are you a clairvoyant or something?" she teased.

Mr. Ferguson laughed, his attention on the floor numbers as they lit up on the digital monitor above the doors. "When you get to be my age, you just notice things. I see untapped potential in people, and I

96 Jenny Hale

know when they're living the life they're meant to live. It's present in their eyes and the shape of their smile."

She nodded, still skeptical of the old man. "Am I living the life I'm meant to live?"

He pursed his lips, knowingly. "Not yet." He gave her a wink.

The doors opened and he pushed the walker into the therapy wing and went on his way. She'd chalked him up as a senile old man, but his words lingered.

Henry was already on the sofa when Stella entered, his shoulders tight and that straight face he made already set. The interest in his eyes as he watched her walk over unnerved her. With a steadying breath, she kept her concentration on the unpacking of her computer and starting it. But feeling the weight of his stare, she peeked over the laptop at him.

"Are you gonna give me the chance to see what you're typing about me?"

"I don't mind sharing what I type. It's nothing you won't be able to read later. *After* your therapy maybe." She broke eye contact and focused again on her screen, pulling up the document where she'd been taking notes. In her peripheral vision, Henry leaned back, his jaw tight, his arms crossed. To her dismay, she read her comment from yesterday that was now in Henry's view: *Gonna be a fun morning.*

Would today be any better?

"All right," Ms. Weixel said, coming in and sitting in the chair opposite Henry. "Let's get right to it, shall we?"

Henry squared his shoulders.

"Tell me one thing that happened since we met yesterday that you could say was positive."

He sat, motionless.

Stella typed. *Request: produce one positive instance since yesterday's session. Response: None.*

He pressed his lips into a straight line, tensing as she typed.

"It doesn't have to be anything grand, remember?" the therapist continued.

Not wanting to type anything else to upset him and make this take any longer, Stella's hands stilled on the keyboard, and she kept her face clear of any emotion, trying to blend in to the surroundings, something she'd become great at over the years.

He turned his head just slightly to get a view of her, his face softening a little. His chest filled with air, but he still didn't answer.

"What did you have for breakfast this morning?" the therapist prompted.

He paused, not responding right away, but just as Stella was beginning to lose hope for the day, he said, "Eggs and a…"

"A what?" Ms. Weixel asked.

*A cup of coffee. That was your favorite. You have it every day*, Stella said in her head.

His lips parted and turned Stella's way as if he'd heard her inner thoughts, that look of attentiveness returning. The corners of his mouth twitched upward before he straightened them back out, his attention on Stella as if he could still read her mind. "A cup of coffee."

Stella forgot everything for that one glorious moment as she saw a tiny bit of the old Henry peek through.

He cleared his throat and turned toward the therapist. "How will talking about my choice of breakfast help me remember my life?"

"There's a relationship between thought and action," the therapist said. "By changing our thoughts to positive ones, our actions become positive, our stress is reduced, and we're more open to more robust progress on cognition."

Stella typed Ms. Weixel's explanation.

"So what are you working on?" Henry asked Stella across the room. "Some kind of study of crazy people?"

Stella gave him a look and then addressed Ms. Weixel who nodded for her to answer.

"Not a study. And definitely not about crazy people. I'm a writer for a magazine about brain health, and I'm supposed to be *observing*, not talking." She finished typing the summary of the therapist's explanation.

"Do you know *why* I can't remember?" he asked, despite her statement about being incognito.

She shook her head and looked over at the therapist again, not sure if they should be using his therapy time to discuss his question.

"The documentation we received from Henry's superior stated that Henry may have experienced frequent explosive artillery fire, and that caused what we call 'commotio cerebri.' It's a puzzling condition that can trigger headaches, difficulty concentrating or sleeping, and oddly enough, amnesia. Henry struggled with small memory issues that they'd been documenting, but then during a training exercise—"

Henry cut her off, finishing the story. "The platform I was on gave out, and a large piece of artillery equipment fell on top of me."

Ms. Weixel nodded. "It caused blunt trauma to the head and specialized memory loss."

"Including how to do my job," he added as if it pained him to say it. "So they sent me home."

"But you do have a civilian job now," the therapist pointed out. "You started a landscaping company when you got home, right?"

"Yes," he said. "But there's little to no work in the winter. And I want to do more than that anyway."

"Like what?" Ms. Weixel asked.

"I don't know." His response was riddled with frustration, and he seemed to be closing up again right in front of Stella's eyes.

Earlier, she'd been trying to think of ways not to be near him, but the distress on his face made her wish she could put her hand on his cheek and tell him she was there for him.

"Don't you need to type all that?" he asked, eyeing her laptop.

Her skin prickled from being caught in her thoughts, and she forced herself back to her document where she inputted the term "commotio cerebri" to research more in depth later.

Henry stood up. "I think we're done."

The therapist checked the time on the clock, but finished or not, Henry was already striding toward the door.

"Do you mind if I ask, what the latest research is on how commotio cerebri is treated?" Stella asked Ms. Weixel before closing her laptop.

Henry stopped at the door. "By making me talk about eggs, apparently."

Even though he'd barely given therapy a chance, and she still had nothing she needed for the article, his little joke gave her a flutter of happiness. She would've absolutely expected that answer from him.

"Hey," Henry called from his truck in the parking lot.

Despite having noticed she was near his vehicle, she would have known immediately who the voice belonged to no matter what. The way he said "hey" was the same way he used to say it when she came into a room. The edge he'd had in therapy seemed to be stripped away. She turned around.

"You get all the way here in that?" He nodded toward her Mazda parked a few vehicles down from his.

"Yes, why?"

He got out of his truck and put his hands in the pockets of his jeans, his shoulders tight, as if he wasn't quite comfortable enough yet to let his guard down with her entirely. "You didn't learn anything from the other night?"

"It's not nearly as cold and snowy as it was then." She wasn't going to let his shortness ruffle her. She reminded herself that, given his memory loss, his issues had nothing to do with this particular occasion.

"Even today, the melted snow has frozen over. You shouldn't be out without four-wheel drive."

Stella gestured to the other cars in the parking lot. "Everyone else is doing all right."

He frowned. "At the very least, people around here aren't used to this weather, and you'll need to have a vehicle that can dodge the other cars when they slide around like maniacs."

"I'll be fine," she said, his gruff concern warming her slightly. While he was nowhere near being the person she'd left all those years ago, the old Henry was right under the surface, waiting to push through. She could feel it. "Did you need something, or were you just coming out to judge my choice of vehicle?" She allowed a smile.

A crack formed in his icy facade. He kept a straight face, but she caught a tiny glimmer of something else when he looked at her. "It's lunchtime and I'm hungry."

She folded her arms both to shield herself from the cold breeze and because she was waiting for an explanation as to what that had to do with her.

"If I'm hungry," he repeated, "I thought you might be too."

"Are you trying to ask me out?"

Even though his expression didn't change, the familiar flush he used to get when she flirted with him washed over his cheeks, giving her an unexpected flutter. What was she doing, flirting with Henry Dutton?

"I'm asking if you want to be driven safely through the snow and ice to get a meal."

"Good, because I'm not into going on dates."

He went around and opened the passenger door to his truck, then stood next to it, waiting. "Do you want to eat or not?"

She had every reason to say no. But without answering, she walked over and climbed onto the cold bench seat in the truck. Henry shut the door and jogged around to his side. As he started the engine, the truck coming to life, Stella blew into her hands and rubbed them together, her whole body shivering. He clicked on the heat to full blast, put the truck in gear, and headed out to the main road.

"Where are we going for lunch?" she asked.

He kept his eyes on the road. "Somewhere empty. I'm not big on people."

She looked over at him, his comment surprising her. Henry had always loved being around others. He was voted "Most Likely to Host a Talk Show" in their high school superlatives. "You don't like people?"

"They're exhausting." He put on his blinker and took a left down Wedgewood Avenue.

"But you asked me to come with you," she pointed out. "Why?"

A huff escaped his lips and he shook his head. "I don't know." He pulled to a stop at the red light and turned toward her as if deciding to share a secret. "Actually, I do know."

She held her breath, wondering what he'd say.

"I feel like…" He looked back ahead and the light turned green. As he accelerated, he focused on the road once more.

"What do you feel like?" she prompted him, unsure whether she actually wanted to hear the answer.

"I feel like knowing you will help me know myself. I can't explain why."

Stella offered an apprehensive smile. She could definitely explain it, but she didn't. Where would she begin? And if he did learn their story, she'd have to tell him how it ended, and she wasn't ready to face her reasons for doing so just yet, if ever.

The guilt was already creeping in without that bombshell. He'd only joined the army after she left him. If those events hadn't happened, he most likely wouldn't be sitting beside her right now, having lost so much about himself and his life. Without warning, tears pricked her eyes. She turned toward the window, blinking them away and pretending to watch the icy slush that slipped past.

## Chapter Eleven

They drove along in silence until Henry pulled to a stop in front of a familiar little bar, tucked away on a back road. A string of garland hung around a window that sported a neon Michelob sign. Stella's heart beat so quickly at the sight that she worried it might hop right out of her chest.

"You sure this is the place?" she asked, wondering why, when they had the entire city of Nashville to choose from, he'd picked the bar where he first told her he loved her. The empty parking lot and three sticky-looking tables she could see through the foggy window were exactly as they had been that night.

"Yep." He hopped out of the truck and went around to her side, then opened her door. "I come here a lot after therapy sessions."

Trying to keep herself cool, she hopped down onto the cracked pavement and followed him to the door. He held it open for her and waved an arm ushering her through, a gesture he used to do all the time. But he didn't even know that.

She went into the dark, musty, bar-style restaurant. The muffled sound of pans clinking in the back filtered through the small room under the twang of country Christmas songs, just as it had that night when they'd stopped on their way home from a basketball game in the

city. It had been the only bar with an open table after the game. Stella
slipped into the memory of it.

"I tried to tell you when we were in line for popcorn," he'd said as
they entered the little bar. "And again at halftime."

"Tell me what?"

He ignored the waitress and stopped Stella right there in the middle
of the restaurant. "And then I wanted to tell you when we were walking
across the parking lot." He reached out and took her hands. "I'm crazy
about you."

His smile, his flushed cheeks, had stolen her heart.

"I can't live without you. I love you, Stella. There, I said it." Then
he stood as if waiting for the verdict, his chest rising and falling with
anticipation.

Stella looked around. The whole place was watching. She leaned in
as if she were going to tell him something, but instead pressed her lips
to his and then everything faded away but the sensation of absolute
perfection in his embrace. When she'd finally come to once more, the
whole place was cheering. That night had sealed the fate of that lone
bar, and it had become their spot. It was the place where they made
all their life plans, drawing sketches of their dream house on the paper
napkins, deciding how many dogs they were going to have, and debating
whether the animals would be allowed on the furniture.

And now, fifteen years after his big announcement, nothing about
the place had changed but the staff. "Y'all seat yourselves," a waitress
called from the back near the open kitchen pass-through.

Henry chose one of the booths across from an artificial tree adorned
with a few sparse strands of silver tinsel.

"Why do you come *here* of all places?" she asked, genuinely curious.

He pursed his lips, his gaze unsteady as he searched for the right answer. "It's quiet and easy to avoid people here. And I have a cloudy memory of… something. Just a flash. I keep coming back, hoping it'll surface." As he sat down, Henry spread his fingers against the tabletop to lower himself onto the bench seat. His hands were more weathered than they had been, evidence of hard work etched into them.

"But you can't remember?" she asked with bated breath.

"It's hard to say, but being here also just feels normal. It's one of two memories that are right on the edge of my mind."

"What's the other one?"

"I have this weird vision of a wooden door."

"That one?" She pointed to the door through which they'd entered.

"No, the one in my memory is a light maple."

A rush of recognition washed through her, and she had to work hard to keep her emotion from showing. It wasn't the memory of their time here, but it was very possibly another memory of *her*. As if all their memories were woven together somehow.

"A maple door? That's the whole memory?"

"I think so. But I'm not sure. Like I said, it's foggy." He grabbed his menu and brought the conversation to a halt, his expression seeming to convey that his inability to give her a solid answer was somehow his fault.

Stella picked up her menu and perused the fare, wondering if he was recalling the same memory she had of that door.

All those years ago, Stella had come out of the market on the main road in town to find Henry leaning against his truck, wearing his work boots and a dirty pair of jeans, a smug smile on his gorgeous face.

❄

"I made something," Henry had said from across the street. "I wanna show you."

She pointed to her chest, pretending to ask if he was talking to her.

He raced across the street and scooped her up, spinning her around and throwing her over his shoulder like a sack of potatoes. "Of course I'm talkin' to you! Now come with me because I can't wait to show you this." He set her down by his truck and tucked her hair behind her ear tenderly.

With a giggle, she climbed in, sitting close to him on the old bench seat. He shifted the truck into gear and then put his arm around her shoulders, his other hand on the wheel.

They drove the short ride to his family farm. He stopped the truck at the old woodshed and opened the door. She stepped down into the field of buttercups.

"You ready to see what I made?"

"Yes," she said, leaning over and kissing his cheek.

Henry took her hand and led her inside. Leaning against the work bench was a gorgeously stained, substantial maple door with a frosted window at the top and an iron handle.

She ran her fingers over it. "This is beautiful."

He nuzzled her neck. "You like it?"

"Yes," she laughed, wriggling away, her arms covered in goosebumps. "What's it for?"

"To keep the cold out."

She pursed her lips and folded her arms, making him chuckle. He went in for a kiss and she dodged him brightly.

"I mean why did you make it?" she asked.

"Oh, that…" He took her hands the way he liked to do. "It's the door to the house I'm gonna restore for you." He kissed her fingers. "It's the door that's going to pile up with snow. The door that will hold our Christmas wreath. It's the door that will watch our little family grow over the years."

She wrapped her arms around his strong shoulders and looked up at him. "I love you."

"I love you." He leaned down and kissed her lips, and it didn't matter if they ever had a house to restore; she couldn't imagine anything better than being married to him.

Realizing that she'd been staring at her menu for way too long, lost in thought, Stella sneaked a peek at Henry over it. He hadn't seemed to notice her drift away to happier times. She took in the unassuming softness in his eyes and the slight breath coming through his lips as he perused the lunch choices.

Right then, the guilt came rushing in and settled like an icy spear in her heart. She couldn't stop the reoccurring thought that this was all her fault. She'd been young, and at the time, in the haze of grief, she'd thought staying grounded in that town was a prison sentence for them both. But now she wondered if she'd been wrong. Together, they'd woven the fabric of both their lives and now, so many years later, it felt impossible to unwind it and start again.

He looked up and she quickly diverted her attention to the list of salad dressing options.

"Is it odd that from the minute I met you I've gotten the name 'Marie'?" he asked.

She swallowed her remorse, keeping her surprise inside for his benefit. "That's my middle name. I'm Stella Marie. You used to call me that sometimes." He'd started calling her that when they moved in together. She wasn't sure why, but she'd been fond of it.

"Stella Marie," he said while he studied her, as if trying the name on for size. His brows pulled together, and he looked back at his menu.

"Does it jog any memories?"

He shook his head.

The waitress came over and set two glasses of water on the table. "Y'all know what you want, or you need a minute?" She reached for the pencil above her ear.

"I'm ready if you are," Stella said, addressing Henry.

"I'll have the double burger, hold the onions, extra tomato," he said, clearly distracted by Stella, who'd subconsciously mouthed the last three words of his order, the feeling of them on her lips like breathing after being under water.

"And a beer," he continued. "Whatever you have on tap."

Stella set her menu on the table and slid it toward the waitress. "I'll have a regular burger and whatever beer he's having."

After the waitress left them alone once more, he asked, "How do you know what I eat? Did you stalk me at mealtimes?"

She laughed, glad his sense of humor remained, but then a wave of anxiety slithered down her neck as she considered how to answer that question.

"We were really close once," she said.

"How close?"

Unsure how much to tell him or the right thing to do for Ms. Weixel's approach to therapy, she tried to answer truthfully, but without actually divulging very much.

"We were... *a thing* at one time."

That glimmer of curiosity she'd seen in his eyes returned, and the corners of his mouth curved slightly upward. "I could see that."

His response shocked her, sending a sensation of exhilaration through her, despite her indecision about her feelings. "You could? How?"

"I feel close to you somehow. You don't exhaust me."

Before she could respond, the waitress brought their beers.

"So you live with your mother?" he asked after the woman left again.

"Oh, no. I'm just visiting." Stella told him about her father, her sister, and how she'd returned to help her mom. "I hadn't realized until Mama called how important it was to come back and be together for Christmas as a family, but now it's fractured." She took in his blue eyes, the idea of her broken family so much bigger than he knew.

For the first time, the hardened wall he'd built up slid all the way down. Her story seemed to have impacted him.

"I feel like I don't have much of a family either." He frowned, scooting the salt and pepper shakers tighter together.

Yes, she knew.

"My mother and father have both passed on, and I live on the grounds with my sister, but I don't remember the last fourteen or so years with her." He rolled his head on his shoulders slightly, giving away the tension the situation caused him. "It's taxing to spend every moment with the same person and have no clue about who they've become. Sometimes I see sadness in Mary Jo's eyes, and I feel responsible somehow for not remembering."

"It's definitely not your fault."

"That's why I agreed to go to therapy, even though it's a waste of time."

Without thinking, Stella leaned across the table and took his hand. "Give it a chance."

He peered down at their fingers.

She pulled her hand back, angry with herself for the impulsive gesture. "I'm sorry," she said. "I shouldn't have been so forward."

"It's okay. I didn't mind. It just startled me, that's all." A glimmer of the old Henry peeked through. He shook his head. "You knew me well, yes?"

"Yes."

"Then maybe you can answer this for me." He leaned toward her on his forearms. "I don't understand why I chose to join the military. I keep hoping that I have some deep-rooted history of courage, but I can't find any evidence of it. And while I love my country, I don't think I have the temperament for battle. Yet, apparently, I was involved in combat. Do *you* know why I enlisted?"

She swallowed against her dry mouth and grabbed her beer, taking a heady drink. "I, uh… I wasn't around when you enlisted."

"It makes me feel like I don't really know who I am."

The waitress cut between them once again with two overflowing plates of food. "Here ya go," she said. And the moment with Henry flew away as if the woman had brought a gust of wind with her.

"Thank you," Henry said, his expression thoughtful.

She wanted to make everything better, to ease the pain she'd inflicted, the pain that was now worse because of her. Then an idea came to her.

"Hey, wanna come over to my mom's with me after lunch? It would give you a break from things and all the heaviness with your sister."

He pinched a fry and tossed it into his mouth as he seemed to consider the offer.

"My mother and I haven't seen you in years, so we'd be getting to know you again anyway. No pressure. And I'll bet we can convince my mom to bake Christmas cookies. She's just itching for a reason."

He allowed a little grin. "All right."

As they ate lunch together, she had no idea if having him over was the right thing to do. She knew a part of her wanted to make things up to him. But what she didn't want to admit to herself was that there was another part of her that didn't want to leave his side.

Henry dropped Stella off at the hospital to get her car, then he followed her home. She tried not to look at him through her rearview mirror during the drive, because every time she did, a tiny seed inside her wanted to pick up where they'd left off, and she knew it wasn't possible or beneficial to either of them.

After she arrived home, she left her car and waited in the driveway. Henry pulled to a stop behind her and got out. Wondering why he didn't step up to meet her, Stella turned around to find him surveying the house. She considered whether he was testing his memory to see what he could recall about the place.

"How long did we date?" he asked, his breath puffing out into the cold air as he walked up to her.

She shut the car door. "Officially, a little under a year, but we knew each other our whole lives." She neglected to divulge the year they'd been married.

All of a sudden he stopped, pausing in the driveway.

"What is it?" she asked.

He pointed to the third upstairs window on the right, squinting up at it. "Did that window ever have a crack?"

She grinned at him. "Yep. Thanks to you."

He shifted on his feet, the curiosity returning.

She pointed toward a tree near the window. "See that big oak tree right there? I used to climb down it after dark to see you. When we were seventeen, you tossed a rock at the window to get my attention, and it cracked the glass. You worked extra hours at the roofing company to pay my dad back for it."

A slight twitch of amusement showed at the edges of his lips. "Did you end up climbing out that night?"

"Yeah. I didn't tell Mama and Pop about the window until the morning."

He allowed a smile then. "What did we do?"

"We laid on a blanket and looked up at the stars."

"Mm." He nodded. "I should probably do that more often."

"Yeah, me too," she said, the world slowing down as she considered the idea. It had been quite a while since she'd lost track of time while enjoying something so simple. For so many years, her life had been made of schedules and timelines. Stella took that moment to acknowledge the feeling of their slight bond just now as the two of them agreed on something. It felt good to be on the same side. She nodded toward the front porch. "Come on in."

When she walked into the living room with Henry, her mother's eyes widened. She set down the towel she'd been using to dust picture frames.

"Hello," she said with a questioning smile.

"Look who I brought home from work today," Stella said, unwinding her scarf.

"I'm the subject of her next article on crazy people, apparently."

His voice was teasing, but withdrawn and quiet, different from what she'd seen a minute ago. It was as if they'd entered the real world again and he'd closed back up. He laid his coat on the edge of the sofa.

"I told you in therapy that it has nothing to do with being crazy," Stella said.

He scratched his head. "It feels like I'm crazy. It's pretty weird when everyone else knows more about you than you know yourself."

"My dear boy," Mama said, throwing a hand to her chest, "I'll bet."

"I was hoping we could bake some Christmas cookies or something," Stella said to lighten the mood. After all, that was the point of this visit. The last thing she wanted to do was cause Henry more stress.

Mama brightened. "Absolutely. I never turn down a chance to bake." Her mother nearly danced across the room. "Let's see what ingredients I've got."

Stella and Henry followed Mama into the kitchen. Henry's gaze roamed the whitewashed wooden cabinets then moved to the wide island and the basket of onions and potatoes that Mama must have been washing earlier. When they'd first gotten married, Mama didn't like not having Stella around the house, so she'd asked them over for dinner all the time. Henry used to help prepare it. The new Henry was always observing, and Stella could only imagine how hard he was searching for answers.

"Is any of this ringing a bell at all?" she whispered to him.

He shook his head. "Only from when we were younger, and it's still fuzzy."

It seemed as if any minute he was going to make an excuse to leave, and she told herself to stop asking about his memories. If he remembered something, and he wanted to tell her, he'd say so.

"Good," she said.

He turned to look at her, questioning.

"It'll be like that brand-new chapter in a book you've been waiting to read," she explained.

His shoulders relaxed a bit, and he offered the tiniest hint of a smile, but then something pulled his attention away. "What's that?" He walked over to the table. The diamond necklace she'd found was laying there.

"I thought I put that in the safe."

Mama leaned toward them, a measuring cup in each hand. "I got it out to take another look. The story is so interesting."

"What's the story?" Henry asked.

"It's a necklace I found on the floor at the airport," Stella replied. "It looks similar to one we saw online."

"I was reading more about it," her mom said.

Stella gave Henry a quick rundown of what she'd researched so far about the Hastings family and the stillbirths.

Henry gingerly picked up the piece of jewelry, draping it across his palm. He flipped the small pendant over and squinted at the inscription.

"Can you read what it says?" Stella asked.

"I can't make it out." He put it back down on the table.

Mama set the measuring cups on the counter and joined them at the table with her phone. "I wanted to see if I could find anything else on it," she said. "And I discovered another story."

"Oh?" Stella offered an empty chair to Henry, then took a seat next to him. "What did it say?"

Mama slid her finger down her phone's screen until she reached the article. "Here it is. Most of the beginning is the same thing we read earlier, but this part is new."

"Tell us," Stella said.

"Well, the diamond was stolen in 1773 by a small-time pirate named of Samuel Morgan, who frequented the trade route between England and the Americas. When the Hastings family were on their yearly voyage at sea, even though they considered it bad luck, the necklace was included among the valuables they took with them.

"In the middle of the night, Samuel Morgan sneaked onto the ship and stole the diamond, along with the Hastings' other jewels and a huge haul of goods heading to port to be shipped to the colonies. He took a liking to the Christmas Diamond, claiming it for himself and clasping it around his neck. But the moment he wore the stone, *his* luck turned. The next day, according to legend, a massive heatwave began, and his men ran out of food at sea, most of their goods spoiling and becoming inedible in the high temperatures. Another boat fired at them, the cannonball hitting the stern of the ship, nearly sinking it, and causing him to divert his voyage to a remote island where he spent months repairing the damage.

"When they finally arrived at the Massachusetts Bay colony, starving and exhausted, nearly half his fleet had caught yellow fever and died. One of his crew had heard the story of the Christmas Diamond and he was certain at that point that the stone was bad luck, so he traded it with a merchant named Charles Worley for all the food the man had. Then he nursed the remainder of his crew back to health and left, never to be heard from again."

"You don't think all that bad luck is true, do you?" Henry asked, obviously skeptical.

"I have to wonder," Mama replied. "Listen to this. It's thought that the rudimentary repairs to the ship were no match for a summer storm that swept over the Atlantic that year, and the boat sank. What are believed to be remnants of the wreckage were found in 1987 about 1,250 miles from port in the Americas, but the scientific analysis isn't conclusive."

"Of course it isn't conclusive," Henry said, inspecting the diamond again.

Stella leaned into his view. "You don't believe the story?"

"Not a chance. If the ship was, in fact, real and went down, it had nothing to do with a diamond necklace."

"I do think our Christmas Diamond is probably just an old piece of costume jewelry, but it does make me wonder. I haven't had great luck since finding it," Stella said. "My car went into a ditch and my sister isn't here when she should be."

"Even if it was some rare jewel, why would a necklace have anything to do with those things?" Henry said.

"Because it wasn't given in love?" Stella chuckled at the ridiculousness of her statement.

Henry laughed for the first time since their reacquaintance, and she relished the familiar sound.

"And that matters?" He rolled his eyes.

"One of the articles said that if the Christmas Diamond isn't given in love, it casts a spell on the one who has it, cursing them with bad luck," Mama said.

"Anyone can find any reason to believe something, but that doesn't make it true." Henry picked up the necklace again. "If it's even genuine at all, this is nothing more than a fancy rock. It has no power over anyone."

Mama reached over and inspected the pendant as it swung from the chain in Henry's fingers. "It does look real... Has the airport called?"

"Nope. If it is legit, I can't get it to its rightful owner. Yet even worse luck." She eyed Henry playfully.

He shook his head disbelievingly and set the necklace back on the table.

"You're right. It probably doesn't have any power at all. But just in case it *is* bad luck, I'd sure like to give it back to whomever it belongs." Stella slid it away from her.

"And what happens if it's given in love?" Henry asked, a derisive grin on his lips signifying that he was only playing along. "Do you get *good* luck?"

"I don't know," Stella replied. "Maybe someone will call after the holiday, and we'll never need to find out."

Henry laughed again, lifting her spirits.

"Should we start baking?" Mama asked, rising from her chair.

"Yes!" Stella stood alongside her mother.

"All right," Henry said, following suit. "But be careful with that thing in here." He waggled a finger at the necklace. "You might burn the cookies."

"Oh, you think you're funny now." Stella grinned at him.

What she didn't want to admit to herself was the fondness that bubbled up at the joke, reminding her very much of the boy she'd known.

# Chapter Twelve

After they'd eaten their weight in warm snickerdoodles, right off the baking sheet, Mama shooed them out of the room and hung back in the kitchen, insisting Stella and Henry relax while she cleaned up the mess from baking.

Henry sat on the sofa next to Stella. "I don't think I can fit another bite in my stomach."

A log popped in the fireplace, embers dancing up the chimney. Stella scooted over to put a slight distance between them.

"You mentioned that it's just you and your mom here," he said, the orange light from the fire dancing in his blue eyes. "What about your dad?"

"He passed away in January."

"I'm so sorry."

His sympathy brought her emotions to the surface. She shoved them down to that special place inside her, where she'd gotten good at keeping them. "I worry about my mom," she said, her voice low so it wouldn't carry. "She's here all alone... He was her high school sweetheart." When she said the words, she had to look away from Henry, the parallel hitting too close to home. While hers and her mother's love affairs had started the same way, they'd had very different endings.

"High school sweethearts, huh?" Henry asked, as if the same thought had somehow crossed his mind. "I do remember having a crush on you."

Her heart pattered. "You do?"

"Yeah. That's another thing that's baffled me."

"How so?"

Henry scooted closer to her, filling in the small space between them. "When did you leave Leiper's Fork for good?"

"When I was eighteen."

"How many years ago was that?"

His line of questioning made her nervous. "Thirteen years, I think."

"That's when I enlisted in the army."

"I wish I knew why you decided to join the army specifically," she said, trying to allow the two events to remain separate until his brain decided to connect them.

"It's a respectable thing to do. I keep trying to find meaning in that. Was that why I joined, you think?" Henry asked.

"It absolutely is honorable to serve your country."

"Perhaps I was looking for adventure."

"Maybe. But I must say, traveling overseas wasn't ever really your thing. You always wanted to stay around here…"

"Yeah…"

And then the reason hit her: he'd been running, just like she had. They'd both run to the ends of the world to avoid facing what they'd lost.

She was so deep in thought that she'd missed the fact that the two of them had fallen into silence.

Henry spoke first. "Thank you."

"For what?" she asked, his comment jarring given her thoughts.

"For today. I feel… like myself today. Whatever that means."

"I'm glad. If it helps, you seemed more like yourself today to me too."

His chest rose with a calm inhale and he nodded, his gaze remaining on her. "I should probably get home." His words didn't match the message of affection in his eyes.

Stella decided it was probably a good idea. She stood to allow him to exit, and Henry followed suit.

"Hey, why don't I pick you up for therapy tomorrow?" he offered. "We can ride together."

Her answer was on the tip of her tongue, but she didn't trust that it was the right one.

"It's fine," he said, reading her indecision right away. "Just an idea—"

"No," she stopped him. His disappointment was more than she could endure. She'd already caused him enough. How bad could it be? They were just carpooling to Vanderbilt—no big deal. "I'll ride with you."

"Great." He pulled out his phone. "Do I have your number?"

She leaned over to view the screen as he typed her name, her details popping right up. "Text me when you're on your way tomorrow."

"Okay."

Henry went to the kitchen to thank Mama, then Stella saw him out. Mama was still in the kitchen doorway when Stella shut the front door and turned around.

"You okay?"

Stella fell back down onto the sofa, her mind in a muddle. A part of her felt as though she was eighteen again when she was with him, but the rational side of her kept ticking off all the reasons she definitely wasn't still that girl.

"I don't know. Should we switch gears and talk about the parade?"

"I suppose," Mama replied, not sounding terribly excited.

Stella got back up and retrieved her laptop from her room. She set it on the coffee table and plopped back on the couch. While Mama got comfortable bedside her, she brought up the parade website, and logged in.

"With fewer entries this year, we need to decide on an order for the participants so we can spread out the different types of vehicles, floats, and acts. Then we need to figure out what we're going to do about Santa."

Worry filled Mama's face, settling in the little wrinkles on her forehead and between her eyes. "What will we do without Santa?"

They both fell silent at the double meaning in the question. For many years, Pop had always been Santa.

*"I'm right here with you."*

The memory of her father teaching her how to ride a bike came to mind. It was a Christmas morning, and she'd come into the living room to find a shiny, purple bicycle.

"When you feel like you're falling, put your feet out and catch yourself," Pop had said.

She'd wobbled along while he held the back of the bike.

"I'm falling!"

"Put your foot out," he reminded her.

Stella gripped the handlebars, dipping precariously to one side. "I'm not strong enough."

"I'm right here with you," Pop assured her. "I've got you." He'd reached out and supported her, keeping her upright.

"Keep me steady."

She sent the thought to Pop now as tears surfaced in her mother's eyes. Stella wrapped her arms around Mama, giving her a squeeze. "We'll be okay," she said, hoping it was true.

❄

Later that evening, on her way to the market to grab a jug of milk for
Mama, Stella stopped at Smokey's, the little restaurant on the corner,
to take a break and be alone for a little while. A no-frills establishment,
Smokey's served black coffee in thick mugs, and if you wanted cream,
they'd bring out a jug of milk from the kitchen. When she stepped
into the warmth of the place, just past the little Christmas tree with
ornaments in the shape of little snowflakes, she saw Henry's sister,
Mary Jo, sitting alone, fiddling with a plate of food, but not seeming
to eat any of it.

Stella made her way over. "Hi," she said, unwinding her scarf and
letting the tails hang down over her shoulders.

Mary Jo looked up, the stress on her face clear as she attempted
to smile. "Hey."

"You okay?"

Mary Jo reached over and pulled out the chair beside her, offering
the seat to Stella. "Want to join me?"

She'd originally come to be alone, but given the sadness in her old
friend's demeanor, Stella placed her coat and scarf on the back of the
chair and took a seat. One of the waiters came over for her order.

"Just coffee," she told him. After he left, she addressed Mary Jo.
"So what's going on?"

"It just doesn't seem like Christmas this year." She lifted her mug
and took a drink, closing her eyes as she swallowed. "I feel like I've had
to mourn Mama's death all by myself because Henry is so consumed
with everything. And then, with his memory loss and the way he's
managing his stress, I'm on edge all the time. I thought when he started

the landscaping business it might help, but it hasn't. Now that we're in the winter months, he's not working at all, and you know how he likes to keep busy."

Stella's heart ached for Mary Jo. The laugh lines from happier days had turned downward, her friend's expression grim. "I'm so sorry you're having to deal with all this by yourself."

"Maybe having you back for a little while will make things better with Henry. He still doesn't feel like my brother, but he has seemed more relaxed since you arrived."

Stella shook her head. "It would be nice, but I can't promise any miracles. Although I did get him to bake snickerdoodles with me and Mama."

Mary Jo's eyes rounded. "You did?" She laughed. "You couldn't even get him to bake cookies with you when he *did* remember his past!"

Stella grinned.

"You were always his rock, that grounding force that could settle him down."

The waiter slid a mug of coffee onto the table in front of Stella. "Milk?"

"Yes, please."

He hustled off behind the bar and grabbed the jug and a spoon, returning and setting them on the table. "Just pass it back to the bar when you're done."

Stella nodded as she poured the milk into her mug.

"He never stopped waiting, you know," Mary Jo said, the lighter moment sliding away.

Stella set the milk on the table and stilled her hands. "I didn't want him to wait," she said, emotion catching in her throat.

"He didn't even try to move on. I used to get upset with him for that, and our arguing about it got pretty heated, but I let it go because he was usually on leave and I didn't want to spend our precious time fighting."

Tears brimmed in Stella's eyes. "He wanted lots of kids," she said, knowing, but not bringing it up to Mary Jo, that she wasn't able to offer him that. "I thought he'd find someone wonderful who could give him a house full of children."

Mary Jo shrugged. "He just closed in on himself after you left."

"I don't know if I made the right decision in leaving the way I did," she admitted. "But I am who I am because of it." Elbows on the table, she pressed her fingers into her eyes. "Marriage is an awful lot to put on someone at eighteen. Life is a mess, isn't it?"

"It sure can be." Mary Jo grabbed the milk and poured some in her cup. "Don't be too hard on yourself. We all had big dreams, you know. You're the only one who actually did something about them."

Stella looked up from her coffee mug. "What were *your* dreams? You never told me."

Mary Jo leaned on her fist, her elbow propping her up. "I always saw myself somewhere else—maybe on a beach or an island—but I never really knew how I'd get there. That's why I called it a 'dream' instead of a 'plan.'"

"You'll never know what you might want if you never take that step and see."

Mary Jo sat up straighter and smoothed the napkin in her lap. "Life has gotten in the way. I felt like I needed to be there for Henry after you left, and then we lost Mom and now Henry's accident…" She shook her head. "It's just not my time."

"I'm so sorry. I didn't know…" She couldn't help but wonder if she'd stayed, would Mary Jo have been able to take a chance on the life she'd wanted? Stella wished she could make it up to her somehow. But where would she even begin?

✳

"Stella, would you come here for a minute?" Mama called from the front entryway that night.

Relieved, Stella had just sent off her first article to her editor and now had been trying to begin an outline for her second. She set her laptop aside and got up off the sofa. When she reached the open, two-story entryway, her mother's head was tipped back as she squinted at a brown spot on the ceiling.

Stella walked underneath it to get a better look, and when she did, a drop of water plopped right onto her cheek. She wiped it away. "Looks like a leak."

When Stella was a baby, her father had remodeled this part of the farmhouse, lifting the ceiling two stories. The only thing on the other side of that wet spot was the roof.

"The melted ice must be coming in," Mama said. "How am I supposed to fix that?"

Stella knew what her mother wasn't saying: how were they supposed to fix it without Pop? "I'll see if I can find someone to take care of it. Right now, let's get a bucket and some towels to protect the floor."

"I've got some old towels in the closet that your dad used to use to dry off the cars after he washed them." Mama strode to the door in the hallway, drew out an armful, and brought them over. "He's got a bucket in the back garage." Her voice broke on the words.

"I'll go get it." Stella gave her mom's arm a squeeze of support. Then she slipped on her boots.

When she opened the front door, the night air blew in like an icy slap in the face. Crossing her arms to keep warm, she jogged around the side of the house, and down the little stone path that was still covered in a frozen sheet of ice. The quick momentum she'd built to manage the cold slowed to a stop when she reached the detached garage where her dad had spent so much of his time. She eyed the latch, imagining his strong grip around it.

"Come in." Pop's words blew on the wind, as if her mind were playing tricks on her.

She remembered one winter day when she was around ten years old. She had opened the metal latch and called Pop's name above the whine of the buzz saw.

"Come in!" he'd called to her, lifting his safety goggles, the little space heater going full blast in the corner. "Watcha up to?"

"Just coming in to see you," she'd said, climbing onto one of the workbench stools and fiddling with the line of screwdrivers on the table. "What are you making?"

"I'm fixing the wooden edge of the screened door for your mama…"

Now Stella stood in front of the closed entrance to the garage, her hand on the frozen latch, wishing that when she opened it she'd find Pop under his lamp inside, fixing that wooden frame. She lifted the cold metal until the door opened. The space was musty, dark, void of the life that had filled it on so many of her younger days. She clicked on the light, the beam only serving to illuminate the emptiness.

A shiver ran down her spine as she stood in the cold space. Where had her family gone? It was as if Pop had taken it with him when he'd left this world. She had to admit that if she'd been asked as a girl, she'd have had a different vision for where she'd be at this time in her life. But she'd also done a good job of ruining the family she'd been building. The sting of tears came yet again, and she tried unsuccessfully to blink them away.

After sucking in a cold breath, she located the bucket she'd come to get, turned off the light, and quickly locked the garage back up, deciding then that she needed to try harder to reach Lily. If she was going to accomplish one thing this Christmas, she was going to put her family back together.

When she got inside, she dialed her sister's number.

"I've tried three times to call Lily and I can't get her," Stella said, frustrated by the time Mama came into the kitchen where she was sitting.

Mama grabbed a Christmas cookie and nibbled it, sitting down at the kitchen table.

"I wish she'd come home. She's supposed to be here."

Mama pulled a napkin from the holder in the center of the table and set down her half-eaten cookie. "Let's do something to get our minds off it." She slid the necklace toward her. "Why don't we research the Christmas Diamond a little more? Maybe we can find a museum or something that might be able to help us figure out whether we're in possession of an antique or not."

Stella ran a finger over the blue stone. "Why are you so interested in this necklace?"

Mama's gaze remained on the gem. "I don't know... Something about it speaks to me."

"What do you mean?" Stella grabbed a cookie and took a bite, the sugary crunch of the outside giving way to a soft, spicy inside—a reminder of Christmases past and happier times.

"Remember when you came home for Christmas last year and your dad and I didn't spend a lot on gifts because he was sick?"

"Yeah."

"He promised to buy me something special. He never did, and I guess a part of me wishes for something lovely this year." She picked up the pendant and held it up to the light. "This is so pretty. I almost hope no one claims it."

"All right." Stella decided to humor her mother. If no one claimed the necklace, she'd leave it with Mama when she went to her next assignment. "What should we search for?"

Mama set down the necklace gingerly and reached for her phone. "What about Charles Worley? We could see if there's anything on him."

"Who's he again?"

"He was the merchant that Samuel Morgan, the pirate, gave the diamond to." She was already typing on her phone and scrolling through the results. "Nothing. Let's try… 'Christmas Diamond Charles Worley legend.'" She put her phone between them and a small list of sites came up.

Stella pointed to a particular article that caught her eye: *How Much is the Christmas Diamond Actually Worth?* "Click that one."

Mama tapped the link and started to read. "'Charles Worley, a local merchant in the Massachusetts Bay colony, took the stone to a fellow colonist who'd been a jeweler back in London. He told the man he'd been hiding it in a small trunk in his bedroom and hadn't let a soul know he had it.'

"'The jeweler, named Edward James, assessed the diamond at two carats.'" Mama's eyes rounded and she looked up from her phone, lifting the diamond again and turning it back and forth in the light. "Want to guess how much the Christmas Diamond was worth?"

"A lot, I'd imagine."

Mama kept reading. "'Today, the jewel is estimated to be worth upwards of *twenty thousand dollars*. The merchant immediately had the jeweler engrave his family name on the back. Over the years, the inscription has been worn down, but evidence of it remains...'" Mama gasped. "You don't think..."

Stella flipped over the diamond to reveal the inscription they hadn't been able to read. "If it was a good replica, they'd attempt the inscription as well, right?" Stella countered. "I'll bet it's a Christmas trinket someone was bringing to a relative or a friend, and it slipped out of their shopping bag on the way to their plane." Stella stopped talking when Mama's face filled with disappointment. "You never know, though," she said, hoping to cheer up her mother. "What else does the article say?"

Mama resumed reading. "'The day after the merchant took the necklace to the jeweler, the merchant went missing. It was thought that, given the poor conditions in which he lived in the colony and with this opportunity for trading such a possession, he ran off in search of someone to buy it from him.'" Mama clicked off her phone. "We could take it to a jewelry store in Nashville and have it appraised. Then we'd know for sure."

Pop's voice floated into Stella's mind. *"Humor her."*

That had been his mantra when Stella was growing up. "Mama wants to paint the back room green, but I think it should be cream," she'd said.

He'd said, "*Humor her.*"

"Mama insists on planting tulips in the corner of the yard where we all accidentally drive over the grass."

*"Humor her."*

"Mama wants us all to take a family portrait, even though were all stuffed from Thanksgiving dinner."

*"Humor her."*

She'd asked him once, "Why do you always humor Mama?"

Pop had answered, "Because when we're all gone, it won't matter what the thing was she'd wanted; what will actually matter is the happiness we gave your mother when we said yes."

"I could take it when I go into the city tomorrow for Henry's therapy session."

Mama brightened, the same way she had when she'd bought the green paint. "That's a great idea."

# Chapter Thirteen

"Before sunrise, a plunking sound woke me up, so I got out of bed to figure out what it was. The bucket under the leak was nearly overflowing. I switched it with the biggest baking bowl I have and went back to sleep, but with the rain and ice overnight, it's almost to the brim already," Mama said as she padded around the kitchen in her slippers and bathrobe the next morning. She gestured across the room to the living area. The bucket was drying on a towel by the fireplace. "We've got to find someone quick."

"Okay, let's do that first thing."

Mama stopped and looked at Stella as if the sight of her had just registered. "Are you already working?"

Stella was dressed and sitting at the table, typing on her laptop. "I'm trying to get some time in before heading to Vanderbilt with Henry." She'd sent a request to her editor, Amy, asking if she still had the old project files from one of Stella's former research topics on brain function. The email she'd been waiting for had just popped up. "I made coffee."

"You're an angel." Mama went to the counter and pulled a mug from the cabinet.

Stella opened the message. The email, in fact, contained the latest research that she wanted to consult.

While Mama heated a pan on the stove for breakfast, Stella took a sip of her coffee and scanned the experimental study about the correlation between magnetic brain stimulation and memory improvements. The data was encouraging. Several subjects reported progress using the strategy.

"Want any eggs?" Mama asked.

Stella shut her laptop. "No, thanks. Henry's picking me up in a few minutes." She tucked her laptop under her arm. She couldn't wait to talk to Henry about the study. After slipping the laptop in its case, she grabbed the diamond necklace for the appraisal, clasped it around her neck, and slipped it under her shirt.

By the time she'd grabbed her coat, Henry had pulled up. Stella called goodbye to Mama and headed out the door.

As she approached his truck idling in the drive, she pointed light-heartedly to a wreath made of pine that was wired to the grill of the old pickup. Henry's stoic expression didn't change, but she could've sworn she saw a hint of pleasure in his gaze.

"Sprucing up for Christmas?" she asked as she climbed in.

"Mary Jo thought it was a nice touch."

She grinned at him. "I agree. It could be your 'something positive' today."

Henry rolled his eyes.

Her lips parted to begin to tell him about the article, but having not spoken to the therapist about it, she decided against it last minute and buckled her seatbelt. Plus, she was just starting to get to know him again. Part of her wanted to build more experiences with him to show him that she'd grown and matured before he tried a new strategy to repair his memory and he remembered what she'd done.

"Do you think you could swing by a jewelry store before taking me home later?" she asked.

He glanced at her before turning his attention back to the winding road in front of them. "Sure. Why?"

Stella pulled her collar open to reveal the necklace. "Mama and I thought we should get this appraised to see if it's real or not."

"Aren't you worried that wearing it will bring you bad luck?" he asked with a sarcastic tone.

"Not if it's a fake." She lifted the stone to inspect it again.

"You think it is?"

"Yeah," she said, tucking it back under her collar. "Why else would it be on the airport floor and not a soul seems to be looking for it?"

"I've never believed in all that hocus pocus anyway."

"You never do." She caught herself as she spoke. She realized his comfortable demeanor made it easy to slide back into how she'd once felt about him.

She worried he'd tense back up if she offered any banter. Instead, to her relief, he seemed to relax into the drive, his shoulders loose and a neutral softness upon his lips. Mary Jo's assessment came to mind: *"He has seemed more relaxed since you arrived."* She couldn't deny the feeling of affection that swelled at the thought.

When they reached the hospital, Henry hung back, his pace matching her short strides. He held the door open for her, and he seemed genuinely pleasant. He even greeted Ms. Weixel when he walked in, which caused her to send a surprised and delighted look over to Stella behind his back.

"So, Henry, do you have any positives for me today?" she asked, clicking her pen and sliding it into her pocket.

Stella sat in her chair across the room and opened her laptop.

"I had a nice drive into the city this morning," he replied.

Stella's hands stilled, and she peered over at him. Had he actually offered a decent answer today?

"That's great news," Ms. Weixel said, as she took her seat across from him. "What about the drive was nice?"

"I was in good company." Henry's gaze flitted to Stella.

Her pulse rose as she typed his answer, keeping her eyes on her screen.

"Who was with you?" the therapist asked.

"Stella and I rode together this morning."

"Oh, that's really great."

"And I had eggs with coffee."

He eyed Stella, sending her stomach into a somersault. What was in those eggs this morning? He'd let Mary Jo tie a holiday wreath to the grill of his truck, and now he was answering the therapist's questions. Who was this new Henry?

"Well, I'm delighted to hear that. And I'm glad to see you actively participating in your therapy."

The session went on without a hitch and Stella documented it all, the whole time wondering what had gotten into Henry. His behavior was different today, very familiar.

"I'm going to give you a little homework to complete before tomorrow," the therapist said at the end of their meeting. "I'd like you to do one new thing. Something you haven't done before—your choice—and report back in our next session."

❄

"Could we call the trip to the jewelry store something I haven't done?" Henry asked while maneuvering the truck out of the parking lot.

Stella shivered on the cold bench seat, rubbing her arms through her coat, trying to get warm. "I'm not sure that counts."

Henry turned up the heat. "That's what I get for complying with her ridiculous therapy. Now I have homework."

"It doesn't have to be stressful."

"What would I possibly be able to do right now that I haven't done before?"

He had a point. She and Henry had spent their entire lives in the area. There wasn't a whole lot they hadn't done. "Maybe we can search for something here in Nashville. I'm guessing there's at least one new tourist attraction we haven't gone to."

Henry shook his head. "I'm not really up for all that." He turned out of the hospital parking lot and came to a stop at the stoplight. "I was hoping to just go home."

"All right then. Why don't we go to the Christmas tree farm? You can play a new game or two and call it a night."

"That's not a bad idea. And it's on the way home, so it wouldn't take too much time. Would you mind going with me?"

She definitely didn't mind helping with his therapy, and she loved the idea of spending more time in Leiper's Fork. She'd been all over the world and seen so many things, yet there was a nostalgia about that little spot called Christmas that felt as if it were a part of her.

"I don't mind at all."

"Perfect. Thank you."

He followed the directions on his phone to the jewelry store and turned at the next light. His attitude today reminded her of the old Henry, and she had to admit she was curious to find out if he'd show any other signs before they parted for the day. But with every step forward, she knew she was one step closer to having to face her demons. He was starting to let her in, and the last thing she wanted was to hurt him a second time. Not after everything he'd been through already.

After a few more turns, they pulled into the parking lot of a small jeweler.

"Moment of truth," she said, touching the diamond that hung around her neck. "I hate to burst Mama's bubble. She's convinced it could be the real thing, but I'm nearly sure this will prove that it's not."

"I guess we'll find out." Henry opened the door for her, and they walked inside.

Stella unclasped the chain and approached a clear case full of shiny diamonds. She laid the necklace on the glass top just as the jeweler approached them.

"May I help you?" he asked, his hands clasped behind his back.

"I'd like to get this appraised," Stella said.

With a polite nod, he pulled a piece of black velvet from the cabinet and laid it on the counter. Then he placed the necklace on top of it, the center diamond and its surrounding smaller stones shining under the lights.

"It's a lovely piece."

"We're trying to determine if the stones are real. And, if you can tell, how old it is."

The man pulled out a loupe and placed it against his eye, then peered through it as he lifted the stone closer and turned it over. "The inscription on the back is difficult to read, even with magnification... I'll need seven days or so to get a full workup on the stones." He set down the tool and wrapped the necklace in the velvet pouch. "The cost of an appraisal is fifty dollars."

"All right, that's fine."

The jeweler handed Stella a small clipboard with a form for her contact information. She filled it in then passed it back, along with her credit card. Henry's gaze remained on the diamond as if he were lost in thought.

After completing the transaction, the jeweler handed Stella her card and receipt. "Great. I'll give you a call when it's done."

She slid the ticket into her pocket. As she left, she couldn't help but take one final look at the jeweler as he took the necklace to the back of the store. Then, switching gears, she turned to Henry. "Homework time."

He gave her a halfhearted grin, his mind clearly elsewhere. He held the door open for her and they climbed into his truck.

"I wish I could remember you beyond our childhood," he said, putting the truck in gear and backing out of the parking spot.

Unsure how to respond, Stella wondered if knowing their story would matter to the man he was now. Memory or not, he'd changed over the years, just as she had. In a way, they'd been given a clean slate, even if it was against his will.

"You know, I could spout off a list of experiences we had together to help you remember—some wonderful and others not so great. But I guess none of that will help you right now because, at the end of the day, your feelings and new experiences are more important, since you can draw on them to move forward."

He didn't reply, but he seemed to be listening. Then he shrugged. "It would just be nice, that's all."

When they arrived in Leiper's Fork, Henry drove to Christmas and parked. They got out and made their way past the red trailer decked out in festive holiday accents, heading toward the booths. Stella followed his lead.

"Are you hungry?" he asked.

She cinched her coat up around her neck to ward off the cold. "A little."

"What's your fancy? My treat. Cotton candy or corn dogs?"

His question took her back to better days, giving her a punch of wistfulness. "Corn dogs."

"Well, apparently, we're at the perfect spot." He guided her toward the booth that boasted the best corn dog in town. Since it was quite possibly the only corn dog in town, she had no choice but to believe them. Henry offered the attendant a few bills and the man handed him two giant corn dogs on sticks. He handed her one. "Fine dining for sure."

She laughed, glad his humor was surfacing easily today. They meandered through the aisles of trees for sale, their bright red-and-white-striped tags flapping in the icy breeze.

"Where to?" She bit into the crispy outer shell of cornmeal surrounding the hot dog, the sweet and salty taste reminding her of childhood.

"I have no idea," he replied. "Let's just walk and see where we end up."

They strolled past a booth with floating rubber ducks. "Oh, I used to love this game," she said between nibbles. "You played it with me when we were kids, remember?"

The corners of his eyes creased with his look of affection, and she knew he did remember. "I would use all my money, trying to win the big bear for you, picking duck after duck and comparing numbers, but we always ended up winning trinkets."

She laughed.

Henry was busy looking around. "Nothing here feels like something I *wouldn't* have done."

"I'm assuming you just have to do something new to you at this moment."

He squinted at the booths. "Everything here seems too easy. Maybe this wasn't the best idea."

Delighted to hear he was, in fact, taking the assignment seriously, she asked, "It's probably the best we've got—we'd decided that."

"I don't know…"

"Do you have any other ideas about where you could go or what you could do?"

He grinned at her and shrugged. "Nope."

They resumed strolling through the row of booths the way they used to. The ringing of winning bells and cheerful holiday music carried her thoughts to the old days when she came here with her dad, and it made her miss him right then.

Pop's voice entered her mind. *"It's fun even if we can't all be together."*

She remembered one Christmas when Lily had broken her arm and didn't want to go. A thirteen-year-old Stella had been so disappointed when her sister couldn't join them, but Pop had tried to lift her spirits. He'd put an arm around her and said those words to her. Then he reminded her that Lily would want her to have a good time.

Henry pointed to the ducks as they walked by a second time, pulling her out of her memory. "This game's probably rigged."

His chuckle gave her a flutter. His arm brushed hers and she had to fight the ache in her chest. Out there, walking in their familiar territory—the place she'd loved to meet him after school every Christmas—she wanted to lean against him, put her head on his shoulder, and walk arm in arm like they used to, but she checked herself.

"I bet the bear's number isn't even on the bottom of one of those ducks," he said.

She looked into his blue eyes. "I think it is."

He stopped walking. "Why?"

"I guess I always have faith it's in there somewhere."

She wasn't referring to the ducks anymore, and she found herself straddling the line between following her heart and acting with her head. She didn't want to start something she wasn't ready for, and she still didn't know if she had the guts to tell him what they'd been through. But all he had to do was smile at her, and she found herself slipping back into the girl of her youth.

As if her musing had sent a message into the universe, Henry paused at the Hula-Hoop booth, staring at it, his brows pulling together.

Oh, no. Given her recent line of thinking, Stella prayed he didn't want this to be his homework. She wouldn't be able to manage. She held off on finishing her corn dog to use it as an excuse for moving along to the next booth— they couldn't hoop together if they were both holding their lunch, right?

His gaze moved to the hoops hanging on the wall. "We've done this before, right?" His eyes slid from the hoops back to her, a mixture of affection and interest in them.

Her heart nearly stopped, and she held her breath. "Yes." She waited for him to give her more information about exactly what he remembered.

"Meet me at Christmas." The words came off his lips on a whisper. He faced her. "You met me here once."

"You remember?" she asked, her pulse rising.

She didn't want him to remember yet. She was just getting him back. She'd been afraid since the day she walked into Vanderbilt and found him there that if he remembered their later time together, she might lose him again. Would that be for the best? Stella had a whole life outside of Leiper's Fork, and Henry certainly didn't need her mucking up his new life. Maybe without the terrible memories of her, he could finally move on.

"It's vague," he replied, cutting into her inner dialogue, "but it feels closer to the surface than the other memories."

The way he was looking at her unnerved her.

"Will you come back to my house with me?" he asked.

She wasn't sure that was a good idea, given this new development.

"I know what I want to do for my homework."

"Why are you suddenly such a good student?" she asked.

"What?"

"Out of nowhere, you're answering Ms. Weixel's questions, doing your homework—it's a one-eighty from the man who saved me from the ditch my first night here."

His jaw clenched, his gaze shifting as if he were wrestling with something. Then he said, "You make me want to do better; you make me *want* to remember."

Guilt and uncertainty mixed within her like a toxic cocktail.

He held out his hand. "Come back to the cabin with me. I'm serious. I might need your help."

She knew she shouldn't say yes, but if she did, perhaps it would help him get the last fourteen years back, and if it did, they could finally move on from it. She was being selfish, anyway, swimming in those old feelings for him when she knew good and well that she could never give him what he wanted.

"All right."

He nodded toward the remainder of her corn dog. "Bring your lunch with you."

"That's okay. I'm full anyway." The food had settled like a brick in her stomach, and she tossed the rest into a nearby bin.

They made their way to Henry's truck, hopped in, and drove the few minutes to the farm, parking outside the guest cabin.

"There's a woodshed out back," he told her, shutting off the engine. "I haven't gone in there since I've been home, so it's something I haven't done."

She got out and shut the truck door. "Why haven't you been in it?"

"It feels strange, being here—like I'm living in someone else's house, even though Mary Jo said I lived here before. I feel I should still be in the main house in my old bedroom." He walked beside her down the stone path leading to the woodshed. "This shed, however, was something I did use every now and again—I remember that. I just haven't felt like going in."

"So why now?" she asked.

"When I saw that game of Hula-Hoops, I remembered more about the door."

"I don't follow."

He stopped outside the shed. "I remembered a note I'd put on the door at the house that said 'Meet me at Christmas.' You and I used to leave notes on the door for each other."

Her skin prickled. "Yes, we did."

"And I wanted to give you a new door, the maple door I'd been working on. I think I made it here in the shed, and I thought having you with me might jog more of the memory."

He tugged on the large barn door and slid it open. Right in front of them, still leaning against the worktable, was the door he'd had been restoring for their farmhouse. It was sitting there as if she'd only blinked and the last thirteen years hadn't happened. The guilt and sadness of that final day and the loss of what they'd had rushed in, and her eyes filled with tears.

"What does this mean to you?" Henry asked.

She blinked, trying to clear her tears. "It just... hit me hard. It's been a long time since I've seen it, that's all."

He squinted at her, clearly not buying that as the full answer. "Why does it make you emotional, though? What's the connection?"

She gazed into his blue eyes, formulating her opinion of how to approach this. Being with her was proving helpful for him, and while she didn't know if she was ready for Henry to remember *everything*, she had to do what she could to help him.

"Look, I could tell you, but I'm afraid that if you know things because I've told you it might muddy the waters of your actual memories. Already, you remembered a note on the front door of the house—that really happened. And I do have a connection to this door—you're right about that too. But I'd rather you get to know me in real time and remember our past on your own and not based on a handful of memories that only one of us can recall."

He stared at the door, looking dejected, clearly trying to work out whether he agreed with her approach.

Unable to handle the sight of his disappointment on her account, she decided to tell him about the study from her email, praying she was doing the right thing. "I learned about a new form of therapy that uses magnetic brain stimulation to improve memory."

He slowly turned to her, his face aghast. "What? You're not putting magnets in my brain."

"I think it uses pulse-technology, but even still, what's the alternative?"

"Hanging out with you seems to be working pretty well."

Just then, her phone pinged with a text. And then with a second. So she checked it to be sure everything was okay.

"It's my mom, reminding me we have a leak in the ceiling. She says she called and left messages with a few repair companies, but she's not getting any answers." Stella responded to Mama that she'd help her out when she got home and returned her phone to her pocket.

"Where's the leak exactly?" Henry asked.

"In the main entryway. We think it's coming from the roof."

"I have a ladder. I could take a look. At the very least, I could put a tarp on it until after Christmas."

"You'd do that?"

"Sure."

She couldn't deny the little thrill that coursed through her as he looked at her, and she wondered what the coming days would hold for them.

# Chapter Fourteen

"I found you a roofer," Stella said when she walked into the house, nodding to the truck parked outside their front window.

Mama peered through the glass as Henry leaned over the tailgate and pulled a ladder from the truck bed. His breath billowed out around him in the cold as he strained to carry the massive ladder to the porch and lean it against the roofline.

"It feels off not to see Pop climbing up to check things out," Mama said. "He'd have gotten up there and fixed it before any of us even knew it was leaking. He spent so many days working on this house."

"He loved doing it," Stella said.

When her father finally told them he had cancer, it was already too late. Stella had been angry with him for that. He'd waited on purpose, so as not to spend his days grieving. For eight months, he dealt with the business of dying without sharing it with a soul. During the day, he spent time with Mama, called Stella and Lily for long chats, and did things around the house. At night, he worked on getting his affairs in order, made files of investments and bank statements, and wrote down all his passwords.

*"Life isn't about dying. That's just one day. It's what we do with all the other days that matters most,"* he'd said in his last moments, the words echoing in her mind now.

Seeing Henry outside made her wonder what Pop had been like at their age. The son of two lawyers, Pop had grown up wealthy, but he'd chosen a simpler life, working with his hands and living out in the countryside. He jumped right into life as if he couldn't wait to live it. By the time Pop was thirty, he had children already. With the right person, Henry could've been like Pop and had kids by now. Henry would've made an amazing father. Before she'd left, he'd been so patient. Once, when they were at church on Sunday morning, the Sunday school teacher had burst into the hallway in a panic, unable to find a little preschooler named Matthew. She could recall every detail of that moment.

"I'll look for him," Henry had said.

"He didn't want to be left in Sunday school. He's afraid of strangers," the woman called after him as he took Stella's hand and scoured the hallways.

They finally located the little boy outside in the churchyard. Henry dropped Stella's hand and paced slowly over to him. "Wow, you're so lucky," Henry said, walking beside the boy, his attention on the ground as he moved slowly around.

The little boy looked up at him. "Why?"

"Well, you're standing in a patch of clover. If you find one with four leaves, do you know what it means?"

Matthew's eyes rounded. "Good luck?"

"Nope. It gives you your shield."

Matthew scratched his head and then plopped down in the center of the clover. "What kind of shield?"

"The bravery shield. When you find a four-leaf clover, you become fearless. Nothing will scare you. Not Sunday school, not the teachers—nothing." Henry reached down and plucked a clover and handed it to the boy. "It's your lucky day."

Matthew gasped, taking the four-leaf clover into his tiny hands.

"No one can stop you now. You're invincible."

"I am?"

"Yep. And the other kids might need you to help them. A few of them might be scared. Think you can walk in with me and help me keep everything under control?"

The little boy took Henry's hand, and Henry delivered him to the classroom.

"I can take it from here," Matthew said.

Henry raised is eyebrows. "You sure?"

"Yep." The little boy held up the crumpled clover and then put it into his pocket.

"Okay, you take care of this room and I'll make sure everything's all right with the others."

Stella knew right then that he'd be a wonderful father.

❄

Mama opened the front door. "Hey, Henry!"

The ladder rattled against the gutter as he straightened it. He nodded a hello. Henry was a lot like her father in temperament—Pop had always loved him as a son. A tiny piece of her wanted to believe Pop had sent Henry back to them, but she knew it probably wasn't true. And she still had her big secret looming, the guilt of leaving Henry unaware still pelting her from the inside.

Pop's voice returned as if she hadn't heard it the first time: *"It's what we do with all the other days that matters most."*

Mama beckoned Henry inside. "Come in out of the cold for a minute, and I'll show you where the leak is."

Henry entered and his gaze flickered to Stella. He flashed her a smile before he focused on Mama.

"See it there?" Mama pointed to the brown spot in the ceiling, a drip hanging precariously from the surface, ready to drop into the bucket any second.

"All right," Henry said, rubbing the scruff on his face. He went back to the door. "I'll take a look on the roof and see what I can find."

"Thank you, dear."

"Yes," Stella added. "Thank you."

While Mama went back to the ironing she'd been doing, Stella took a seat on the sofa, across from the fire, her mind full. What did she really want to happen at this point? Was she leading Henry on in some way, only to go back to her regular life and break his heart again? Could she withstand her own heartbreak? Christmas would end, and Stella's work would resume. She'd fly out to some country that was inevitably too far away to keep in touch like she'd want to, and she and Henry would either drift apart or suffer some sort of dramatic split that wouldn't do either of them any good.

Stella mentally paced through a normal day in her life: researching long hours, drinking cup after cup of coffee on trains and in the backs of cabs while she found commonalities in various studies, comparing her findings from the subjects in her research at whatever hospital she was visiting. She'd drop her things the minute she got home, the windows dark from the night sky, then under the yellow light of a foreign kitchen in whatever flat she was staying in for that month, she'd write.

In her adult life, there were no lingering remnants of the long days of her youth spent barefoot in the creek out back or bandaging her sore fingers from climbing trees with Henry all day. She barely remembered the wind in her hair from riding Delilah, the old horse on his farm, or holding her hand out the window of his truck. In the faraway places she traveled, the night sky was silent and still, unlike the star-filled skies of Tennessee with glimmering moonlight and lightning bugs.

Who was she really? And what did she want? *Pop, I need you*, she called out in her mind.

*"You have everything you need for every decision you want to make,"* he'd said once when she'd been trying to decide if she wanted to go away to science camp or spend her Saturdays working her first high school job. *"But you have to reach out and grab the things you want and hold on to them."*

Henry came back into the house, his strong hands pink from the cold. "I think I found the issue. Looks like a shingle cracked in the snow and the seal under it is damaged."

"Do you know how to fix it?" Stella asked, waving him into the living room.

"I think so." He walked over to the fire and spread out his fingers in front of the flames, but he didn't sit down. "For now, I'll put a tarp over it. I'll see if I can find the supplies in town, and I'll come back to repair it tomorrow. I should probably get back."

"Okay," Stella said.

The corners of his lips turned up just enough to make her heart patter before he let himself out. "See ya tomorrow."

"Yes, we'll see you tomorrow."

After he got in the truck and turned to drive away, he threw his hand out the window, just as he had every time he'd come over when they were young, and despite her trepidation, she couldn't help but be excited to see him again.

Later that night, Stella sank into the bubble bath she'd drawn, trying to quiet her thoughts with the warmth of the water and the fizz of the bubbles. But her mind was still racing after the day's events.

It was totally natural to feel something for Henry, she reasoned. After all, she'd been married to him. And he evidently recognized their strong connection. He was opening up around her, and he seemed to enjoy being with her. It made sense that their bond would surface in his memory when she was around.

She liked being with him enough that the idea of staying in Leiper's Fork floated into her consciousness. But she knew that was ridiculous. She'd worked hard for her job, and she couldn't imagine leaving it only to have him finally remember what she'd done and never speak to her again. Even if he forgave her, how could they move forward, given her inability to have children? Henry's words rang through her head, making her wince. *"I want a house full of little boys and girls who look just like us."* She could never give him that.

Sometimes she let herself wonder about their child, who he or she would've been. She contemplated the changes in her life. What would she be doing right now if she hadn't lost the baby? Who would she be? Would she be happy? Would Henry?

Stella closed her eyes and plunged her head under the surface of the water, her ears filling until the sound of her movement was muted, bubbles of air escaping her nose. She held her breath in the wet cocoon, trying to focus on that moment and nothing else, but it was proving difficult. There were no right answers for any of this.

She came back up for air and bathed, methodically rubbing the stress from her skin. When anything bothered her over the years, she'd always gone to Pop. He'd listened to her childhood worries about her grades at school or where the teacher had sat her in class. She'd told him all her fears about how she didn't know what to do when she grew up. He'd listened intently to every single thing, offering reassurance and helpful advice every time.

"I miss you so much," she whispered into the empty bathroom as she moved the bubbles around her. "I wish you were here, Pop. I don't know what to do."

*"You always know what to do."*

She grinned to herself, remembering one time when she'd confided in him that she couldn't do math.

"I have to understand this and I don't know how to do it," she'd said, staring helplessly at the math problem in front of her without a clue how to begin to tackle it.

"You always know what to do," Pop said.

"How can you say that?"

"Because you are equipped with everything you need to solve any problem. You just have to trust yourself and work at it."

She looked back down at the problem and took in a slow, steadying breath. As she studied the numbers an idea came to her. "What if I multiply these two first?"

"Go for it." Pop gave her a supportive pat on the back.

She started working the problem, and before she knew it, she'd gotten to the end of it. "The answer is thirty-seven?" She checked the key in the back of the book.

"Boom. Thirty-seven." Pop clapped his hands together in satisfaction.

"Stella?" The stifled sound of her mother's voice came from the other side of the bathroom door.

Stella, who'd slipped back under to wash away the tears spilling down her face, surfaced and rubbed the water from her eyes. "Yes?"

"Henry's here."

"What?" She stood up, bubbles sliding down her skin as she reached for her towel. Wasn't it after nine? "Why?"

"He says he remembers something." Mama's voice was quiet. "He's a little agitated. I offered him some cookies, but he said he didn't want any."

Stella wrapped the towel around her and stood in the middle of the bathroom, paralyzed. What did he remember? Her mind spun with the various answers to that question as she ran a comb through her tangled, wet hair and then dressed in her fuzzy pajamas on autopilot.

When she got to the living room, Henry was sitting on the sofa, facing the fireplace. He stood immediately and came over to her, an intensity in his eyes she couldn't decipher.

"I'm going to go to my room to read," Mama said, clearly excusing herself for their benefit, although Stella was hoping Mama's presence would soften the blow of whatever Henry was about to say. "Anyone need anything?"

Stella shook her head.

After Mama left, he took another step toward Stella, invading her personal space. "We were married." It wasn't a question, but rather a statement, a fact. "Why didn't you tell me?"

"I... Um..." she stuttered, feeling faint.

He reached for her hand and opened it, palm up, then placed his closed fist on top of her fingers. He released what he was holding, and his wedding band fell into her palm. Then he sat on the sofa and hung his head.

Stella moved closer to him. "What, exactly, did you remember?" Her inhales were shallow, as if she'd suddenly lost the ability to take a full breath.

His cheeks flushed, surprising her. "I got into bed like I always do and shut my eyes," he said, peering into the fireplace. "But tonight was different. I had this overwhelming feeling that if I opened them, you'd be under the covers next to me." He shook his head. "I remembered I had a wife who slept beside me every night. And I remembered that person was you." He ran his hands through his hair in frustration, making her flinch. "I remembered I had a ring to prove it," he continued, "and, trying to convince myself that I wasn't delusional, I got up and fished around my top dresser drawer, and in the back of it my fingers hit a wooden box and I knew I was right. I pulled it out and there it was—the wedding band."

Stella held up the gold band, her aching eyes filling with tears once more. She tried unsuccessfully to blink them away. She hadn't seen that band since the day she left. "Do you remember anything else?" she asked, her voice too weak to come out as more than a whisper.

"No," he said, sounding defeated. Then he looked up at her, vulnerability written on his face. "What happened to us, Stella?"

She hesitated, wondering if she should say anything, and if she did, what exactly she would say.

"And don't give me that bull about me needing to remember myself," he said, his jaw clenched. "I deserve to know."

Stella rubbed her eyes, buying time. "You've remembered a lot today. And it's late. Why don't we get a good night's sleep and..." She knew how weak the suggestion sounded.

"I asked Mary Jo and she wouldn't tell me. She said you needed to do it."

Stella swallowed. "We were really young..." That was all she could get out, the rest of the words stuck in her throat, the absolute anguish of that day hitting her like a tidal wave.

"Something happened, Stella. I can tell by the way you're acting and by the way Mary Jo looked when I told her."

Her lips parted. She wanted to say something to put him at ease, but what? "Why does it matter? It was in the past."

"Why does it matter?" he roared. He stomped across the room and peered out the window at the black sky then whirled around. "We didn't work out, did we, Stella?"

She stood there in her pajamas feeling more vulnerable than she ever had. This was her moment to fix what she'd broken, and she had no idea how to do it. "No, we didn't. It was a long time ago."

"You're the first person I've felt halfway normal with since the accident, and when I go home at night, all I want is to see you again. Then I find out you and I *didn't work*..." He went back to the sofa and sat, dropping his head. "Did I do something wrong?" he asked without looking up. "Did I drive you away somehow?"

"No!" The shock of his question sliced through her, and she had to sit down next to him before her knees gave out. Although his pain was misdirected, seeing the hurt on his face took her back to that awful day.

"It was me, wasn't it? I know I'm not the easiest person to be around."

"No. No, it wasn't anything you did," she blurted, gripping his ring. "We got an annulment. I wasn't eighteen when we got married."

"You were in high school?"

"No. I skipped the fourth grade, so I graduated at seventeen."

"Why didn't we just get married *after* you were eighteen?"

"I… went off to Stanford and you joined the army."

He shook his head, his shoulders dropping. "It doesn't make sense."

"What doesn't?" she asked, hanging on to the quiet between them.

"That memory of you beside me in my bed felt like me and the life I'd choose for myself way more than anything I would've done in the army." He got up and paced to the fireplace, facing the stockings Stella and Mama had hung.

Stella sat there in silence for a moment, his statement slamming her. "You loved being married. You were always a family man," she said quietly, more tears surfacing. "Before your accident, you had an endless reserve of patience, and you wanted… a whole house full of kids." Saying the words out loud brought a deluge of tears for what she hadn't been able to give him. In that moment, she wished she could've given him his dream.

He turned toward her. "I thought you weren't going to tell me anything about myself." His eyes were full of tenderness.

She realized then that she held the key to who he was, and their dance of information was pulling him closer to her, something she wasn't entirely sure how to manage. "I don't have any right answers. I'm trying—"

"Well, given that you research this stuff for a living, if *you* don't have answers, I sure don't," he said, his signature humor surfacing beneath the intensity of the moment. He sobered quickly. "You make me want to remember every single detail."

She stared into his blue eyes and drank in those familiar features, taking in the comfort of having him on the sofa where they'd spent so many hours talking and giggling as kids. Her heart ached for those old days, but his confession was a double-edged sword. She had the urge to run once more, like she'd had when she left that day, but there was nowhere to go this time. She was forced to face the issue head on.

*"There's nothing better than family,"* Pop had told her just before she left. She could hear him again. *"I'm not sure you'll find anything that's better."*

"Maybe we should just start over…" she said. "We're different people now. Can't we start again, right now? Maybe be friends?" She offered him the gold band.

He took it from her and put it in his pocket. "I'd like that." He gave her a warm smile. "I'm sorry I burst in so late. I just needed to know… I'll let you enjoy what's left of the night."

As Henry stood, she rose and grabbed his arm, not wanting him to leave, but also not having a good reason to ask him to stay. She dropped her hand, and they faced each other, caught in limbo between their old lives and their new ones.

# Chapter Fifteen

Running a little late after working and not having heard from Henry that morning, Stella decided to drive herself to the hospital. During the drive, she went over ways to approach the therapy session today. It would be difficult to sit silently in the back of the room, but she knew she needed to remain as professional as possible.

"Stella, I'm glad I caught you," Dr. Astley said as she clipped toward her in a Vanderbilt hallway. "I tried to call you this morning."

Stella stopped and checked her phone. Sure enough, she had a missed call. "Oh, I'm sorry I missed this." She put her phone back in her purse. "What's going on?"

"We've had a slight change."

Stella shifted the weight of her computer bag on her shoulder, her mind still full. "What do you mean?"

"I've got good news and bad news. Which do you want first?"

"Good?"

Dr. Astley slipped her hands into the pockets of her lab coat. "Okay, the good news is that I got you another subject for your article. His name is Herbert Ferguson."

"Oh, yes! I met him in the hallway. That's great." But something on Dr. Astley's face gave her pause. "And the bad news?"

"Henry Dutton has left our program."

Stella's shoulders fell, her bag slipping to the crook of her arm. "What? Why?"

"He called this morning and said he didn't want to continue."

What in the world was Henry doing? He was so intent on regaining his memories, and he'd been progressing well. Why would he decide to just quit therapy? It made no sense.

"I'm sorry you came all this way this morning. Mr. Ferguson isn't coming in until later today."

"That's okay," Stella replied, although nothing about the situation with Henry was okay. "I'll come back later."

"All right. He's coming in at three o'clock."

"Thank you for letting me know."

"No problem."

Stella immediately exited the hospital, got into her car, and drove straight to Henry's. She bumped along the gravel road between the main farmhouse and the cabin, parking out front next to his truck. After hopping out and bounding up the steps, she rapped on the front door.

"Henry!" she called, knocking. When no one answered, she peered through the window to find that the light in the kitchen was on. She knocked again, harder. "Henry! It's Stella!"

Finally, the door opened. "Is something on fire?"

She put her hands on her hips. "You know why I'm here."

He opened the door wider to allow her to enter. She walked in, the familiar scent of burning wood and cedar wrapping around her. The old wood stove flickered orange and sent out a wave of heat through the room.

"Have a seat." Henry gestured to the sofa she'd picked out when they went furniture shopping at the second-hand store in town. The decision had been between this one in the muted burlap tan or a striped one with a stain on the middle cushion. "Want something to drink?"

"No, Henry. I want an answer." She sat down, shrugging off her coat, the Christmas tree gleaming in the window opposite her. "Why did you quit therapy?"

He opened the door to the wood stove and threw another log on the fire. "I was following your advice."

"What?" she asked, exasperated.

"You said that maybe I should just start over. Which means I don't need that ridiculous therapy. It wasn't helping anyway."

"You didn't give it a chance."

"We'll have to agree to disagree on that point." He clapped the log debris off his hands.

"Henry. You're starting to remember. I've seen it, plain as day."

"But if I don't *need* to remember because I'm starting over, then why should I go?"

"I meant with us. *We* should start over. Regardless of our past, we are different people now. That's all I meant."

"Done." He sat down next to her.

"Okay," she said, trying not to focus on those blue eyes. "Now, shouldn't you return to therapy?"

"No." He rubbed his hands down the thighs of his jeans, shaking his head. "Therapy wasn't working. You are. So if you want to help me remember, all you have to do is come over." He opened his arms wide, a grin on his face. "This is the new therapy location. Unless you want to get coffee. Then we can call the coffee shop in town the new location."

"You're not funny," she said, half-heartedly.

His grin only grew—the spunky, mischievous boy he used to be peeking through and making her more flustered. He was a far cry from the Henry she'd found when she first arrived, and she didn't want to think for one second that it had been only her presence that changed him. Because if that were true, it would only be a matter of time before she let her feelings slip and something more happened between them. Because she certainly didn't trust herself with him.

"This isn't like skipping school in tenth grade. This is important," she said.

"No, it's not. There are many ways to find peace and healing. I'd prefer to find those things here in my cabin with you at my side."

"But the medical team has proven methods that work."

"It's a bunch of malarky."

She grunted in frustration. He'd always been stubborn, and she knew full well that he wasn't going to do anything he didn't want to do. "You need to do this, Henry."

"Why? For you and your article?"

"That's a low blow. This doesn't have anything to do with my work. Mr. Ferguson has agreed to be my new subject anyway." Truth be told, she wasn't sure how she would bridge the two cases to get a full article, and it would be even more difficult if Henry didn't return to therapy. Her entire future with the magazine hung in the balance.

"Well, my therapy today is to go outside into the woodshed and mess around with that door. I think I'm gonna make something out of it."

Her heart plummeted into her stomach, but she tried not to let it show. "Make something out of it?" she repeated, trying to keep her voice even. She knew the door would never adorn that restored farmhouse for the two of them, but there was something so final about cutting through the wood and turning it into something else. "What are you going to make?"

He pursed his lips in an adorable way. "I have no idea. But I feel like it's what I should do. It sounds… fun."

"That makes sense. The last year I lived here, you took up woodworking," she said. "Maybe you subconsciously remember that."

He blinked, his brows pulling together as if he were inwardly trying to validate her statement. "I do enjoy it. More than landscaping."

She stood up, still frustrated that he wasn't giving therapy a chance. She gritted her teeth. "Well, I'll leave you to it."

"All right," he said as he walked her the few paces to the front door. He opened it, and she walked out into the winter air. "Sure you don't want to putter around in the woodshed with me?" Something in his eyes begged her to stay.

"That might be a good activity to do alone to explore your interests. I'd just distract you."

The corner of his mouth twitched upward. "Yes. You would."

She grinned despite trying not to show how much she enjoyed his banter. "Bye."

With a chuckle, he shut the door.

Full of nervous energy, she trekked through the frozen field to the main house and knocked on the back door.

Mary Jo answered.

"You said to stop by," Stella said.

"Of course. Come in." Mary Jo ushered Stella inside and beckoned her over to a small sitting area next to the breakfast nook. "What's up?"

"Henry being Henry."

"What's he done now?" She brought over a candy dish of wrapped peppermints, placing it in front of Stella, then sat down across from her in the gingham-cushioned wicker chair matching the one Stella was in.

Stella grabbed a mint and untwisted the ends, then popped it into her mouth and took a minute to let the crisp sweetness sit on her tongue before answering. "He quit therapy."

Henry had mentioned he'd gone to therapy for Mary Jo, so Stella expected his sister to be outraged. Instead, her expression was blank, as if she were chewing on the idea and deciding how she felt about it. "He never really subscribed to it," she said at last.

"I know it isn't a quick fix, and Henry isn't a terribly patient person these days, but I study the mechanics of the brain for a living. There are proven benefits to sticking with therapy."

"Did he say why he quit?"

"He thinks being with me is more helpful."

Mary Jo smiled, which only made Stella more exasperated.

"He might not be wrong," his sister said.

"And what happens when I leave?" Stella asked.

Mary Jo's face fell. "You're planning on leaving?" But before Stella could answer, she shook her head. "Silly question."

"I'm only here for Christmas. For Mama. I was never planning to stay." As she said the words, that feeling of being caught between her old life and her new one came tumbling toward her, and she wondered again what she really wanted. It was all a muddle.

Mary Jo grabbed a peppermint, the cellophane wrapper rattling in the silence between them. She got up and made herself a cup of tea, offering one to Stella, but Stella declined.

*You can always reinvent yourself.*

Pop's voice always seemed to fill the silence lately.

She'd called him from California during her first week away at Stanford and asked, *"What if I get this degree and it isn't what I'm supposed to do with my life?"* That had been his answer.

Why had she thought of that memory? Did she have some deep desire to reinvent herself?

"I'm glad Henry chose not to go forward with therapy," Mary Jo said, breaking the silence when she returned with a steaming mug that smelled of jasmine and honey.

"Why in the world would you be glad?" Stella asked.

"Because he's making a decision; he's doing what feels right. He hasn't done that in a long time." She set her mug on the small table between them. "He isn't saying he won't go just to be obstinate. He's saying he won't go because he thinks there's a better way."

Stella considered this. "But what if he's wrong?"

Mary Jo gave her a challenging look. "What if he's right?"

"I have no idea how I'm going to get the article done," Stella admitted to her mother after telling her the latest on Henry. She sat at the kitchen table and stared at the two measly paragraphs she'd written. "Henry only just started to be cooperative in the sessions, and I didn't really get a whole lot even then. Now I have to start over with an elderly man named Herbert Ferguson. I'll have to line up a whole new angle of research to support what I observe in his sessions."

Mama was getting yet another sheet of cookies out of the oven, and Stella wondered if all the cookie baking was her mother's way of occupying herself so she wouldn't have to think about Pop's absence.

She set the pan on a trivet on the counter and faced Stella. "Maybe you could just write the entire article about Mr. Ferguson."

"Maybe."

While Mama slid her spatula under the cookies to transfer them to the cooling rack, the sweet scents of cinnamon and sugar filling in the air, Stella checked her email. Her mind was only half on the task when she opened the most recent correspondence from her editor. The message landed in front of her like a gift from above.

Hey Stella,

I saw this piece and thought it might be good to consult. Hope you're doing well out in the hills! Got everything crossed for you for that President's Award!

Happy holidays,
Amy

The pressure of the award mounting, Stella took a deep breath, clicked on the attachment, and read the title of the literature review: "Effects of Chronic Stress on Memory." Interested, she scanned down to the findings: "Higher levels of stress were associated with more incidents of memory loss when coupled with a traumatic event or injury." She immediately connected the description to Henry and how he'd changed since she arrived. Her mind spun a hundred miles an hour as she considered how she could use this to support the anecdotal records from Henry's therapy.

"So the happier he is, the better chance he has to remember..." she said to herself, scanning the summary. "That fits perfectly with Ms. Weixel's approach, but it also..."

"What's that?" Mama asked.

"My editor might have just saved my butt." She opened the document with her notes from Henry's sessions. "And Henry might just be on to something."

Mama set her spatula on the counter and lowered herself in the chair across from Stella, clearly interested. "What did you find?"

"This article explains how memory loss can worsen with stress."

"He has been under a lot, I think, given what Mary Jo told me."

"Henry swears he doesn't need therapy because he remembers more when he's with me. Which makes me think that, for some reason, I bring his stress down."

"So being with you really does give him the chance of remembering."

"Yes. If his anxiety is reduced, there's a greater chance of success, which now makes absolute sense. The therapist was trying to get him to think positively."

But then the indecision that had plagued Stella reared its head once more. She really wanted to start over with him, maybe create a friendship first, the way she'd planned… But the more time she spent with him, the more she fell back into her old feelings, and from the way he looked at her sometimes, she was willing to bet he felt those old feelings too. If she spent more time with him, he was likely to recover his memories more quickly, which could change everything. Could she find a gentle approach to tell him what happened in her own way before he remembered how she left? Should she?

"How lucky was he that you decided to come home now," Mama said.

"Yeah…" Her answer withered on her lips.

"Speaking of luck, any news on the necklace?"

"The jeweler said it would be a few days."

"The story behind it is just so intriguing. I've been reading more about it."

With no answers, Stella welcomed the change in conversation. She closed her laptop. "Did you discover anything else?"

Mama grabbed her phone and typed. "I did! Let me see if I can find the article I read last night…" After a bit of scrolling, she said, "Here we go. I searched for 'Christmas Diamond jeweler' and look what I found." She set her phone on the table between them.

Stella leaned over and read the section.

The jeweler, Edward James, couldn't let the diamond go without knowing its entire history. He believed the fate of the diamond could be different, and he hired a detective to help him find the merchant, Charles Worley, to tell him. Mr. Worley hadn't gotten far, settling in a remote area of Rhode Island, but when Edward's detective located the home, he was met by an estate agent who was packing the man's things. To his disappointment, the merchant had just died.

Worried the diamond might fall into the wrong hands, Edward went to pay his respects. While there, he searched the rooms, found the trunk, and pocketed the diamond. He was thought to have gone to London briefly, where he'd hidden it away. He returned to Boston, and his detective located the Hastings family who'd originally lost it. He began to investigate the history of the diamond under the guise of writing a newspaper article about it. It was during his time with the family and others in the city where he learned the true story of the diamond—the account we have today—which he'd written down in his journal.

However, Edward James's strong faith led him to a different conclusion about the diamond, which he also wrote down in his journal. His core belief was that we're all made of love, as is everything in the universe, so if we want good luck from the diamond, we have to treat it with love. He likened the diamond to a stowaway or a lost child, and vowed to give it with intention and to proclaim that it was a token of only love. When he married, he retrieved it from its hiding place in London and gave it to his soon-to-be wife. He made his intentions clear and told her it was not just any symbol, but a physical representation of the love he had for her. The journal ended with that last entry, and no one knows the exact fate of the couple or the diamond. Some accounts say they lived happily ever after.

"Maybe *we* have it now," Mama said with a wink.

Stella shook her head. "I doubt it very seriously."

But even though their necklace was probably nothing special, it was nice to see her mother interested in something. It seemed to fill the silence that had permeated the house since they'd lost Pop.

# Chapter Sixteen

Later that afternoon, Stella was feeling nostalgic. She left early for Mr. Ferguson's therapy session and took a detour into town. When she reached the diner she used to work at, she pulled into the parking lot and got out. She put her mittened hands on her hips and took in the snow-dusted, one-street village, thinking about Pop and her life here.

This sleepy town had been her whole world before she packed up and left for Stanford. Its quirks had been her every day. She recalled long mornings spent with Lily and Pop at the farmers market on weekends while Mama cleaned the house, and then they'd bring down their biggest quilt and settle in the grass at the Lawn Chair Theater, an old log structure with curling vines adorning its walls, to hear the up-and-coming Nashville musicians who were usually only one signature away from absolute stardom.

*"It's good to be home, isn't it?"* She heard Pop's voice in her head as if he were walking beside her. He'd said that every time they came back to Leiper's Fork after leaving for any amount of time. She could still feel the warmth of his genuine delight when he returned to their little town.

"It is good, Pop," she said quietly as she paced down the street, past the local art gallery, heading toward the woods where she and Pop liked to search for honeysuckle in the summers. "I miss you so much."

*"I'll never leave."* The memory of his return after one particular beach vacation surfaced, making her smile. *"Five days is enough time to be away,"* he'd said. *"I'll never leave."*

Wishing Pop could be there to hold her hand like he had when she was a girl, she kept walking along the edge of the woods, as far as she could go, and then made her way back to the sidewalk, past the local bar, the boutiques selling the latest in western wear, and a couple of lunch spots she and Lily used to visit together. All their windows glittered with shiny holiday decor.

Not only had she given up Henry, but she'd pushed away the absolute charm of this town, and she appreciated it so much more, now, after being gone.

"I wish you could be with us, this Christmas," she whispered to Pop, praying he could hear her and know how much they loved him. With a weight on her heart, she walked back to her car and started her second trip of the day to Nashville.

After a briefing with Dr. Astley, Stella arrived at Mr. Ferguson's therapy room. The contrast to her first experience with her last subject was stark. The room was quiet, decorated the same way, with a sofa by the window that sat on the edge of a small rug. Two chairs were placed opposite the sofa, where Mr. Ferguson sat beaming, his hand raised in greeting.

"Hello, there," he said, leaning over to move his walker so she could get by, even though it wasn't in the way. "Lovely to see you again."

"Same." Stella smiled and sat down in the back of the room, then retrieved her laptop.

Mr. Ferguson's therapist, Ms. Barnes, walked in with her own small laptop. "Good afternoon," she greeted them. "Herbert, this is Stella Fisher. Since you signed the release, she'll be observing us for an article she's writing for *Brain Borders Magazine*. Your name and all your information will be kept strictly confidential."

"Yes, we met." Mr. Ferguson wriggled his fingers for a second hello.

Stella smiled at the old man.

"Since we're a few minutes early," the therapist continued, "do you mind if I give Stella a little more background on your case before we get started?"

His bushy eyebrows bobbed, his old eyes sparkling. "Not at all."

"Thank you." The therapist sat down and twisted around toward Stella. "Herbert has what we call a mild cognitive impairment."

Stella opened her laptop and pulled up a blank document, then started entering notes.

"We are watching his symptoms to make sure he isn't experiencing the early onset of Alzheimer's, which was his initial concern."

"So far, so good," Mr. Ferguson added brightly.

Stella gave him another grin and went back to her notes.

"He enrolled himself in the program due to concerns of general forgetfulness." She addressed Mr. Ferguson. "Do you feel comfortable explaining your early symptoms to Stella?"

"Of course." Mr. Ferguson shifted on the sofa. "I have a cat named Lucy. I started to panic at times, wondering if I'd fed her or let her inside for the night. One night, I had to get out of bed, just to check. She was always fine, but it was enough to worry me. But as the weeks went on, I struggled terribly with things like remembering my family members' full names, my birthday…"

"That sounds stressful," Stella said as she typed quickly before giving him her full attention again.

"You can't imagine." Mr. Ferguson cleared his throat, his beard wobbling with the quiver of his lips. "Lucy is all I have…"

Stella glanced at Ms. Barnes.

"Herbert lives alone and has no family, so Lucy is his only companion."

Stella closed her laptop, her interest getting the better of her.

"I do have the people from my church. After my wife passed away last year, I've needed their support."

"I'm so sorry. I lost my dad about a year ago."

Mr. Ferguson gave her a sympathetic nod. "I try to keep positive. I swear the more positive I remain, the better my memory is."

"I actually just read an article about that," Stella told him.

Mr. Ferguson nodded. The man's sadness was evident and Stella could tell he wanted to talk about his wife, but it was time to get started, so she shrank back in her spot and allowed the therapist to take the lead.

Mr. Ferguson's session was uneventful. He complied, answering all questions asked of him. He was open, kind, and good spirited. Stella found herself typing madly to compare him with her experience with Henry in therapy, the article she'd read the night before guiding her thoughts.

When the session had ended and they were parting ways, Stella felt drawn to Mr. Ferguson. She had a million things to do, but he clearly needed someone. And she understood a little of what he was going through with the loss of his wife.

"I'm sorry if this isn't appropriate, Ms. Barnes, but, Mr. Ferguson, would you like to do something today? Maybe we could take a slow stroll through one of the museums or art galleries."

The excitement in his eyes revealed how lonely the old man must have been. "I'd love to," he replied excitedly.

Ms. Barnes nodded. "I think that would be a wonderful idea."

Mr. Ferguson canceled the bus for seniors he usually took home and the two of them crossed the street from the parking deck.

"Oh, look at that!" Mr. Ferguson pointed to a white horse-drawn carriage covered in fairy lights and red bows for the holiday. It twinkled against the gray city sky.

"Let's take a ride. My treat." Stella had lived outside Nashville her whole life, but she'd never taken a carriage ride in the city. She started to open her purse, but Mr. Ferguson batted her hand away.

"Absolutely not. I'm paying." He pushed his walker down the sidewalk toward the carriage. When they made it safely to the other side of the street, he pulled a wad of bills from a weathered wallet and paid the coachman. The man folded his walker and slid it in the front of the carriage, then helped them both into the back. Before Stella knew it, she was moving down the main streets of Nashville, enjoying the Christmas decorations, while the horses' hooves clopped against the pavement. Tiny bells on the sides of the carriage jingled, adding a festive feel that was only now taking hold. She'd been so caught up in work and grief that she hadn't stopped to really take in all the festivities.

"I love it here," Mr. Ferguson said.

"Have you always lived in the area?" she asked.

"My wife, Margaret, and I moved out to the countryside a few years before she died. She wanted a place where she could sit on her porch and watch the sunrise in the mornings. We sold everything we had in Nashville, including the upholstery business I owned, and retired in the Tennessee hills, right next to a peaceful little brook that she fell in love with. Sometimes I still go out there and take walks beside it, but it's been getting harder lately." He patted his hip.

"It sounds beautiful."

His lip began to wobble again, and he leaned forward to address their driver. "It's chilly. Do you have a blanket?"

The coachman handed him one, and Stella covered their legs, bunching up the rest of it at their waists.

"This will be my first Christmas without her," Mr. Ferguson said. The creases in his forehead deepened as he blinked away his emotion. He turned toward the garland-draped buildings, all lit up for the holiday. "We never had children, and I don't know how I'll get through it alone."

"I understand. This is mine and my mother's first Christmas without my dad, and my mom's having a tough time."

As she told Mr. Ferguson about Mama, Pop's voice whispered a message he'd always taught her growing up. *If I teach you anything at all in this life, it's to be kind. We're all one big family, really.*

She considered this. "I have an idea. Why don't you spend Christmas with us?" she asked.

Mr. Ferguson shook his head. "Oh, no. I couldn't intrude on your family time."

"We're all family, really," she said, using Pop's words.

Once, when they were in Nashville walking to one of the live shows that Pop used to take her to, they'd passed a man on the street. He appeared to be homeless, but he didn't look like the rest of the homeless people she'd seen; he'd seemed lost instead of hopeless.

Pop had stopped and asked the man, "What's your story?"

The man said, "I came to Nashville to play music, and I ran out of money. Now I have nothing, but I won't go home until I make it."

Her father gave the man all the cash he had—one hundred thirty dollars.

"Why did you give all your money to him?" she asked.

"We're all family, really," he'd told her.

"Please, Mr. Ferguson. We'd be happy to have you," Stella said, the clopping of the horses sailing back into her consciousness.

"Well… Ask your mother first," Mr. Ferguson said.

"Done. I'll let you know tomorrow." She smiled at him, glad to have asked.

Mr. Ferguson stroked his beard. "You're an angel, I think."

She chuckled. "Definitely not."

"For me, you are."

She didn't offer a rebuttal. His comment stayed with her through the rest of the ride. When they returned, Stella offered him a lift home, but he told her he'd called a car to pick him up, so she waited with him until it arrived and helped him over to it.

"Are you all right to go home on your own?" she asked. "Is your hip okay after all the bouncing in the carriage?"

"Oh, yes." He gave her a wide smile. "Spending time with you made me feel like a young man again."

When she left him, despite everything she had going on, she felt a little lighter too.

❄

When Stella got home, she went straight into the living room to let her mother in on the last few hours. "Hey, Mama, I sort of invited an old man to our house for Christmas."

"Oh?" Her mother's eyebrows lifted as she tossed a log into the fire, sending sparks up the chimney. Just then the oven buzzer went off and Mama moved toward the kitchen. "Who is he?" she asked over her shoulder.

Stella followed. "He so lovely." She told Mama all about Mr. Ferguson. Just thinking of him filled her with joy. "He smiles all the time, unless he's thinking about his wife, Margaret."

"He sounds like a nice man."

"Sorry I invited him without checking with you first, but I think he's lonely and I felt bad for him."

"He's welcome to come over." Mama grabbed the oven mitts and slipped them on.

"I'm glad he won't have to be alone for Christmas—"

A loud pounding sound radiated around them, distracting Stella from the conversation.

"What's that?"

Mama pulled a bubbling casserole out of the oven and set it on the counter. "Henry's in the attic."

"Henry's here? Where's his truck?"

"He parked in his spot around back."

Mama's response surprised her, and she took in a deep breath to ward off the affection for him it caused. When they were growing up, to leave space in the driveway for Mama and Pop, Henry used to pull behind the house and park next to the maple tree. For his eighteenth birthday, her father added gravel to the area just for him.

"How did he know about his spot?" she asked.

Mama brushed her hands on her thighs and gave her a knowing look. "He said he remembered."

A tingling sensation ran through her. "What, exactly, did he remember?"

Mama shook her head and shrugged helplessly, then dipped a serving spoon into the casserole. The air filled with the hearty scents of butter and potatoes.

"What's he doing in the attic?"

"He's seeing if he can fix the broken shingle and seal by crawling through the rafters. With no tether." Mama's lips pressed together—her annoyed face.

Stella rolled her eyes. "Henry's always gone through life as if he's invincible."

"I *am* invincible," he said as he came into the room. He offered her a cautious look of amusement, making her stomach flip. "I laid a tarp over the insulation in the attic, just in case you have any lingering drips. But I fixed the shingles—once I got up there and really checked, there were a couple of them." He walked over next to the Christmas tree and fiddled with one of the ornaments. "I'd let it all dry for a week or two and then paint over the water stain on the ceiling. You should be good to go."

"Thank you so much, Henry," Mama said.

"No problem."

His cheeks were slightly pink from the cold, making him look entirely too handsome. Stella wanted to put her hands on his face to warm them up. The thought surprised her, and she turned toward the steaming dish on the counter.

"Stay for dinner, Henry," Mama said, offering him a plate. "I'll pay you in chicken casserole."

"Done." He took the plate from Mama, dished out a helping of casserole, and handed it to Stella before getting another plate out of the cabinet, evidently remembering where they kept the dishes.

The slack in his shoulders and the ease of his movements as if he remembered every day he'd spent at their house, took Stella back to their youth, nearly stopping her in her tracks.

"Hey, Stella, after we eat, want to go over to the Christmas lot? I heard there's a band playing in the pavilion."

The invitation felt like a nudge from Pop after walking through town earlier, reminiscing about the bands they'd watched together.

"Sure." She turned to Mama. "Wanna go with us?"

Mama shook her head. "Oh, no. You two go and enjoy yourselves. I've got laundry to do." She gestured toward the table. "Y'all sit, I'll get us some sweet tea."

Henry pulled out a chair for Stella and, as she took her seat, he went to the counter and dished casserole onto a plate, offering it to Mama before getting his own.

Mama took three glasses from the cabinet and began filling them with tea. "So, Henry, what are you and Mary Jo doing for Christmas?"

"I'm not sure," Henry replied, sitting down next to Stella with a full plate. "We haven't really talked about it."

"Well, you're more than welcome to come here if you get bored. Stella's invited her new friend, Mr. Ferguson, over, since he's by himself this holiday."

Henry gave Stella a curious look. "Mr. Ferguson from the hospital?"

"He's my new subject," Stella replied. "He's such a sweet man, and his wife passed away this year, so I thought I'd be nice and spread some holiday cheer."

Henry gave her a crooked grin. "That's thoughtful of you."

"You know Stella," Mama said, "Always wanting to help people."

When Henry didn't respond, Stella looked over at him, only to find those eyes on her, full of fondness.

In that instant she got a glimpse of what it might have felt like if she'd never left.

※

"Y'all have fun," Mama said to Stella and Henry after they'd cleaned up the dinner dishes.

Henry placed his hand on Stella's back, guiding her to the back door. "Yes, ma'am."

Stella grabbed her coat and went outside. "Mama said you remembered your parking spot." She climbed into Henry's truck.

He started the engine, and snow flurries began to flutter, landing softly on every surface and swirling on the wind. "Yeah."

"Do you remember anything else?"

He put the truck in reverse and twisted around to check behind them before he pressed the gas. "Not too much."

His answer didn't settle her like she'd hoped it would. She couldn't get a read on him to determine if he recalled anything else about their history.

The gravel spun under his tires. He backed right up to the tree the way he'd always done, with perfect precision—she could reach out her window and touch the bark, but he'd never once hit the tree. It was as if he'd remembered exactly how to maneuver in that tight spot. He put the truck in drive, went around the front of the house, and they were off, heading down the lane for the main road.

The drive to Christmas was short. Henry parked the truck and hopped out, then strode around to Stella's side to meet her. The twang of country Christmas carols floated toward them as they made their way to the makeshift venue, erected in a nearby barn. The dark-red doors were flanked by glittering Christmas trees with lights strung above them.

He ushered her inside. Space heaters warmed the entire barn, soothing her icy skin. A band played on the stage, behind a row of hay bales, and the thumping of the drums echoed in her chest.

Henry gestured toward the bar lined in swags of red and green ribbon. "Want a drink?"

"No, thank you." The alcohol wouldn't settle well in her stomach, given her nerves over being with him. The closer he got to being the Henry she knew, the more unsure she became in how to act around him.

"All right then."

The band kicked in with a slow tune, which slowed down her busy mind and soothed her a little. He walked around behind her and took her coat by the shoulders, guided it off, and placed it on a nearby stool with his.

"Let's dance." He held out his hand.

She eyed him, uncertainty swimming through her.

"It's *therapy*."

The other option was to talk, and she wasn't sure she was ready to do that either. With him remembering more, he might have questions. So she took his hand and they walked onto the old wooden dance floor. He held her waist and she wrapped her arms around his neck, then swayed together like they hadn't missed a beat. It was everything she could do not to look up at him, so she turned her head and put her cheek on his chest, breathing in his woodsy, spicy scent. She closed her eyes, the feel of the moment like heaven. The tenderness in his grip, the steadiness in his breathing—it all felt so natural.

*"Give yourself grace."* Pop's voice floated in on a memory from a time she'd struggled with a bad grade at school because she hadn't studied

as much as she should have. *"Remember, we can't change what's done. What matters most are the choices we make today."* Her gaze landed on a nearby table, a Santa hat sitting there all alone. He used to wear a hat just like that the whole week before he was Santa in the parade. It was as if Pop were there somewhere and had just taken it off. The sight of it felt like he was leaving her a reminder of him, even though that couldn't be. He certainly couldn't have met her at Christmas this year, could he?

She kept her head resting on Henry's chest, trying not to let herself worry about things too much, and just enjoy this moment with Henry, dancing. That's what Pop would've told her to do.

When the song ended, she'd calmed down, thanks to hearing Pop's words and feeling the gentle movements of Henry's hands as they'd swayed together. She'd helped Henry, but in a way, he'd helped her too. Being with him and facing him made her feel as if things could somehow work out and be okay.

The band kicked in to a gritty, folky tune, the fiddle going a mile a minute. Henry took her hands and spun her, making her laugh, before pulling her next to him and moving to the music. That deviously gorgeous smile she'd always known had returned, and she couldn't help but fall prey to his charm. As they moved around the dance floor, only then did she notice a few familiar faces of people in town, gathering and smiling. Mary Jo was at the edge of the floor. She waved and then clapped along to the music, alight with merriment at the sight of them. Marty, the old farmer from down the street, threw up a hand to them with his wife, Penny, bopping along beside him. Other neighbors and townsfolk she hadn't seen in years were watching them as well, as if she and Henry were putting on a private show.

"Look at those two," she overheard Penny say to one of the church ladies on the other side of her. "I didn't think I'd ever see the day."

Dancing with Henry made Stella feel more alive than she had in years. She couldn't remember the last time she'd stopped working long enough to do something spontaneous. She'd been so busy trying to keep herself from noticing the loss of this very feeling that she hadn't been able to enjoy herself in over a decade. When she stole a glance at Henry, his wide smile told her she wasn't the only one. That angry man she'd encountered when she first arrived had all but vanished.

The band finished the song to the cheers of the small crowd, and Henry gestured toward the bar. She followed him to a tall table with a candle flickering inside a mason jar.

"Sure you don't want something to drink?" Happiness sparkled in his eyes.

"Oh, all right," she relented.

He held up a finger and jogged to the bar, returning quickly with two beers. He set one on the table in front of her. "That was fun," he said.

If she didn't know better, she'd think she was standing opposite eighteen-year-old Henry again by the lightness in his manner.

"Yeah, it was."

He took a swig of his beer and placed the bottle on the table. "I wanted to tell you I'm sorry."

"For what?" If anyone should be sorry, it was her.

"I know you have work to do. I shouldn't have downplayed that. And I also know that, by leaving the therapy program, I might have screwed it up. It wasn't intentional." He pouted adorably. "If you want me to go back so you can finish your research, I will. But I just don't get much out of it."

"I do think traditional therapy can be helpful," she said over the music. "But I'd hate for you to go through with it for my benefit. I'd much rather it be for your own."

"I don't find it helpful at all. It's slow."

"It's a process."

He shook his head. "Ms. Weixel wanted me to think positively, to"—he held up his hands to make air quotes—"'open up those channels in my brain' to see the silver lining." He leaned across the table toward her. "But the thing is, there wasn't anything positive in my life until you came back."

She was starting to see what he meant. She hadn't allowed herself to feel anything before—the loss of her first love, sadness about her dad, or the pain of losing a child.

"I understand. But what will you do after the holiday when I leave? Have you thought about that?"

He picked up his beer, but didn't drink it, his jaw clenching as he looked out over the crowd on the dance floor. "No." His face softened and he reached out for her hand. "Can we just take it day by day?"

That was all she could do, given the fact that she wanted to stay in this moment with him for as long as possible.

# Chapter Seventeen

The night before, after Stella came home from the Christmas lot with Henry, she and Mama had finished a few more preparations for the parade, assigning vendors tasks to help organize it, and emailing the final lineup to the participants. But they still had no Santa.

Stella laid on her bed as the morning sun peeked through the winter clouds and pondered alternative final float ideas, but the truth of the matter was that everyone expected to see Santa on the last float. When no other options came to her, she got up, grabbed her laptop, and went in search of breakfast.

Mama was at the kitchen table in front of a box of tissues, with one balled in her hand. "Oh, I'm so sorry," she said, blinking furiously and clearing her throat.

Stella sat next to her and put her hand on her mother's knee. "Mama, what's wrong?"

"I'm okay. It's just a low day." Mama rubbed her forehead with her fingertips. "I miss your dad so much that I feel like I won't make it through. I close my eyes, and I swear I feel him standing next to me, but when I open them, no one's there. My world is so empty without him."

Stella wrapped her arms around Mama's shoulders, her own pain welling up. "I know. Sometimes, I swear I can hear him talking to me.

And yesterday, there was a Santa hat sitting alone on a table at Christmas and it was all I could do not to look around for him."

Mama smiled through her tears. "That doesn't surprise me. He was *always* talking, and if he could, he'd have left that hat just for you."

A tear slipped down Stella's cheek. "I feel I've missed out, being gone so much. I wasted his last years."

"You had no idea they'd be his last."

"I wish he would've told us how sick he was."

Mama nodded, blotting her eyes with her tissue. "I'm so sorry. I didn't mean for you to start your day with this."

"I think starting my day with family is pretty great, actually." She gave her mother a squeeze, wishing Lily could be there as well to comfort their mother. But she dared not allow the utter confusion over her sister's absence to creep in—she had enough emotion to manage at the moment.

"I'm so glad you're here." Mama gave her a meaningful look before she cleared her face and stood. "So. What's on the agenda today?"

Stella rolled her shoulders. "I need to work on my second article. I've got to see if I can iron out the slant I want to take so I can get the premise over to my editor for approval. I'm close, but I need to do a lot of research."

"That sounds like it might call for sugar. Let me know later if you need a plate of cookies to get you through, and I'll fix one right up." Mama winked at Stella, clearly trying to lighten the mood she'd set. "At least it'll be quiet for you here. We're out of salt, and I'm going to run to the store. Need anything?"

"No, thanks. I'm okay."

"All right. There's cereal in the pantry, and we've got plenty of eggs if you want to fry some up."

After Mama left her alone in the kitchen, Stella opened her laptop and pulled up her notes. She stared at the page from Henry's therapy, trying to find the perfect intro to tie it into Mr. Ferguson's. She opened a blank document and began typing: *Memory loss comes in many different shapes and sizes…*

Just then, the faint sound of her phone ringing in her bedroom filtered into the kitchen. She loped down the hallway to get it. When she reached her room, she scooped it up and saw her sister's name.

"Hello? Lily?"

When there was no response, she checked the screen. She'd missed the call. She must have answered it just as her sister hung up. She quickly dialed back but got a message saying the call couldn't be completed. Her shoulders slumped and she dropped onto her bed. Mama needed family around her and, while Stella was doing the best she could at keeping her spirits high, she needed the whole family together. She couldn't help but wonder again if her absence had set the tone for the family and, looking up to her, Lily had followed her lead. Considering the last year, she'd squandered the time, and now she could never get it back.

Christmas wasn't going to be the same without Pop and Lily, and she wasn't quite sure how to get through it. *And* with Mr. Ferguson possibly coming, would they all be clouded in grief for their loved ones? Her mind full, she struggled to get back into research mode. She sat on her childhood bed, trying to keep her attention on the task at hand.

*"Step away for a while."*

When Stella had been studying for her final history exam in high school, she'd broken down in tears with Pop, concerned there were too many dates to remember. He'd taken her over to her pottery wheel and lumped one of her clay balls onto it.

*"Step away for a while and do something you love. The joy will release your stress and all those dates will have room to filter in."*

The buzz of the doorbell pulled her attention from the memory. She peeked out the window to find Henry's truck in the driveway. She got up and went to answer the front door.

"Hey. I know it's Saturday, but I thought we could have a therapy session." The corner of his mouth twitched upward in that charming way of his. He stepped inside and shut the door. "Have you eaten? We could go out for breakfast."

Stella had to hone in on the depth of her inhale to keep the flutters at bay. With every day that passed, he felt more and more like Henry.

"I haven't, actually," she replied, unable to turn him down. "I could do with stepping away from writing for a little while too."

Henry grabbed her coat from the hook near the door and held it out so she could slip her arms into it. "Are you having a hard time?"

"I think I have an angle. And I have one piece of research. I just hope there's more out there."

"Maybe we can talk about it over a plate of eggs and bacon." He opened the door, his truck still running in the driveway.

Stella locked up and got in, the old vinyl seat warm from the heater. They drove down the road to Smokey's. Once inside, they took a seat at one of the tables by the window. The owner, John Purdy, also known as Smokey, brought over a couple of laminated menus. He eyed the two of them, clearly interested in the fact that the town lovebirds were back together after their decade-plus hiatus.

Stella greeted him. "Hey, Smokey."

"Nice to have y'all back. I didn't think I'd ever see you 'round here again," he said to Stella.

"Why's that?" Henry asked.

"Miss Stella left outta here in a hurry, and you weren't far behind."

An older man wearing a tattered John Deere cap and bibbed overalls called over from the bar. Stella recognized Mr. MacAvoy, the owner of a strawberry farm down the road. He'd always let Stella and Lily run through the fields and eat their weight in fresh strawberries, right off the runners. His wrinkled cheeks lifted into a smile, and he gave her a little wave.

She waved back, warmed that he'd remembered her.

"Special's shrimp 'n grits," Smokey said before heading back to pour coffee for the old man and his friend.

Stella scanned the choices, but she was wondering what she was doing there with Henry. He was confusing her. She needed to get her work done—work she'd left all those years ago to do, work she'd poured herself into and, until now, absolutely enjoyed. Henry wasn't making this easy. How was she ever going to win the President's Award when she had no article written? All she had to do was write one more incredible article to set her apart from the other candidate being considered. But it was easier said than done with everything going on in her personal life.

"He-ey," Henry said, waving in her peripheral vision. "You're a hundred miles away. You okay?"

"Yeah," she replied, attempting to shake off her contemplations.

He squinted at her. "What were you thinking about? Was it what Smokey said about leaving?"

"No, just work."

He stared at her.

She sighed. "I'm up for an award, and if I get it, it comes with a big promotion. But I have to knock it out of the park with this article to win it."

"You want the promotion?"

"Yes. I've worked really hard for it. All I've done for the last thirteen years has led up to it."

Henry was contemplative and she wondered if he, too, was thinking about how muddled things were between them.

"You have better things to worry about, though," she said, brushing it off. "Let's focus on your therapy."

"All right. Well, first things first." He signaled to Smokey. "Could we get two coffees?"

Smokey eyed him, a grin surfacing. "Want your usual?"

A flicker of uncertainty shone in Henry's eyes, but he replied, "Yes."

"Sure thing." Smokey went behind the bar and pulled two heavy mugs from the rack above him.

Stella leaned in. "Your usual is coffee with milk, and you always ask for a biscuit."

His gaze moved across the blue-and-white gingham tablecloth, seeming to think this over. "With butter on both sides of the biscuit."

Stella smiled. "Yes," she said nodding. "You remembered."

"Yeah, I did." He gave her a little smirk that sent her stomach flipping.

"That's amazing."

Excitement danced in his blue eyes, and she couldn't help but be excited for him, even if it meant they might be getting closer to facing the music. Eventually, they'd have to.

He peered at the menu. "Do I get the same thing here every time?"

"Yep." She purposely didn't look at her menu so she wouldn't give away a single clue.

As Henry ran his finger down the choices, Smokey brought over the coffee and biscuits then left them alone once more. "Definitely the bacon sizzler."

Stella broke out into a huge smile. "You remember that too?"

"No," he said with a laugh. "But it sounds perfect."

She laughed. "Fair enough."

"Henry's been cracking jokes and everything," Stella told her mother when she got home.

Mama closed the book she was reading and set it on the coffee table. "You always did bring out the best in him."

Stella tried not to think too deeply about her mother's statement because it hurt too much to believe it. Had she missed out on something wonderful by leaving? "You and Pop brought out the best in each other too."

Mama stared in the direction of the mantle. "Yes. We sure did."

"I feel like I've failed Pop," Stella said. "I set a terrible example for Lily by running off. Look at her now."

"She seems happy," Mama said.

"But she could have included us. It's my fault she hasn't." Stella plopped onto the sofa next to her mother.

Mama offered her the other side of the blanket she'd draped across her legs. "You put too much pressure on yourself. Your sister has made her own choices." Mama was quiet for a minute before continuing. "I've always wondered why you ran off so quickly. It was like you did a one-eighty in a single day. You were happily married to the love of your life, and then all of a sudden you were off to Stanford."

Stella's face heated with shame for not telling her mother everything. "I got scared," she admitted.

"Of what—happiness?"

"Of…" She couldn't finish the thought. She still couldn't say out loud that she was afraid she'd be a hinderance for Henry because she couldn't have his children, that he'd always wanted a house full of them—his own, and that she'd thought that by leaving, she would free him up to have that. "Of my shortcomings," she finally verbalized.

"You had no shortcomings to us or Henry."

Tears filled Stella's eyes as she mustered up the strength to explain. "There's something important I never told you. Something that happened before I left." She'd never told a soul, and she struggled to get the words out. If only Pop could've been there right then for support.

*"I'm always here."* The memory of his words from the day she left Leiper's Fork came back to her. Stella took in a deep breath, channeling his smile as she told her mother about the miscarriage and diagnosis that prompted her to leave. Everything spilled from her lips as if it had been waiting to be told, each word lightening her burden a little more than the last. When she finished, she squeezed her hands together, intertwining her fingers the way she used to do with Pop when she held his hand.

"Oh, Stella… Why didn't you tell us?" Mama asked, tears streaming from her eyes. "We would've been there for you to support you."

"I just couldn't. It was too overwhelming."

"Did Henry know?"

She shook her head. The tears became a deluge. "My whole life was ripped away in that one moment at the doctor's office, and if I tried to talk about it, I would've crumbled." Her heart broke again for the life she'd lost. "But the pain is still very real."

"My sweet girl. I'm so sorry." Mama swept her up in a hug.

It was the first time she'd allowed herself to grieve. The fear of never having a family of her own, the sadness of losing a child, and the loss of her future with Henry had come tumbling out. Yet another part of her felt relieved; it was easy to after telling Mama. Yet Stella hadn't ruined *her* life or broken *her* heart.

"You have to tell Henry," Mama said quietly.

"I don't know if I'm ready." Stella laid her head on Mama's shoulder and wept.

But maybe Mama was right. Henry deserved to know why she'd abandoned him, no matter how difficult the situation would be.

# Chapter Eighteen

Stella spent a few hours at the town library, researching and working on her article after her talk with Mama. She felt lighter and able to focus. When she returned home, Henry was sitting on the porch steps, waiting for her. She pulled up next to his truck and parked her car.

When she got out, he stood and slipped his hands into his pockets, bunching up his thick coat at the waist of his jeans.

"Hey."

His pensive look gave her pause, but she forced herself to move past it. Anytime he wasn't openly grinning, she worried he'd remembered. The caution in his look right now made her wonder.

She climbed the steps, her fingers brushing the greenery-draped railing, and met him on the porch. "Didn't get enough of me this morning?" she asked lightheartedly to test the waters.

He grinned easily, the old Henry beaming from his face, and she had to remind herself to breathe as relief flooded her.

"I was wondering if you'd want to come over to my house for a little while. There's something I'd like to show you."

That was a difficult question, but she replied, "All right," and followed him to his truck.

The ride to the cabin was quiet and the silence felt heavy, as if he wanted to tell her something but was waiting until they arrived. When they got inside the cabin, she couldn't stand the suspense one more second.

"What did you want to show me?"

He gestured for her to sit down on the sofa, then lowered himself next to her. Their legs were too close, and her heart pounded as she fought to keep her emotions steady.

She swallowed, slipping off her coat and draping it on the arm of the sofa, keeping her head turned toward him so she couldn't see their former bedroom.

"Did you remember something else?"

He nodded.

"What?" she asked, nearly breathless.

"I remember *you*."

She felt light-headed, her conversation with Mama still front and center in her mind. "What about me?" she asked carefully.

He reached over and took her hand, holding it in his, gazing down at it as if it were a find he'd only just discovered. "I remembered how much I love you, and it all made sense."

"What made sense?"

He looked at her. "From the moment I met you, I've felt drawn to you. You light up my days—and they've been pretty dark." The corner of his mouth twitched upward.

There it was: that expression as if he could swallow her whole with one adoring look. She couldn't break his heart again. She had to tell him right now before things went any further. Her pulse racing, her vision blurring as she considered how to begin, she let her gaze roam to the bedroom door, and a little slip of white from the corner of their bed made her feel as if she were under water.

Henry followed her line of sight. He stared at the bedroom door silently as everything inside her screamed in agony at what she was about to say.

"Henry, there's some—"

"I remember something else too."

"Wh-what?" she asked, straining to get the word out before it strangled her.

His head tilted to the side, his lips falling into a serious position. "I remembered holding you in our bed." He looked back and forth between her and their room. "I remember looking at you in the dim light. You floored me every time you climbed into bed without a stitch of make-up, your hair down around your face—I didn't know what I'd done to be so lucky. I felt like I'd won the lottery."

She tried to combat the prick of tears as her long-buried emotions climbed to the surface. "It was a long time ago, Henry."

"You keep saying that." He caressed her hand, winding his fingers around hers the way he used to when they watched movies cuddled up on the sofa. "And I know. But I never stopped loving you. I remember." He gripped her hand and stood, pulling her up with him. "I want to show you something." He grabbed her coat and handed it to her.

She followed his lead, and they went out to the woodshed behind the house.

"I've been busy," he said before tugging open the large barn doors.

When the light from outside illuminated the space, Stella gasped at what was in front of her. She grabbed his arm, her knees feeling as if they'd give out.

"I'm not sure why I chose this, specifically, but the idea wouldn't leave me. So I repurposed the door."

Tears spilled from her eyes, her heart feeling as if it would jump right out of her chest, the sorrow from all those years ago ravaging her. There, in front of her, was the most gorgeous child's rocking chair with a bright red bow. She ran her fingers over the thin arms, then the seat, and finally the little slatted back. The chair rocked gently under her touch. All the lost years and the loss of their child came tumbling through her and she let out a sob.

Henry jumped into action and wrapped her in his arms, his embrace devastating her even further.

"What's wrong?" he asked. "I hope you don't think I'm suggesting anything by this," he said, his eyes wide and unstill, as if only just realizing what it might imply.

She pushed against him, putting space between them. "I—I have to go." Disappointment flooded her when she realized *this* was the moment and still, she couldn't tell him. It was too hard. She broke free and rushed through the doors of the woodshed, gasping. The frigid air burned her lungs. She put her hands on her knees, trying not to collapse.

"Stella, what's going on?" Henry came up next to her and laid his hand on her back, but she pulled away, stumbling through the slush.

Thirteen years had passed, yet the pain wasn't any easier to manage. She angrily wiped her tears, trudging toward the cabin as he followed, not having a clue where she was going. Henry had driven her there, and he'd have to take her home, but she knew he wouldn't without a conversation first. Her temples pounded. She grabbed the door handle and let herself inside, the house they'd shared only serving to make her feel more suffocated.

Henry grabbed her arm gently and turned her around. "Stella. What's happening here?"

"I can't…" The words were caught in her throat, the insecurities and feelings of inadequacy that she'd pushed down all those years ago, wrecking her.

Henry guided her to the sofa. The heat from the wood stove scorched her icy, tear-streaked cheeks.

"What really happened to us, Stella?" he whispered.

She sniffled, taking a long breath in through her mouth. "I need some time," she managed.

He caressed her hair, running his hand down her head and onto her back. Then he pulled her into him. Her muscles lost their tension, giving up the fight. She pressed her cheek to his chest, breathing in his woodsy scent. Then she cried as he held her, the anguish she'd ignored for so long, finally releasing. As the pain tumbled out, she realized that she'd pushed herself to the limit, traveling, researching, striving for success to prove to herself that she was worth something even though she couldn't achieve what she'd wanted most—a family with Henry.

*"You are enough, Stella,"* Pop's voice whispered in her mind. This time, it wasn't attached to a memory; it was as if she could hear him now, in this moment, speaking to her. *"You've always been enough."*

Pop's words and Henry's embrace together gave her strength. When she'd cried all she could, she looked up at him. "I'll tell you everything, but I need some time to figure out how I want to do it."

He nodded, his concern for her clear in his expression, and she wondered by the interest in his gaze if he already had an inkling of what she would soon tell him.

She stood and smoothed her shirt, then ran her fingers through her hair, pulling out the tangles. "Could you take me home?"

"Sure," he said, so many questions behind that one word. He took her hand, raised it to his lips, and kissed it. "I'll wait for you."

And the terrifying part was that she knew he absolutely would.

Later that night, still trying to get over her visit to Henry's, Stella opened her laptop as she sat at the old desk Pop had used when he paid bills. He'd always paid with mailed stubs and paper checks until Mama took over. Her mom hadn't been able to come anywhere near the desk for a while, but for Stella, it had a different effect. It comforted her. After hearing Pop's voice today, she wanted to be close to him.

She opened her email to find one from her editor.

Hi Stella,

I hope you're enjoying your holidays and getting so much work done!

I wanted to send over your next assignment. I'm giddy that I was able to secure a placement for you at Asklepios Hospital Barmbek in Hamburg, paid for by one of the American Brain Foundation grants I applied to. You'll be part of a research team, and they're funding eight weeks! The study focuses on rare neurological diseases, so get going on the preliminary research. They have a patient with vertical gaze palsy that I'm dying to hear about.

Your flight is scheduled out of BNA in Nashville, departing at 9:00 a.m. on December 27th. You'll fly into Hamburg International and stay at the Hotel Atlantic until we can secure a flat. After five weeks, you'll travel on to Helios Krefeld Hospital for the final three weeks.

Steven asked me to send you, specifically—"the best we've got," he said. The team is thrilled for you. He can't wait to read your brain injury articles. The first article is ready to go. Just waiting on the second from you. Hoping to have it before the holiday.

Let me know if you need anything special for your stay, and I'll get Margie to organize it for you.


Happy holidays,

Amy


Stella rubbed the pinch in her shoulder and leaned on Pop's desk. A single line kept going through her head: *He can't wait to read your brain injury articles.* Steven. As in Steven Rotrosen, judge of the President's Award.

After being home and with everything regarding Henry, her life felt as if it were two distinct halves: the one where she'd run from herself and the one where she was being forced to face it. Both were pulling on her, and she wasn't sure which direction to take anymore.

# Chapter Nineteen

After a late Sunday breakfast, Stella helped Mama clear the dishes, and the two of them settled on the sofa, watching TV, where they stayed until the afternoon. With everything on her mind, Stella relished the quiet. She'd closed her eyes and tried to ignore the hum of *It's a Wonderful Life*, when the phone rang with an unfamiliar Nashville number. She answered it.

"Hello, Miss Fisher. We've finished the appraisal of your pendant, and we'd like to arrange a time for you to come pick it up. We're open a few hours today if you'd like to stop in."

Luck certainly hadn't been on her side with or without the necklace, but she wasn't so sure she wanted to bring it back into her home. Mama looked over at her questioningly.

Shaking off her superstitions, she answered, "Of course. I can be there in about a half hour if that works."

"Yes, ma'am. That's perfect."

"All right. See you soon." Stella ended the call and looked at Mama. "That was the jewelry store. They said the appraisal for the necklace is ready."

"Did they say if it's valuable or not?" Mama asked.

"No, he didn't say," she replied. "Want to come with me?"

Mama brightened, her eyes widening in excitement. "Absolutely."

Her mother's enthusiasm warmed Stella. "You always see the bright side of things," she said.

Mama put her arm around her. "I have to. I've dealt with enough grief to know that the world can be so dark sometimes. If I piece together all the little dots of light, eventually I'll have sunshine. It's tough sometimes, but I have to make a point of it."

Stella let her mother's words sink in. She wished things could be different with Henry, wondered what her sister was doing without them, and longed to have Pop by her side, but she still had a lot to be grateful for.

"You know what? You're so right." She linked her arm in Mama's and they made their way to the door.

Northbound I-65 was congested with holiday traffic heading into Nashville, but Mama's presence brought a lightness to the journey. They chatted, played Christmas music, and neither mentioned any of the things weighing them down; they were determined to piece together the light. Even so, Stella wondered how her mother would react when the jeweler burst her bubble and told them the necklace wasn't worth a thing.

They finally arrived, parked, and went inside. An air of anticipation sizzled between them—Stella could feel it.

They walked up to the counter and Stella introduced herself. "We're here for the appraisal of a diamond necklace." She handed over the ticket.

"Ah yes. Let me go to the back and get it."

The man quickly returned, holding the black velvet case and a file folder. He slipped on a pair of gloves and opened the box, revealing the Christmas Diamond clean and sparkling with a radiance Stella hadn't seen before. The jeweler slid it closer to them, the brilliance of the piece overwhelming after the cleaning. Then he opened the file.

"Our guess is that this dates back to the mid-1700s, although the inscription seems to have been done later. It looks as if it's a family crest of some sort for what we think to be the name of Worley. The stones are all real, and the blue diamond in the center is extremely rare. We value this piece at approximately thirty-five thousand dollars."

Stella's mouth dropped open and she turned to her mother. "That date is in line with the story. And the article said it would be over twenty thousand."

Mama pulled out her phone and tapped on the screen before turning it around to the jeweler. "Do you think it's this one—the Christmas Diamond?"

He took Mama's phone and peered at the screen, comparing the image to the diamond in front of them. "I'd say it looks very much like it could be." He handed the phone back to her.

"Oh, my word. It *is* the real one," Mama whispered.

Stella tried to keep herself together. The jeweler passed the box to her, and she and Mama walked out into the winter cold, although Stella barely noticed the temperature.

"What in the world?" she said, still stunned. She gave the box to Mama to hold so she could get in the car and drive them home. "We definitely need to find its owner. Someone is probably freaking out right now."

Mama sat in the passenger seat, her bouncing knee giving away her manic energy after such a surprise. She clasped her fingers around the box as if it were going to jump out of her hands. "No one left any messages from the airport, right?"

"Right. I'll try to call them again when we get home."

"Good idea." Her mother's gaze moved to the box, her complete shock clear.

They sat in silence on the way home. Stella had no idea what to do with the necklace. Was it really bad luck? What would happen when she brought it back into their house? If only Pop were here; he'd make her feel okay. *Pop, tell me what to do with this thing. Why do I have it?*

No response.

One thing was certain: given its worth, there was no way she could keep it. She *had* to find the owner.

While Mama took a nap, Stella set her laptop at Pop's desk, distracted as she tried to do some work. She opened her browser to research a few of the topics she'd jotted on her list, but her heart wasn't in it. Everything else kept going through her mind—Henry, Lily, the diamond, and she still hadn't found a Santa for the parade in four days' time. Her mind was absolutely whirring.

Feeling the weight of the world on her shoulders, she opened a new email window, ready to ask Amy for an extension. She knew that with their deadlines, she wouldn't be able to give it to her, and Steven was waiting for the article to weigh in on the promotion, but she had no time left and no idea how she was going to get it all done.

Unable to find an answer to her work conundrum, she considered her next move with Henry instead. It was definitely time to tell him. But she still wasn't sure how she wanted to do it. Where should she start? And where would they go from there? Would he hate her for leaving and not telling him why? Stella rolled her shoulders and stretched her arms.

Needing Pop's presence, she opened the top desk drawer and ran her fingers over the pens he always kept right at the front. She took one out and held it, the thought that his fingers had once gripped it warming her. Only a little over a year ago, she'd have found him sitting right there, holding one of those pens, balancing his checkbook or something similarly mundane. He'd had no idea when he sat there so many nights how short his life would be. She placed the pen back in the drawer, missing him terribly.

Then she caught sight of an envelope at the back. It had her name on it, and she immediately recognized her father's handwriting. She retrieved it and flipped it over. It was sealed. What could it be? Should she wake her mother and ask if she knew anything about it? She doubted Mama knew it was there—her mother hadn't been anywhere near Pop's desk. If she'd have found it, she'd have said something. And it was addressed to Stella.

Carefully, she slid her finger under the flap and loosened the seal. With every movement, the knowledge that she was about to read her father's words filled her with joy. She pulled out the single page and took a deep breath as she stared at her father's scratchy handwriting. Steadying herself, she read the note.

My dearest Stella,

First off, I want to say I'm sorry. I know I didn't handle my illness very well, and while I attempted to spare you all from a lengthy diagnosis and battle, I realize, in the end, I might have done more harm than good by not letting you know. If I'd have told you, you might have felt more of an immediacy to make the most of every moment, the way I've felt lately, which could've helped you after I leave. When I am gone—I know you—you'll blame yourself for not spending more time with me. But that's silly.

You have your own life, Stella, and boy do I love to watch you live it. It's much better than seeing you fuss over me.

I spoke to Lily, but I didn't get to say everything to you that I wanted to say so now's my chance.

You and I had different ideas of what your future would hold. I would've loved to see you settle down with Henry. He always made you so happy; you glowed whenever you were around him. I think he could make you happy. But I always let you go your own way, and when you wanted to go off to college and then travel the world, I was delighted to see you spread your wings. However, your short time in this world will be a blip—I can tell you that with absolute certainty now. I want to make sure your choices are based on your happiness. What lights your fire? You only get one shot at life. Above everything else, make sure you've got that one answer figured out.

I also know that when I get to the other side, you'll want to talk to me the way you always used to. My silence will hit you and your mom the hardest. You'll want my advice and I won't be able to give it to you. Please know that I will do everything I can to come back to my family, because my version of heaven is with you, Lily, and your mother. No matter what, if it's at all possible, I'll be right there with you, and I'll try my very best to let you know I'm there.

Love you.
Pop

The words blurred. Stella tore her eyes from the letter, blinking to focus, and looked around the room, wishing Pop would show her that he was, indeed, there, but she was met with silence. She held the letter to her chest, cradling it, yearning for him. She craved his attention, and she longed for one more minute with him to tell him how much she loved him.

She considered her life's decisions, trying to assess if she'd made her choices based on how much happiness they'd brought her. As she reflected, she realized they'd brought her more relief than actual happiness. They'd given her a chance to shine when she wasn't sure she could otherwise. But had they made her *happy*? What did it mean to be happy anyway? She'd been able to travel, pay her bills, escape the sadness she'd pushed away for so long… She wasn't sure she knew what might make her happy. Or at least, she didn't want to admit it to herself, because what could make her the absolute happiest wasn't available to her. Her anatomy wouldn't allow it.

But there were other things, too, that would've made her happy. Lily being there was one. If she allowed herself to dream, she could imagine the perfect scenario. If she could do it all over again, and nothing went wrong, she'd have waited to marry Henry until Pop and Mama were with her. And Lily would have stood beside her like they'd planned as little girls. Mama and Pop would look on lovingly, and they'd all stuff their faces with cake while they laughed into the night. Then she and Lily would find two farmhouses right next to each other, and they'd raise their families—one big happy unit. Happily ever after.

Allowing the daydream caused a lump to form in Stella's throat. Slowly, she folded the letter, placed it on the desk, and turned her focus back to her laptop. Channeling her father, she began anew on her final article before Christmas, deleting the old title and typing a different one: *Is Happiness the Key to Everything?* It certainly seemed to be helping Henry and Mr. Ferguson recover from their brain trauma.

As she worked, the article began to take shape, her fingers moving as quickly as they could to get her thoughts on the page. While she clicked the keys, she knew in the back of her mind she'd need to answer one question in order to finish: *How does someone find that elusive happiness that seems to make everything better?* She put her hand on the envelope Pop had left for her like a little gift from the beyond. Maybe, if she was lucky, Pop would show her the answer.

## Chapter Twenty

After spending most of the next day at the library, finishing up her research for her second article, Stella walked along the hospital corridor on her way to Mr. Ferguson's therapy session, but her mind was on everything else. Right then, she'd been thinking about the Christmas Diamond and whether or not she'd find the owner by the end of the holiday. She'd put it in the safe before heading out this morning and left another message with the claims desk at the airport. She was still trying to clear her mind enough to focus on work when she entered Mr. Ferguson's room.

"Good afternoon," he said happily.

She forced a smile through her haze of introspection. "Hi."

The tiny squint of his eyes told her that her smile might not have been as convincing as she was trying to make it.

"Everything okay?" he asked, studying her.

"Yes, of course." Stella took a seat at the back of the room and opened her laptop, but she could tell Mr. Ferguson wasn't buying it. Thankfully, the therapist came in to distract him.

"Hello," Ms. Barnes said. "How are we today?"

Mr. Ferguson brightened. "Lovely, and you?"

"Very well." Ms. Barnes opened her small laptop and clicked a few keys. Then she nodded hello to Stella before turning her attention back to Mr. Ferguson. "Let's go over some of the goals we set last time."

"Sure."

Mr. Ferguson rattled off a few things he'd been working on while Stella typed. The session went along easily, with Mr. Ferguson complying with the therapist's requests and being absolutely delightful. By the end of the appointment, Stella had managed to get a full page of notes, which would help her finish the article. She'd been slow to finish this one, when she was usually able to come up with ideas in a flash. She wondered if the Hamburg trip might actually be helpful for her. It could help to clear her mind and get her back on track.

When they'd finished the session, Mr. Ferguson asked Stella to walk him out. He seemed pensive on their way to the elevator. "Your mind is heavy with something," he said. "Want to tell an old man what's bothering you?"

Stella shrugged lightheartedly, trying to play off her anxiety. But there was a friendliness about him that reminded her of Pop. "How long do you have?"

Mr. Ferguson laughed. "As long as the good Lord gives me."

The best thing she could do for herself was to try to take her mind off everything for a little while. "Want to come over to my mother's house?"

The sparkle in his eyes gave the answer before he'd even said yes, and she knew all he wanted was to be with people. "I'd love to. Let me call and cancel my ride."

"Great. I'll just text my mom to give her a heads up."

She assisted Mr. Ferguson into her car and helped him fasten the seatbelt around his belly. After she put his walker in the back seat, they drove until the city gave way to rolling hills, horse pastures, and endless expanses still dotted in white from the snowfall. Mr. Ferguson spent the drive peering out the window while Stella tried to keep her mind empty of everything that weighed on her. It would be so easy to get on a plane and go to Germany early and start the next assignment. But she couldn't leave Mama alone for the holiday. She breathed in the winter air, concentrated on releasing her shoulders, and tried to relax.

When they got home, Stella walked Mr. Ferguson to the door, helped him up the porch steps, and then set up his walker once they were inside. Mama had the fire going, and the tree was shining brightly, lifting Stella's spirits.

"Jackson Cole called." Mama's voice sailed in from the other room after Stella latched the door shut.

"Jackson Cole?" she asked, the name slightly ringing a bell.

Mama came into the living room. "Oh, hello," she greeted Mr. Ferguson, holding out her hand. "I'm Anna Fisher."

"Herbert Ferguson." He shook her mother's hand.

"It was a little spur of the moment," Stella said, hanging up her scarf.

Mama beamed, clearly delighted to have company. "I'll make us all some dinner."

"Who's Jackson Cole?" Stella asked again while helping Mr. Ferguson with his coat.

"The grand marshal for the parade."

Stella hung Mr. Ferguson's coat next to hers. "Oh, yeah." She'd seen Mr. Cole's name on the parade list and had copied him on emails.

"He's wondering if we have everything squared away, and he asked where he should deliver the Santa suit." An uneasy look on her mother's face, she gestured toward Pop's Santa hat on the table and the red and white suit hanging in plastic on the kitchen doorknob.

There was an air of loss that tightened Stella's chest at seeing the suit, knowing Pop wasn't there to wear it. She eyed her mother, apprehension setting in. "What did you say?"

"I told him we were almost finished. Because we are, aren't we? And I told him I'd have to call him back with Santa's address."

Stella took in a deep breath, trying to find the calm she'd been chasing in the car. "We need a Santa. Where are we going to find one at this late date?"

Mama chewed her lip and shook her head. "Think Henry would do it?"

Stella let out a sarcastic laugh. "I doubt it very seriously." She redirected the conversation to Mr. Ferguson. "So sorry. We got sidetracked. You're welcome to sit on the sofa. Want some tea or coffee?"

"I'd love a good cup of tea, if you don't mind."

Mama piped up. "Oh, I can make you peppermint tea. How does that sound?"

"Delightful." Mr. Ferguson wriggled into a comfortable position while Stella moved his walker out of the way.

"I'll be back. Stella, do you want anything?" Mama asked over her shoulder.

"I'm okay. Thanks." Stella sat next to Mr. Ferguson.

"So, would you like to tell me what's been bothering you today?" Mr. Ferguson asked.

Stella's chest tightened. "A lot, really, but I don't want to burden you with it all."

"You won't. I'll forget in an hour, and you can pretend you didn't say anything," he teased, giving her a wink.

Stella shook her head, smiling, his cheerfulness contagious. "Not funny."

"Seriously, though, let me be your sounding board."

She didn't want to burden Mr. Ferguson with all her baggage, but something about him made her feel like she could talk to him the way she used to talk to Pop.

"Well, for starters, I'm planning the Leiper's Fork Christmas parade, and I don't have a Santa for the final float."

Mr. Ferguson frowned. "The big guy busy or something?"

"He had a knee replacement, apparently."

His eyes widened. "Oh, no."

"The parade is in three days and Santa has always been the big finale. Everyone expects to see him."

"Yes, someone has to drive the sleigh." He stroked his scraggly beard.

*Beard.*

Stella took in the roundness of Mr. Ferguson's belly and the pink in his cheeks. Before she could ask, he said, "I could step in."

"Do you think you could?"

"With a few more cookies, I could manage."

"Perfect," Mama said, her words breathless as she came in with a plate full of them in one hand while she gripped two mugs of tea in the other. "Here you go." She set it all down in front of them and then grinned at Stella, her misty eyes sparkling. "Mr. Ferguson is our new Santa?"

"Looks like it," Stella replied, hope floating in like a delicate snowflake.

❄

After dinner, Stella drove Mr. Ferguson home. When she got back, she sat down at the kitchen table, staring out the window at the tiny flurries of snow falling against the purple evening sky, the sight barely registering. She'd started to work on her article, but instead, she was busy wondering if Pop could see them. She'd asked for him to solve her problem regarding something he'd been so passionate about—the parade—and magically, she'd found her Santa.

Had he helped today, or was it just wishful thinking? The house felt eerily quiet without him to pull them all together, and she'd liked to think he was still there somehow. She also missed Lily. What was her sister doing right then? Was she giggling with Mateo over something he'd said, the way she used to with Stella? She was probably having a blast in Costa Rica. Stella couldn't blame her for enjoying her life; she was no better, ready to run off to Hamburg as soon as she could. What would Mama do when she left? She pushed it out of her mind.

She picked up the ballpoint pen she'd been using to jot down notes and tapped it against the empty pad of paper, her thoughts jumping to the Christmas Diamond. Given how much the diamond was worth, she had no clue what to do with it, apart from leave it with her mom to watch over it.

Abandoning her article entirely, Stella had another idea. She pulled her laptop across the table and opened the search engine.

"Whatcha doing?" Mama asked as she slid out the chair next to Stella. "Working?"

Stella shook her head. "I'm searching for the legal requirements when finding something that isn't yours… to see what we should do with the Christmas Diamond." She clicked a few keys, then scrolled until she saw a sentence she wanted to read. "This says that, legally, we could keep it until the owner comes forward." She turned her laptop to draw Mama's attention to it. "And that includes property found in public areas. But… It looks like each state has its own rules." She clicked on the state of Georgia since she'd found it in Atlanta. "According to this, we have to take reasonable measures to get the item back to the owner or we face criminal liability."

"Oh, no," Mama said.

"I've called the airport where I found it several times. I think that's *reasonable*. Although, the owner did move through that airport, so I can't help but wonder if there's something else we could do—I just don't know what."

"I have no idea how we'd find the owner."

"Let's see what the particulars are." Stella scanned the article. "If we cannot determine the rightful owner, we have to turn it over to a government agency… and if it isn't claimed within six months, the owner's rights are terminated and ownership reverts to us."

A twinge of disappointment shone in Mama's eyes. "Certainly someone would come forward. I love that necklace already." She laughed. "Even though I have absolutely no need for anything that fancy."

"And it's supposed to be bad luck," Stella reminded her. "We haven't had the best luck since I found it."

Mama smiled. "I've been thinking a lot about that, and I've decided that I'm siding with that ol' Edward James from the article who relied on his faith. We have our own path and make our own luck."

"You think?" Stella wasn't entirely convinced.

"I know." Mama repositioned a little bowl of candy canes she'd set out, lining it up with the two porcelain angels that stood with it. "Your dad and I barely had enough money to live on when you kids were little. With his farming job and me being a homemaker and staying with you and Lily, times were tough. But your pop restored this whole house, board by board. We played games with you kids after dinner, we caught lightning bugs on late summer nights, and we laughed—oh, did we laugh." Mama put her hand on her heart, her expression brightening with the memories. "To an outsider who saw your beat-up shoes and thrift-store dresses, we might look like we didn't have good luck, but we actually had the best luck."

"Are you talking about luck or love?" Stella asked.

Mama pouted and looked over at the empty Santa suit, fondness showing in the flutter of her eyelashes. "Yeah, you're right. It was definitely love."

"How did we end up in different countries, given how close we were?" As soon as the question left her lips, she reminded herself that she was the one who left first.

As if she'd noticed Stella's train of thought, Mama grabbed two candy canes from the bowl and handed one to her. "I wish we could all be together this year for Christmas."

"Pop would've wanted that," Stella said. She peeled back the plastic wrapper and tasted the cool tingle of peppermint, the sugary sweetness doing little to overcome her guilt for not spending more time with her family.

# Chapter Twenty-One

Stella wasn't expecting anyone the next morning when the doorbell rang. She'd been working on her computer, attempting to build out her argument for the relationship between happiness and cognitive function, comparing her notes from her sessions with Mr. Ferguson and Henry to her latest research. Mama had gone to her weekly yoga class, so Stella got up and rushed past the Christmas tree to get the door. When she opened it, Henry stood on the other side holding a basket full of muffins and biscuits with a big red bow tied on the handle.

"Mary Jo and I made them," he said, holding the basket out to Stella. "She suggested I bring them over."

"Thank you," she said, taking them from him and letting him in.

He peered up at the ceiling. "How's the spot? Has it dried up yet?"

"It looks like it," she said, following his gaze. "It just needs a good coat of paint now."

"I've got some scaffolding back at the house. I could put a little primer on it and then fix it right up."

A flurry of wistfulness overtook her. "You always loved to fix things."

His eyebrows rose with his smile. "Still do, evidently."

Trying to stifle the thrill that snaked through her at the sight of his smile, Stella focused on the biscuits. She held up the basket. "So you baked these? I've never known you to bake anything."

He raised his hands in the air like a fugitive caught in the act. "Okay, I'll admit it. I didn't do the baking. That was Mary Jo. I just pressed the biscuit cutter into the dough."

She shook her head playfully. "So *Mary Jo* made these."

"I was there for moral support, but Green Bay was playing Miami, and the game was tied at the half."

Stella threw her head back and laughed. "That's the Henry I know and love."

They both sobered at the word *love*.

"It's good to see you spending time with your sister and watching football. Those sound like happy moments—a lot different from when I first arrived."

"I'm not the same as I was that day," he said. He shrugged off his coat and hung it over the stairway railing. "You make me want to do better."

"Why?" she asked, legitimately curious. What had she done to help him? If anything, she was messing it all up by being there, muddling both their lives.

He slipped his hands into the pockets of his jeans. "I've been asking myself the same thing. I don't really understand it. When you're around, it's as if I've gotten my best friend back, and I'm whole again. I do remember how I felt about you, but even if I didn't, I swear I'd still feel it."

Her chest tightened with the knowledge of what he'd yet to learn about their history. "Let's go sit by the fire." She led the way to the living room and they settled on the sofa, the fabric warm from the blazing flames across the room. She set the basket on the coffee table. "I'm ready to tell you what happened."

"Wait," he said, putting his hand on her arm, his heavy grip sending a current through her. "What if you don't?"

"I thought you wanted to know."

"After you tell me, will I still feel the way I feel for you right now?"

Her face burned with the answer. "Maybe not."

"Then don't tell me."

She stared at him, full of indecision. She'd been building up to this for so long and now that she had the courage, he'd stopped her. For what? Shouldn't she get it out in the open? What if he remembered how she left on his own? He needed to know why.

Henry got up and assessed Pop's old stereo. "We used to play music on this, yes?"

Adoration for that carefree time in their lives washed over her. "Yes."

He nodded. "It's familiar. May I?"

"Of course."

He clicked it on and fiddled with the knobs, tuning the radio, and stopping on holiday music. "That's better." He seemed to have nervous energy as he walked over to the fireplace and ran his fingers along Stella's and her mother's stockings. He moved to the tree and studied a few of the ornaments.

"I'll Be Home for Christmas" poured from the speakers, filling the room. He stopped in the empty space between the living room and the kitchen, scrutinizing the floor.

"What are you thinking about?" she asked, walking over to see whatever it was he saw, but when she stopped next to him, there was nothing there.

"We used to dance, right here."

If she closed her eyes, she could still feel his arms around her while they swayed to the music. "Yes."

He reached out, his fingertips grazing her waist, asking for permission. She stepped toward him, the two of them like two magnetic poles, and before she knew it she was in his arms, and they were moving effortlessly together like they always had. The sensation broke her heart all over again.

He dipped his head, the stubble on his cheek brushing her skin, his lips so close to her that her skin tingled in response.

"Do you still feel anything for me?" he whispered in her ear.

She couldn't tell him no. Because that wouldn't be true. Her feelings for him had never waned; she'd just pushed them away, trying not to feel anything. The truth was that dancing with him was like coming home. She, too, missed her best friend and the man she loved.

He pulled back to look at her.

She peered into those blue eyes and knew she couldn't deny it. "Yes."

Henry leaned down and gently pressed his lips to hers. An explosion of fireworks shot through her body. She didn't know what would happen in the days to come, but as his lips moved on hers, she wasn't able to formulate a single thought, so she relaxed into the feeling of being with the love of her life.

When they finally slowed, he looked down at her and grinned—that smirk surfacing as if he was up to something. "Hi," he said as if he'd only just seen her.

"Hi." She stared into his eyes, all the good years they'd had rushing back between them.

The music continued playing as they stood together, learning this new version of themselves. Then he grabbed hold of her, dipping her and making her laugh. When he righted her, he said, "I've done that many times before too."

"Yes, you have. What made you remember?"

He shook his head. "I don't know. I just did. Being with you is better than weeks and weeks of therapy."

"You're right. I've been reading about a new theory along those lines. While I still think therapy is ideal, in this case you got lucky and found an alternative to release the memories. But… your memories have all been positive ones. You're still blocking out the negative thoughts."

"It doesn't matter." He clutched her tighter and nuzzled her neck, making her squeal before he let her go.

Mama's voice interrupted them. "Look who I found while I was out and about." She walked in with Mr. Ferguson.

Henry greeted them while Stella helped Mr. Ferguson into the room. "What are you doing on this side of town?" she asked the old man.

"I was lonely, so I thought I'd take the bus out this way and go to that Christmas lot. It seemed so festive, and I thought it might make me feel better."

Mama leaned over to him. "You know you never need to feel lonely. You can always call me."

Mr. Ferguson's face lit up. "Oh, you're too kind."

"I'm alone too, you know," Mama said.

"Not this holiday." Stella put her arm around Mama and gave her a squeeze.

※

Stella sat across from Henry and Mr. Ferguson while Mama pulled a chair up beside her at the table.

Mama shuffled the deck of cards. "What do you say we play Crazy Eights?"

"How do you play it again?" Henry asked.

His question amused Stella. "We used to play this after work to wind down."

"Oh, my goodness, yes," Mama agreed. "You and Stella would come over for dinner sometimes, and you two would play for hours. You were neck and neck, and we never knew which one of you would pull off the win. You kept multi-game scores on pads of paper." Mama gasped. "Hang on." She got up and went over to the kitchen junk drawer and rifled through it. Finally, she pulled out a legal pad. "Look! I've still got your last score card. You can pick up where you left off." She dropped it onto the table, along with a pen.

Henry leaned across the table, pulling it to him. "Looks like I'm winning." He turned the score around for Stella to see. "By two games."

"Oh, you're in trouble tonight. I'll catch up in a jiffy." Stella cut the deck and shuffled the cards once more.

"Neither of you will win with me playing," Mr. Ferguson piped up.

"We'll see about that," Henry said with a playful wink in the old man's direction.

Stella took the pad of paper and started to write their names for the new game, but paused at her sister's name on an old roster. "Have you heard from Lily at all in the last day or so?" she asked Mama.

Mama shook her head. "No, nothing."

That familiar pang of guilt ran through Stella. She just couldn't believe her sister wouldn't even try to come home for the holiday.

"Who's Lily?" Mr. Ferguson asked.

"My other daughter," Mama replied. "She's just eloped, and she's in Costa Rica, we think." Mama smiled, but it was clear to Stella that the gesture was only out of courtesy. She was probably just as dumbfounded as her, even though she hadn't admitted it out loud.

Mr. Ferguson's bushy eyebrows pulled together. "You *think* she's in Costa Rica?"

"We haven't really been able to stay in touch with her due to bad reception. She must be somewhere pretty rural."

Stella considered the fact that they were sitting across from a man with literally no family, and yet they had each other and weren't taking advantage of the time they could be together when, at any moment, it could be too late. She sent a silent message to Pop, asking him to show her what to do. Then she tried to refocus on having fun with the people around her.

# Chapter Twenty-Two

After a delightful night of cards—with Stella winning by one final game before they called it a night—she stayed up late working and was back at it early the next morning, clicking keys and barely sleeping. It was her usual routine when she was nearing a deadline.

The words were flowing easily, the idea of happiness as a cure guiding her like a light in the dark as she highlighted how Henry's mind might have actually been saving him from his emotional trauma by not working, because the mind was meant to seek out happiness. She backed up the theory with her research and the data she'd found in Mr. Ferguson's chart, which revealed that he'd been able to keep further memory loss at bay by maintaining a focus on the positives in life.

Before she knew it, hours had passed and she had written the entire thing. She sent it off to her editor and a weight lifted from her shoulders. She'd had to use others' research mostly, sprinkling in anecdotal evidence to support it, but she'd raised some important ideas about the human condition and how emotions impacted the machine that was the human brain. She was proud of what she'd written, and she thought Amy would be as well.

By the time she hit send, it was almost two in the afternoon. She still wanted one more win for the day, so she called the main number for the Atlanta police department and left a detailed message about the necklace with one of the officers who told her he'd call her immediately if anyone inquired. He also said he'd pass along the information to their community hotline, and he asked her to keep the necklace in the safe until further notice.

With the parade tomorrow, she sent off final reminders to everyone involved and sent one more email to Jackson Cole, letting him know that they had Santa and were taking care of the suit delivery.

Not a second after she hit send, her phone pinged with a text: *Hey.* Henry.

She texted back: *Hey there.*

A second text floated across her screen: *Meet me at Christmas.*

Her skin prickled with his choice of words. The last time she'd seen them was on the note taped to the door of their home together. That December had been their final season of true contentment. January and February were tough for the construction business, and Henry had been working overtime to make ends meet, and she'd picked up extra shifts at the diner. In May she'd gotten sick from working too much, or so she thought at first, and then by June, nothing was the same. She'd gotten on a plane to Stanford, searched for an apartment, and settled in before classes began in the August.

As she stared at the text message, Pop's voice rang in her ears: *"Never miss out on an opportunity to make things better."*

This was the second time she'd heard Pop's words without being able to place the memory. Was she just conjuring his voice now, or was he somehow guiding her? It certainly was a wonderful thought. Real or not, Pop was right. Somehow, this Christmas she'd like to make things better for Henry, and while she wasn't quite sure how to do it yet, she needed to figure it out.

"Mama," she called down the hallway, "I'm heading out to meet Henry."

"All right," Mama called back.

Stella slipped on her coat and jumped in the car, driving off to the tree lot. The whole way there, she talked to Pop, hoping he could hear her. "Are you here, Pop?" she asked aloud. "I wish you could show me." She smiled as happiness bubbled up. "I got your letter. It was good to hear you again. You said you'd try to come back to us. Please try harder."

When she arrived at Christmas, Henry was waiting for her in the parking lot. She cleared her throat and gave him her full attention when he walked over to the car.

"What's up?" she asked as she got out.

He reached for her hand. "Come with me."

She took his hand and followed his lead. "What are you up to?"

He led her to a smaller barn at the edge of the property that the town used for weddings and intimate holiday gatherings. When they went inside, a band was playing for no one.

"Are we dancing again?" she asked, a flutter tickling her chest at the idea of having his arms around her once more.

He walked her to the middle of the empty barn and stopped under a ceiling of beams hung with bundles of pine and holly. There were candles along the floor, surrounding them.

"What is this?" she asked.

Henry took both her hands in his, those blue eyes swallowing her. "I don't know what happened to us, but what I do know is that you are the brightest star in my dark sky. You're the one person who can turn the light on inside me, and I never want to be without you. When I look at you, I see sunsets on the porch swing, long dinners together in the grass out back, and a house full of kids."

The air left her lungs, her insecurities surfacing as if to drown her.

He seemed to catch her trepidation immediately. "I mean… I'm not trying to push you into anything. But we were so good together, Stella. I remember it. It was amazing. But even before I remembered, I knew. You're everything I've ever wanted."

Emotion caught in her throat, but she forced herself to speak. "What if I can't give you what you want?"

The band continued playing, but the whole scene was awkward.

"What do you think you can't give me, Stella? I only want you."

She could barely look at his pleading face. She'd heard Pop's voice telling her to make things better, and she thought she could, but it was all too difficult. She'd achieved everything in life. She followed her dreams and made them happen. Except for that one dream that, for whatever reason, she wasn't allowed to live. A part of her hurt too much for everything she'd lost, a part of her that wanted nothing more than to board that plane to Hamburg. She couldn't face this. Trying to explain would mean she'd have to deal with the reality of what they would face in the future, and their relationship now was too new. Her confession would certainly be too heavy for the two of them to withstand.

"I can't do this, Henry," she said, the words barely audible. "I have to go."

"Don't run away from me," he said, tugging her arm gently. "I planned all this to show you how serious I am. I'll do anything it takes to try again. I *love* you."

She pulled out of his grip. The doctor visit confirming the miscarriage, the diagnosis, the loss of their child—whom she'd wanted to name Clara if it was a girl and Dawson if it was a boy—all of it rushed over her. She and Henry could never simply start over because they had too much history. As she ran out of the barn, tears streaming down her face, she could no longer ignore the loss of the little family they'd been trying to start.

Sure, the traveling life wasn't what she'd wanted to begin with, but it freed her from having to experience all these emotions that still, after so many years, were too much to bear. She stopped down the path from the barn, her hands on her knees, and squeezed her eyes shut, but only succeeded in conjuring up the face their child might have had. The child who would never know how it felt to ride on his or her daddy's shoulders or spin around while Stella made pottery or gardened behind the farmhouse.

In that moment, she knew. She wasn't running from Henry only to save him; she was also running from her own devastation. Because what Henry wanted was what she'd wanted as well.

❄

Stella had spent the last hour in the bathroom, showering to hide her emotional state from Mama. She stood under the hot stream of water praying for relief. She leaned against the side of the shower and let the sobs come, the deluge of hurt and disappointment ravaging her.

Somehow, both she and Henry had been spared Henry's sadness—he didn't remember the worst part of their life together, and she hadn't had to deal with the pain of telling him and seeing how it hurt him. But, in a way, she relived it every time she saw that loving look in his eyes.

She stood in the steamy shower until there were no more tears to cry. When she got out, she wrapped herself in a warm towel, closed her puffy eyes, and breathed in the scent of soap. It was easy to think she could make things better or start over, but, emotionally, she just couldn't yet. If ever.

She needed to get back to a sense of normalcy if she wanted to survive the holiday. It would already be difficult without Pop and Lily, and she had to be strong for Mama. When she felt as if she'd finally gotten herself together, she left the bathroom, got dressed, and went to Pop's desk, where she dove straight into her email to keep her mind busy. To her surprise, there was a message from her editor. She opened it.

Stella!

I know it's the holidays, but I couldn't help myself and I opened your email. I just read over the article and it's incredible. I sent it immediately to Steven and it only took him twenty-five minutes to come back to me to tell me that you're getting the President's Award. I'm so happy for you! So we'll need to push back the Hamburg trip a few days and fly you to New York so you can accept the award and the promotion. Start working on that speech!

Congratulations!
A.

Stella sat back in Pop's desk chair and took in the news. She'd done it. The most challenging article she'd ever written, the one she'd doubted would even come together, had just won her the President's Award. She could leave everything behind, get on a plane for New York and then Hamburg, and never have to deal with any of her issues—

Except… she thought about Henry. He'd come so far in the short time she'd been there, and a part of her still felt like she owed it to him to help him regain a sense of himself. Despite what he said about not wanting to know what had happened to them, she knew she had to tell him whether he wanted to hear it or not. She needed to be completely honest no matter what.

Stella rolled her head to stretch her neck.

*Pop, I need you. I need you to help me know how to handle this. At this point, you probably know everything about what happened, and I'm sorry for not telling you. But now I need you to show me how to deal with it because it's ripping me apart.*

"Hey," Mama said as she came up behind her and stopped a few feet away from Pop's desk. "I'm taking Herbert to the movies and then to dinner. Wanna go?"

"Herbert? Mr. Ferguson?"

Mama smiled. "Yes. He texted me."

Stella turned around to face her mother. "You and Mr. Ferguson are texting each other?"

"We are. It's nice to have him around."

"He reminds me of Pop sometimes. Just a little older."

Mama nodded. "Me too." She peered down at Pop's desk and took a tentative step closer, then touched the surface delicately. It was a clear step forward, and Stella was delighted to see her mom embracing Pop's memory. "So would you like to go?" Mama asked.

"I think I'll stay back, if that's okay." She wouldn't be able to concentrate on a movie in her current state.

"Suit yourself. I'll be home in a couple hours."

After Mama left, Stella put a frozen pizza in the oven, threw a few more logs on the fire, and settled in on the sofa by the light of the Christmas tree. Full of tension, she didn't sit long before she was back up, pacing in time with her thoughts. She went to the safe and took out the Christmas Diamond, hoping its sparkle would lighten her mood.

Even though the necklace had a tumultuous history, somehow, this holiday, she'd been entrusted with its care. In a way, the diamond's owner had gotten lucky. The necklace hadn't been swept up with the trash or thrown into someone's bag never to be seen again. It had been cleaned, shined, made new once more, and it was protected. She placed it back in the safe, feeling a little better.

When the pizza was ready, she took it out and cut herself a slice, then sat at the empty table. She eyed the bowl of candy canes. The stillness of the house drove home Pop's absence, and Stella could truly understand the isolation her mother must have felt. She got up to find her phone to text Lily. The message went through as far as she could tell, but there was no indication that it was being read. Was Lily even thinking about Pop or what her family was doing?

She finished her slice of pizza, then wrapped up the rest. She couldn't do anything about Lily right then, but she could do something about Henry. She shouldn't have run off on him like that. Again. But the rocking chair had caught her completely off guard and her emotions in the barn had gotten the better of her. Now she was more composed, she needed to see him. She grabbed her keys and coat and left the house.

The whole way there, she tried to determine what she wanted. A part of her wondered if she and Henry could be happy, just the two of them. How would he feel about adoption, later down the road? Maybe she could go to therapy herself and deal with her reality of not being able to have biological children. Was she ready for the emotional toll that would take on her? And then there was the big promotion she'd been trying to get for so long at work. How would she navigate that? She certainly wouldn't be fulfilled without the movement of work, but her job required her to travel, and she'd be away from Henry. She also knew

Henry hadn't figured himself out either. Would they spend their days on opposite sides of the world? Could their relationship survive that?

She pulled up to the cabin to find Henry coming out his door with a panic-stricken look on his face. He locked eyes with her as she got out of her car.

"I was coming to see you," he said, his eyes wide and full of… something. He turned around and jogged the few steps to the front door, opened it and stood inside the doorway, waiting for her to come in.

Stella entered and followed him into the living room. Henry shut the door, sealing them into the little space.

"You crushed me today," he said before turning around to face her. "I came home feeling more lost than I have in a long time."

He stared into her eyes with a kind of knowing that froze her in place. She braced herself for whatever he had to say.

"I went into our bedroom and fell on the bed in desperation at the thought of not being with you. And then the pain started to feel very familiar."

Stella held her breath.

"I remembered the desperation. I remembered… Everything."

She opened her mouth to say something, but nothing would come out. This wasn't how she'd wanted to explain herself. Tears spilled down her cheeks. "There's so much to tell you," she finally managed. Then she slumped on the sofa in utter mental exhaustion.

"Why don't we start with the day you left." He sat on the sofa, but kept plenty of space between them, as if the distance would protect him from the hurt she'd caused.

Stella tried to relax her tense muscles.

"We're not eighteen anymore, Stella. I've grown and changed since the last time we talked about this, and, this time, you won't get off so easily. I want answers. I know you still care about me, so why on earth did you leave?"

Stella scooted closer, reached for his hand, and laced her fingers through his. Then she told him everything. As her tears fell, she told him about losing their child and what the doctor had said about not being able to have children."

For the first time ever in her life, she saw tears in his eyes. "We had a baby?"

"Not for very long," she whispered, the anger at her body surfacing.

His jaw clenched as she gave him this new information.

The pain in telling him was almost unbearable but with every word, it was as if the chains that had held her down since she was eighteen were slowly disappearing. No matter what happened to them going forward, at least now he knew.

"I never got to tell my dad," she said, her voice breaking. "He and I had always had a bond because I had planned to do what he had, marry and stay in this town. When I left, he thought I wanted something different, and for a long time I tried to convince myself that I actually did. But, really, I'm the one who's lost. Because my dreams of having a family with you are gone." She squeezed his hand. "You deserve to have your family. I thought you'd get over me and find someone wonderful who could give that to you. I wanted that for you."

Henry wiped a tear off her cheek, his sorrow apparent in the set of his jaw. "Stella… Yes, I did want a house full of kids. But you missed one important detail: I wanted a house full of kids with *you*. My life starts with *you*, Stella."

"Even if I'm broken?" Her lip began to tremble.

Henry gently lifted her chin. "You're not broken. God just wants you to make your family a different way. If having kids is what you want."

He leaned into her space to make his point. "We all have moments where our life can go in two different directions, but we have to do our best to find happiness. I learned that the day you walked into therapy."

His mention of happiness took her back to Pop's letter. Then she thought back to the article she'd crafted. Her being there had changed him entirely. "So did you remember *everything*?" she asked.

He shook his head. But then he placed his hand on her cheek and gazed into her eyes with so much love that it felt as if her heart would burst. "Just the most important part." He wrapped his arms around her and the two them shed a few more tears together. She wasn't sure how long she stayed in his arms, but she knew one thing: that was where she belonged.

After leaving Henry's cabin, Stella spent the rest of the evening sitting in silence, sifting through her life in the house Pop had restored for his family. She wished she could go back and do things differently. She would have faced her pain and told Pop what she was dealing with, and listened to his wise words before making a decision. Maybe things would've worked out and she'd have even gotten married on the porch like she and Lily imagined. But she had to give herself grace. She had been so naive and young, dealing with something so huge. She'd done the best she could at that moment.

She considered the sparkle she'd seen in her mother's eyes when she left for college. The what-if, she was sure, was enticing to Mama, but in the end, her mother had chosen long-term happiness over a fleeting curiosity. That decision had given her the best life and allowed her to spend every single day with Pop—one of the most perfect people Stella had known.

She wished again that Pop could be with them now. She believed this life couldn't possibly be the whole show, and that he was, in fact, somewhere wonderful—maybe even right there with them, but it was hard to believe, given his silence. Pop would make sure they knew he was there—he'd said so himself. Had his voice in her head since she'd been home actually been him? Or was he in the winter wind that blew over her cheeks when she went outside? Maybe he'd find a way to show her.

## Chapter Twenty-Three

"Well, don't you look just perfect?" Stella said as she walked into the living room, the next day, the gray, early-afternoon light filtering in around them.

Mr. Ferguson was in the chair next to the Christmas tree, and he was wearing the Santa suit. It was made from a thick red velvet material with white fur cuffs, black buttons down the front, and a wide leather belt latched by a shiny silver buckle. Mr. Ferguson had incorporated his own beard into the artificial one, and Mama had curled it all in ringlets before adding blush to his cheeks to enhance their rosiness, the way she had for Pop. He planted his bulky black boots on the floor and hoisted himself up, looking both reminiscent of her father and also like the big guy himself.

"Thank you for letting me do this," he said.

Stella smiled. "Of course. You definitely fit the part."

"It makes me feel the magic again. It's been a long time."

"Do you have your hot cocoa?" Mama asked, coming into the room while folding up her red-and-green holiday blanket. She tucked it in the basket they always took with them to the parade.

Stella raised her travel mug. "Yep."

"Great. It's going to be a cold one." Mama was all bundled up for the festivities in her wool cap and matching scarf. She had also filled the basket to the brim with sandwiches, snacks, and cookies to get them through until dinner. "I say we drop Herbert off with the parade procession, help him get into his chair on the float, and then park just outside town and walk in."

"It's a little early, isn't it? We won't need this much time."

Stella's phone pinged with a text from Henry: *Meet me at Christmas. I'll be on the side with the tree lot. No running away this time.*

She bit back a grin and shook her head. "Oh, never mind. We should go."

"The car's already running," Mama said, holding open the door. "What changed your mind?"

"Henry wants me to meet him at the tree lot."

Mama's face lit up and she looked over at Mr. Ferguson. "Oh, yes."

Stella went outside and opened the car door so Mama could set the basket in the back seat, then she helped Mr. Ferguson into the passenger seat.

"What do you mean, 'Oh, yes'?" Stella asked her mother.

"Just that Henry always likes to meet there."

"Yeah, I'd forgotten. We always used to meet him at the tree lot before the parade, didn't we?"

"It's been a while..."

Mama got into the car, and Stella climbed in on the other side. Then the three of them headed to meet Henry.

As they drove into town, Stella considered how much had changed between each request to meet her at Christmas. What had begun as a holiday tradition when they were young and she'd had no idea what lay ahead, had picked right back up, even through hard times since she'd been back, when she battled her past. And now, here they were, meeting one more time at Christmas, everything out in the open and Henry almost completely himself again.

After dropping off Mr. Ferguson and parking the car, the walk into town was long with the crowds, but they made it. When they reached the entrance of the lot, Stella turned around to talk to Mama, but they'd somehow gotten separated. She texted her that she was going to meet Henry and would find her near their usual spot, where they used to watch the parade with Pop.

As she neared the lot, the crowd parted and Henry was standing there, smiling at her. He was clean-shaven, dressed up, a scarf hanging loose around his shoulders, and those blue eyes making her weak. She stepped forward to greet him.

"Follow me." He took her hand, and they walked down a row of trees to a secluded area that had been blocked with cranberry-colored velvet ropes.

"Are we supposed to come back here?" she asked.

"It's fine." He led her through the maze of trees while she wondered what in the world he was doing.

When they reached the end of the last aisle, hidden away from the throngs of people and encircled in Christmas trees, her mouth dropped open. Nestled between the spruce trees, was a rectangular table sitting on a dark-green tweed rug. The table was covered in Christmas plaid with a chair on each end, and every surface held glowing candles and China dishes with Christmas trees painted around the edges. Above the table, instead of the bulb lights that hung above the aisle, was a glass chandelier, hanging on a wire. A space heater sat on each side of the table producing so much heat that she felt toasty, despite the frigid temperature.

There was so much to look at that she almost missed the one tree that had been decorated. Sweeping strands of red wooden beads cascaded through the white lights, and every branch was adorned with clear baubles. When she got closer, she could see that each one held a photo of the two of them inside.

"I found a box of our belongings," he said over her shoulder, sending tingles down her body.

The captured memories—things she'd long forgotten—took her back in time, and one by one, pieced together all the good moments they'd had. Photos of the two of them up in the tree; Henry kissing her cheek as they sat inside his truck; them in their green-and-gold high school caps and gowns, raising their clasped hands in victory. There was even one where he held a water balloon precariously above her while she lay unsuspecting in the sun. As she took in the photos, each one representing a treasured slip of time, she felt at peace with the past and ready to take her first step into the future with Henry.

She reached out to lift one of the baubles into view and tears sprang to her eyes. "This time we went fishing with Pop was one of my favorite days."

"You caught the biggest fish that day."

She looked up at him in utter shock. "You remember that one?"

He waved his hand at the decorations. "All the photos on this tree are memories that have come back to me since you got here."

She turned to face him, taking time to soak in this Henry, this man.

"Have a seat?" He pulled out a chair for her.

Stella complied, the warmth from the heaters allowing her to remove her coat. It gave her a chance to admire the frost-covered trees surrounding them without worrying about the cold. This area, tucked away from the gathering crowds, was like a dream.

A tuxedo-clad waiter appeared from behind one of the trees carrying a tray with a silver domed serving dish. He uncapped it and placed a plate in front of Stella. "Your lunch is buttermilk fried quail on a bed of open-fire grilled asparagus."

She tried to hide her grin as she looked up at Henry. "I had this once before and loved it. It's from that fancy restaurant you took me to."

"For prom."

She laughed. "Yes."

"You wore that dark-blue sequined dress, and I couldn't take my eyes off you."

The man in the tuxedo placed a second plate in front of Henry and then left them alone once more.

Stella set her cloth napkin in her lap. "This is amazing."

"I wanted to do something special for you. I tried to take you dancing, but you ran away, so I figured I needed to weigh you down with a chair and good meal this time."

She laughed at his lighthearted way of softening the explanation of the previous night, but then she sobered. "I'm sorry I always run away when things get hard. I'm going to try not to do that anymore."

The silver flecks in his blue eyes gleamed in the candlelight, and he gave her an adoring smile.

After they ate, she turned her attention to the baubles. "We had a great life, didn't we?" She looked back at him.

He nodded.

"Look at all those memories."

"You missed one," he said, then stood up and reached deep into the tree. He pulled out a box that hung from a red velvet string.

Stella gasped, a tear escaping down her face when he opened it. She blotted her eye with her napkin.

Cushioned inside on a little tuft of more red velvet was her modest gold engagement ring with the little diamond chip embedded in silver on the top.

Henry opened the ornament and took out the ring, pinching it between two fingers and holding it between them. "The band is back at the house. I was wondering if you'd like to wear this ring as a promise that we'll see where we go from here—together."

"I'd love to." She held out her hand.

He gently took it across the table and threaded the ring onto her finger, peering down at it fondly. "It's finally back where it's always belonged."

Stella moved her finger under the light of the chandelier against the gray sky, the little diamond shimmering. How long it had been since she'd worn it…

"Right now, this is just a reminder—no pressure of any kind. It's a reminder of how much I adore you."

She couldn't deny their bond and how he seemed to make everything better. But would he really want to settle for less than everything he wanted, just to have her?

"Stella, I'm going to ask you to do something that I never got to ask last time."

"What is it?"

"Let *me* be your answer to whatever you have to deal with in life. I'm strong enough to handle it."

She could see forever in his pleading eyes. It felt like catching her first breath in years. She took his hand. "I want nothing more than to try again. But I need a little time," she said, looking at the ring. "Not to think about what you just said, but to figure out the *rest* of my life."

"Don't take too long." Henry squeezed her hand. "I don't want to spend a single minute more without you." He raised her hand to his lips and kissed it. "Our future—whatever we might make of it—starts now." He checked his watch. "It's about time for the parade."

With an air of festive excitement, she held Henry's hand as they left the gorgeous table behind and made their way back into the crowd, weaving through people to the side of the street where they could see the first floats were already coming down.

The eclectic grouping started off with the local police department, the sheriff leading the way in his cruiser with its blue lights flashing as he tossed candy from the open window. He blipped his siren at a few kids who cheered him on. Next came the Boy Scouts, all wearing their uniforms and Santa hats as they sat on bales of hay in a trailer pulled by a tractor, followed by the girl scouts who were singing "We Wish You a Merry Christmas." An antique Cadillac rolled by with its top down and the local insurance salesman, Marty Johns, was sitting on the back, dressed as Elvis. Then came a pedal tavern with two rows of townspeople pedaling and drinking hot cocoa while throwing T-shirts that said, "Get your Christmas on."

The local animal shelter employees all wore matching green sweatshirts that said, "Bring home a little love this Christmas" while they walked a pack of dogs all dolled up in red scarves and reindeer antlers and let the parade goers sneak a little pet here and there.

The high school band lifted everyone's spirits with a jazzy rendition of "Jingle Bell Rock," their drumbeats pounding in Stella's chest. As they all moved in unison, dancing while marching through the street, Stella couldn't help but wish that Pop could see this.

Stella's favorite grouping was the alpacas from the nearby farm, walking with their handlers. They clopped along wearing red bow ties. After that, Mary Jo walked with the Junior Rodeo Association, the three rodeo girls decked out in white fringed shirts and cowgirl hats while riding their horses, one of them from Henry and Mary Jo's farm.

One of the local fire trucks bleeped its horn as it roared down the street, the firefighters throwing peppermints and candy canes to the crowd. The local distillery also came riding through with a banner. Their driver wore a foam hat in the shape of a whiskey bottle.

In the middle of it all, Mama found Stella and Henry when they'd finally reached their old parade-watching spot. "There's nothin' quite like this, is there?" she asked, handing them each a peppermint.

Henry chuckled. "Definitely not."

The three of them wrapped up in Mama's blankets to keep warm. The parade was just as lovely as it had been when Pop planned it, and Stella wondered if he'd been with her all along.

After the local ballet school and baton twirlers, when the final float emerged, Mr. Ferguson looked absolutely perfect as Santa Claus sitting on his red velvet throne, waving his gloved hand with a long list of names of all the local children in his lap that trailed to the bottom of the float, curling at the end, the float pulled by horses dressed as reindeer.

"Ho, ho, ho! Merry Christmas!" he bellowed, and all the kids cheered and danced in the street behind him. When he saw the three of them in the crowd, he winked. It couldn't have been more perfect.

Feeling absolutely full of love, Stella grabbed Henry's hand. He smiled down at her before they turned back to the confetti-strewn street while the crowd filled it, celebrating the holiday. *We did it, Pop*, she said into the air. *Did you get to see it?*

When the festivities began to wind down and everyone was heading toward their cars and homes, a beautiful red cardinal flew past them and landed in the center of the street. The red bird, perched there in the white and green confetti, was the picture of Christmas.

"Look," she told Mama and Henry, pointing to it.

"Isn't that lovely?" an old woman behind them said, leaning over Stella's shoulder, clearly noticing it too.

"Yes," Stella agreed.

"You know, it's thought cardinals are our loved ones coming back to us," said the woman.

Just then, the bird flew right toward them and then away.

Mama gasped and Henry squeezed Stella's hand. Stella couldn't help but wonder if Pop had been right there with them. In that moment, Stella realized that Leiper's Fork was exactly where she needed to be.

# Chapter Twenty-Four

The next afternoon, Stella ate her lunch while talking on the phone with Amy. Last night, after the parade, and after telling Henry that she would figure out how to stay in Leiper's Fork, Stella had emailed her editor to let her know that she needed to make some changes. After receiving Stella's email, she'd asked her to call—holiday or no holiday.

"We can't lose you," Amy said. "You're the best of the best."

"I don't want to quit—I need the job. But I don't want to travel like I have been. I'm happy here." She ran her thumb over her old engagement ring. She had no idea how she'd make ends meet, where she'd live, or what would happen between her and Henry, but she knew Henry made her feel whole. She wanted to stay and see where life took them.

"Let me talk to Steven, but I don't know what he'll offer."

"All right."

Needing Pop right now, Stella ended the call and opened his letter. She read over his words: *my version of heaven is with you, Lily, and your mother*. She didn't have a version of heaven on earth like Pop had. She'd been so focused on work that she hadn't imagined one for herself. She wanted to feel the love of her perfect person while she had her family around her.

Speaking of family, she was really starting to worry about her sister. She'd been awfully quiet, and that wasn't like her. What was going on?

She picked up her phone and sent Lily another text. Then she stared at the screen, waiting for something—anything—to come through.

Nothing.

Today was Christmas Eve. What would this Christmas bring? While the new developments in her life gave Stella hope, there was still so much unsettled. However, the more she thought about it, the more she couldn't get her mind off Henry. Even if nothing else worked out, he was the one shining light in her path. For some unknown reason, she'd been given a second chance, and now as an adult she knew the full weight of leaving. *Pop, if I choose what makes me happy, the rest will follow, right? Can you send me some sign that I'm making the right decision?* She looked around the room, sharpening her hearing for an answer right when the doorbell rang.

Stella went through the living room to answer it, and Mama met her in the entryway.

"Who could that be?" Mama asked.

Stella opened the door and gasped. "Lily!" She threw her arms around her sister, knocking the bags out of her hands. The man beside her scooped them up.

Lily giggled and wriggled free. She was tanned, her hair longer than usual and pulled back at the sides. "This is Mateo," she said, giving the man a kiss on the cheek.

"Come in, come in." Mama ushered them out of the cold and pulled Lily in for a hug, her eyes full of tears of joy. "My sweet girl. I didn't think we'd see you this Christmas."

"What do you mean? I told you on the phone we were coming."

"We couldn't hear a thing you were saying," Stella told her. "The lines were broken and none of our texts went through."

Lily gaped at Mateo. "Oh, no. I wanted to call you when we landed, but my phone had died and Mateo's accidentally got packed in his checked bag. But I thought I was talking to you in Costa Rica. You couldn't hear me?"

"No," Mama said, taking their coats and hanging them by the door.

"So, you didn't hear anything about what we have planned?"

"Only that you got married," Mama replied.

Mateo spoke up in a deep voice, his accent thick. "Well, yes. We got married, but only for my side of the family. We still want to have a wedding here."

Lily took Stella's hands. "I wouldn't leave you and Mama out of our wedding. We wanted a little ceremony on the front porch—nothing fancy, just us."

Tears of relief pricked Stella's eyes—relief that Lily had remembered, that her sister hadn't abandoned them, and also that Stella's behavior hadn't impacted her decision to stay away.

Lily raised Stella's left hand, saw the ring, and sucked in a breath. "Noooooo," she said with an excited shake of her head. "I know this ring. Are you and Henry…?"

"We're taking things slowly," Stella replied, but she couldn't hide her sizzle of excitement.

Lily squealed and pulled Stella in for a bear hug, the two of them laughing like schoolgirls. "He *has* to come to the wedding. Then we'll *all* be there…"

As Lily trailed off, they looked at each other wistfully. Stella knew by her sister's face they were thinking the same thing: they'd all be there except for Pop.

Mama clapped her hands as if clearing the air. "Let's have wine!"

They sat around the table together, and Lilly started filling them in on meeting Mateo and how they got engaged.

"He was in Chattanooga for work," she said.

Mateo held his glass of wine as he looked adoringly at his new wife. "I saw her in a coffee shop and couldn't leave without talking to her. Six months later, I served her a coffee at that same shop, but it had a little something extra tied to the handle."

"It was so pretty," Lilly said, showing them her sparkling diamond ring. "He'd tied it to the handle of the mug with a red ribbon. Then out of nowhere, a violinist walked through the shop and stopped at our table, playing just for us. Mateo got down on one knee and proposed."

"That's just lovely," Mama said, sighing dreamily and leaning on her hand.

"My grandparents were unable to travel, so we decided to have two weddings: one in Costa Rica and one here."

"I was so worried you weren't coming home," Stella said. "It wouldn't be Christmas without you."

Lily reached out and squeezed Stella's hand. "I knew the calls were choppy, but you didn't get *any* of my texts?"

"I got the one with the photo, but nothing else."

Lily pulled her phone from her pocket and scrolled through the endless texts—an entire play-by-play of events. "In all the excitement and craziness of the wedding, I was texting so quickly that I didn't even look to see…" She scrolled a bit more. "These were all undelivered. Oh, my goodness."

"My family is from a remote village," Mateo said, "so we don't have a lot of modern conveniences. Like cell phone service."

Mama fluttered her hands in the air. "It's neither here nor there. You're home now. And we want to see all the photos." She beamed. "This is going to be a wonderful Christmas after all."

Stella sat on the sofa with Lily, Mateo, and Mama, scrolling through the wedding photos on Lily's phone. "Those gray peaks are the Talamanca Mountains," Lily said, turning the phone so Stella could get a good look at them.

"My family lives in the valley there," Mateo added, pointing to the small dip between the mountains.

"It's so rural and unspoiled. Everywhere you look, there's green. And cutting through it are enormous waterfalls. Mateo's whole family lives in these little huts that look like tree houses. And here"—Lily swiped her finger along the phone screen to select another photo—"are the dancers from our wedding."

Stella leaned in to see three barefoot women with the bottom ruffles of their brightly colored skirts in their fists as they danced. They each had their hair pulled back tightly in a bun and vibrant, matching flowers in their hair.

"They're gorgeous."

"I know," Lily said. "It was just… magic. Mama, look at this." Lily scooted closer to their mother to show her another photo.

They shared stories, Lily telling them all about her busy flights to and from Costa Rica, and Stella filling in Lily and Mateo on the mysterious necklace she'd found at the Atlanta airport on her way home. She'd gotten it out of the safe, and they'd all ooed and ahhed over it.

They'd all settled in around the fire when the doorbell rang.

"I'll get it," Stella offered, crossing the room.

She opened the door to find Henry with a mischievous look in his eyes.

"You busy? I have a Christmas gift for you."

"You do?"

He nodded. "Come with me."

She swallowed, trying unsuccessfully to slow her heartbeat. "Actually, can you come in for just a second?"

He gave her a curious look. "Sure."

Stella took his arm and led him into the living room. "Look who showed up."

Lily turned around. "Oh! Hi, Henry." She got up and gave him a hug. "It's so good to see you."

He stared at her for a tick, a smile emerging, and then said, "Lily. It's so great to see you."

Lily introduced him to Mateo, while Mama turned on the TV to football highlights while the men shook hands. They started talking about sports, Mateo explaining how he'd missed the last two playoff games he'd wanted to see due to their travel.

Stella cut in. "Henry wants to show me something. Is it okay if I leave for a little bit?"

"Of course," Mama said.

"Okay, I'll be back soon." As they walked to the door, Stella said, "I wish I'd known. I haven't gotten you anything."

"*You* are my gift," he said, his blue eyes sparkling.

Stella popped up on her tiptoes and gave him a kiss. Then she put on her coat and walked with Henry to his truck. "Where are we going?"

Henry put it in drive and bumped along the dirt path leading to the main road. "My house."

They drove the short distance, but before turning onto his street, he pulled over and put the truck in park. "I need to put this on you." He produced a red handkerchief. "To cover your eyes."

She turned so he could slip the bandana over her head and tie it in the back. "You're full of surprises these days."

"You inspire me."

The truck began to move again, and Stella guessed by the turns and then the terrain that they'd entered the main road to the farmhouse and were stopping in front of it. Henry put the truck in park and got out. Stella clasped her cold hands in her lap and waited. Her door opened and his warm fingers caressed hers as he guided her out. Then he walked her across the cold ground. She stumbled over something—a tree root?—but he quickly caught her. "I've got you," he whispered in her ear.

They came to a stop and Henry moved behind her. "I remember that you like to sprinkle sugar on your strawberries," he said, the scent of him nearly intoxicating. "I remember that you have to flip your pillow in the night because you prefer the cold side. I remember that you're silliest first thing in the morning." He took off her blindfold.

Stella's vision, cloudy at first from being obstructed, cleared, and she tried to figure out why this particular object was leaning against the old oak tree. "A door?" It was stunning—even prettier than the one before—a Craftsman with three beveled glass windows at the top and a decorative wooden ledge underneath them.

"I promised you a farmhouse," he said. "And I never got to make good on that promise."

She looked at him, still trying to connect the dots.

"You know all those things I remembered about you?"

"Yes…"

"I also remember how you always wanted a farmhouse exactly like this one." He turned her around, and her knees almost buckled. Somehow, he'd managed to wrap an enormous red ribbon all the way around the main house and then tie a massive bow the size of his truck at the front door.

"What does this mean?" she asked, breathless.

"I spoke to my sister. She'd love it if we took the farmhouse. She thinks it would be the perfect place for us."

Stella's mouth fell open. When she'd collected herself, she asked, "Where will Mary Jo live?"

"Well, when she isn't traveling, she wants to live in the cabin out back."

Stella threw her arms around Henry. "We really get to live here?"

He kissed her lips. "If you want to. And, since the first time was annulled, I've also got that gold band and will make good on it anytime you want me to."

Pop's voice blew in on the wind. *"Go on, Kiddo."*

Stella couldn't think of anything better. "First Lily and now this… It's the best Christmas ever. If only Pop were here to see it." She tried to channel his voice once more, hoping for another cardinal or some other sign, but nothing came. "I wish he'd show us if he's here," she admitted.

"Maybe he's busy planning some grand way to do it—that would be his style."

Stella smiled at the idea.

Henry moved behind her and wrapped her in an embrace as they stared up at the home that would soon be theirs. Everything she'd ever wanted was right there in her grasp.

She turned to face him. "I want to wear the gold band, but this time, I want to do it right."

"Okay." He kissed her again, and she couldn't believe she'd get to feel that for the rest of her life.

When they got back home, Stella asked Henry to stay, and they started preparing for Mr. Ferguson to arrive. Stella had called Mr. Ferguson to ask him to Christmas dinner and then stay the night. She'd offered to come get him, but he'd said he could get a ride over with a neighbor, heading in that direction. From that moment on, they all were busy preparing the guest room, setting out dishes of cookies and little hors de oeuvres, and placing crystal bowls of candy on the tables in the living room. While they prepared, Stella and Henry told Mama, Lily, and Mateo about Henry's Christmas gift.

Mama blinked, her eyes glistening. "I remember after you left for Stanford, your dad sat down in this chair, baffled." She ran her hand along the wingback chair next to the fire. "He said, 'I always imagined her married to Henry and living in a farmhouse nearby. I'm going to miss her so much.' He'd be beside himself with happiness."

"Well, we've *almost* given him his wish," Henry said. "Stella and I have decided to get married and have it be legal this time."

Lily gasped. "Oh, my goodness!" She drew both Henry and Stella into a big squeeze of a hug. Then she pulled back. "You could get married with us on the porch at Christmas—like we always planned!"

"As in tomorrow? Christmas Day?"

"Got anything white to wear?" Lily asked with a giggle.

Stella's mind went back to the satin dress in her closet. She was still about the same size. "Actually, I might." She turned to Henry. "Any chance you can get those space heaters over to the porch by tomorrow?"

"If I get to marry you, yes."

Mama clapped her hands excitedly. "Oh, my! We've got a double wedding to plan!"

By the time Mr. Ferguson arrived, they were all around the kitchen table jotting down notes for the quick country wedding they were having tomorrow.

"You all look very involved," he said, leaving his walker and hobbling over to the table with Mama's help.

Mama pulled out a chair for him. "Love is in the air! This is my other daughter, Lily, and her new husband, Mateo. Lily's surprise homecoming wasn't all that was in store for us. We're planning a double wedding for both my girls tomorrow."

Stella piped up. "You're invited."

"My goodness." Mr. Ferguson's eyes rounded. "Nothing like a spur of the moment occasion."

Lily gave Stella a deviant smile. "Oh, we've been planning this for years." She leaned over to Stella. "I think we both have the old and new covered. But we need something borrowed."

Henry was searching on his phone. He had already managed to convince their original officiant, Waylon Evans, to come over and marry them tomorrow, once he determined that he was, in fact, ordained. He looked up and greeted Mr. Ferguson.

Just then, Stella's phone rang. Curious as to whom it could possibly be, she answered it.

"This is officer Miller at the Atlanta police department. I was leaving to go home for the holiday, but I wanted to give you some news on your necklace—it couldn't wait."

Stella shushed everyone and put her phone on the table on speaker. "You've found out something about the necklace?" Stella closed her eyes to focus on the officer's voice as Lily quietly filled in Mr. Ferguson on what she'd been told about the necklace.

"Yes. I thought it was a pretty fitting Christmas present."

Stella leaned in. "What do you mean?"

"We did some digging, and the last owner is deceased. The stone wasn't registered or insured after that owner, at least not that we can find."

"Well someone had to lose it in the airport," Stella countered. "Maybe it belongs to a family member of that person."

"We figured the same. The previous owner is actually from Tennessee. Isn't that where you are?"

"Yes," Stella replied. "Am I allowed to ask the person's name? Maybe we can find out if it belongs to anyone in the family, and I can get it to them."

"Well, you see, the woman who had insured it last had a receipt of sale from 1968 from an antique jewelry dealer in Nashville. Someone by the name of Florence Elizabeth Fisher of Maury County."

Mama gasped, her eyes wide, her face white, and Lily's mouth dropped open.

"That's my grandmother's name," Stella said, stunned.

Mr. Ferguson's brows pulled together. "Your grandmother?"

Lily leaned over to him. "My pop's mom."

Stella began to recount the collision with the woman in the airport. How on earth…

"Well, it looks like it's yours now," the officer cut in. "Merry Christmas."

"Oh, Merry Christmas," Stella said.

When she hung up the phone, they all sat silent, everyone clearly trying to figure out how Stella had managed to get her grandmother's necklace.

"Could someone have been bringing it to you?" Lily asked.

Stella shook her head. "No. It was just me and that stranger who bumped into me. And she didn't seem to recognize it. She thought it was mine already."

"Could your grandma have sold it or given it to someone else and it's just a crazy coincidence that you ended up with it?" Mama asked.

"It seems too crazy." Stella racked her brain for any ideas, combing back through the events that day and leading up to it. Then something came to her. "I've had that carry-on bag since I left for college," Stella said. "I only took it with me to London as an extra bag in case I bought things to bring back. When you called for me to come home, I just grabbed it... Do you think the necklace was somehow inside all this time?"

"Who would've put it in there?" Henry piped up. His phone rang and he stepped away to answer it.

"It's the bag with the flowers, Mama. Remember it?" Stella continued.

"Oh, yes. We've had that bag for ages. I can't even remember how we ended up with it."

"Could it have been Grandma's?" Stella asked.

"Maybe," Mama said with a nod.

"Perhaps she put the necklace in it years ago, and it was jostled loose when that woman spilled her coffee on me?"

"It's a definite possibility," Mama said through her fingers as she covered her mouth, still in shock. Then she sat up straighter. "It could be the something old, something borrowed, and something blue for one of you. But who should wear it?"

Lily was the first to answer. "Stella should definitely wear it since she found it."

Stella shook her head. "No, no. I wouldn't want to single one of us out. Neither of us should wear it."

Then Mama added, "I'll loan you each my sets of pearl earrings as your something borrowed."

"Perfect," Lily said, sitting back satisfied. "What about something blue, Stella? Do you have anything? I have a little blue garter."

Stella considered what she'd brought in her suitcase. "I don't," she said.

Lily clapped her hands. "It's settled then. You wear the Christmas Diamond."

Stella considered its history of bad luck, but her grandma Florence hadn't had any bad luck that she was aware of. "Should I?"

"Yes," Lily replied. "It's your something blue."

Stella still wasn't sure.

Henry returned and clicked off his phone. "The guy who set up the dinner at the Christmas-tree lot said he can bring over a red runner for the stairs and a couple of white chairs and bows. He also knows the guy who owns the lot and he's going to bring over a bunch of trees that haven't sold. They'd go to the chipper anyway."

Stella kissed his cheek.

Pop's voice whispered, *"What's meant to be will be."* Stella smiled, looking up at the ceiling for some sign he was there. But, of course, there was nothing.

As the evening went on, Mama turned on Christmas music in the kitchen. Lily called the town florist, her best friend from high school, who was going to make them both a quick bouquet. Having completed all their wedding duties, Henry and Mateo had settled on the sofa in the living room to watch a football game with Mr. Ferguson.

Mama paused beside the table and put her hands on her hips, a content grin spreading across her face. "We have a full house," she said. "How wonderful is this? The whole family is here."

Stella and Lily both stopped what they were doing and wrapped their arms around their mother.

"I feel Pop here with us too," Lily said.

Mama sucked in a breath. "You do?"

Lily nodded.

"Oh, how I wish he could show us," Mama said.

Stella knew exactly how her mother felt. She, too, wished Pop could somehow let them know he was there. "I found a letter from him in his desk. It was addressed to me."

Lily and Mama both gaped at her, Mama's face shining with a tiny thrill of hope.

Stella told them part of what Pop had written. "If he could show us, he would."

Mama nodded, her eyes glassy.

Lily grabbed their hands. "No matter what, he's here. Even if he can't show us."

# Chapter Twenty-Five

There was a buzz throughout the house Christmas morning as the sisters got ready in Stella's childhood bedroom.

"Is it too wrinkled from being in the bag?" Lily asked Stella, smoothing the satin on her beaded wedding gown.

"It's perfect," Stella replied, getting misty-eyed at the sight of her little sister as a bride.

Lily's blonde locks were pulled up in a loose bun with tendrils framing her face, accentuating the gleam of sheer gloss on her lips. She was a picture of perfection.

"Moment of truth," Stella said, taking her gown out of the closet. She held it out to examine it. The cut demanded a more youthful figure, but when she slipped it on, it fit like a glove and accentuated her mature curves better than she'd hoped.

"Oh, my goodness, Stella," Lily said. "You look beautiful." Her sister came over and tucked a little piece of holly in the pearl-pinned sides of her long flowing hair. "Perfect."

"Are we really doing this?" Stella asked.

Lily giggled. "Absolutely."

They walked into the living room. Mr. Ferguson was the first to see them.

"Wow. You ladies look lovely," he said, causing the others to turn.

Henry, wearing a tuxedo that emphasized his square jaw and made him nearly irresistible, met Stella's stare, and then his gaze slipped down her dress and back up, their whole lives flashing in his eyes. He came over to her. "You look incredible."

"Thank you. So do you. But should you see me before the wedding?"

"It's close enough!" Waylon Evans cut into their conversation. He had more gray in his beard and eyebrows, but his burly grin and denim bibbed overalls were just the same. "This *is* the weddin'. Let's get this party started, shall we?"

Lily called over to Stella. "Did you ever get something blue?"

"I didn't," Stella replied.

Henry leaned into her ear. "Go get the necklace."

"No, I decided I absolutely shouldn't," she replied, her lingering superstition over it taking hold. She'd considered it again while trying to fall asleep last night, but, given the pendant's history, it felt too precarious. This time, everything would be right. She didn't dare risk a single choice in her forever.

He widened his eyes at her, a mischievous look in them. "Yes, go get it."

She shook her head, but he was insistent. Why, she had no idea.

"I have something I need to say, and I want you to be wearing the Christmas Diamond when I say it."

Mateo and Lily were taking their places, and Mama had turned on a low hum of Christmas music.

Stella stared at him, trying to figure out what he was up to. She looked over at Mary Jo for any indication, but Henry's sister just shrugged, clearly in the dark as well about Henry's reasoning.

"Please, Stella. Go get the necklace."

His urging was enough to make her forget about bad luck. "Okay," she relented.

She went to the safe and took it out, then latched the pendant around her neck. *Pop, if you can hear me, please don't let this necklace be bad luck*, she said to herself. His gentle laughter floated into her mind, which was a curious memory to have right then, but it did make her wonder if she was being silly thinking the necklace had any bearing on her current circumstances.

When she went back to the living room, Henry took her hand and called everyone to gather around. "I had something really interesting happen last night, and I feel compelled to tell you all." He turned to Stella and Lily. "I dreamed of your pop."

"What?" Stella said, her skin prickling.

"He was in his little fishing boat, bobbing in the water with the oars inside next to him. He smiled at me and said, 'Tell them I'm here, and then look up the words "the Christmas Diamond and love."'" I woke up right then and couldn't go back to sleep. It was incredibly real. I remembered him so clearly, it was as if he was really there. I don't know what came over me, but since it was the night before my big day with Stella, I felt sentimental. I got on my phone and searched for the Christmas Diamond, and I wrote down the first thing that came up. I need to read it to you."

Mama stepped forward, wiping away a tear. "Is that all he said in the dream?"

Henry pulled a small slip of paper from his pocket and unfolded it. "I think he has more to say." He smoothed out the paper and began to read. "'When the Christmas Diamond was given in love, a new legend was born. The Christmas Diamond resides among the angels, who leave it with the people they want to connect with. The diamond carries a message from loved ones who have passed to remind their families that they are with them even when they aren't seen. When worn, the Christmas Diamond is a sign that the loved one has come to meet them once more.'"

Stella considered how the legend wouldn't have made any sense if her grandmother had bought the diamond and owned it for years, then simply passed it to her son. Unless, maybe her grandmother gave it to him before she died as a symbol that she'd always be with him, which sounded a lot like their grandmother. The fact that it had shown up right at their wedding, when they all needed to know Pop was there, made the message undeniable.

Mama covered her face with her hands, unsuccessfully attempting to keep her tears from falling. "He's right here with us," she said. "This is his Christmas gift. And he gets to see *both* his girls get married like he always dreamed."

Stella glanced down at the diamond and wondered if it was a symbol of his blessing—a blessing he hadn't been able to give her the first time around. A tenderness for these people, her family, filled the air as they stood together, gathered in love. Stella touched the diamond around her neck. *Thank you, Pop.*

*"I see ya, kid,"* Pop's voice whispered, and a lump of happiness formed in her throat.

Waylon led everyone to the front porch. The heaters were on, warming the space. A few snowflakes had fallen onto the red runner leading up the stairs to the front door. The two couples stood under an arch of Christmas foliage with trees adorned with silver bells on each side. Lily and Stella held bouquets made of Fraser fir foliage and red berries.

As the snow fell lightly to the ground, the two couples said their vows, and Stella received the biggest Christmas gift of her life: she got her whole family back.

After changing into her jeans, unwrapping presents, and having a lively Christmas lunch with her family, Stella was unable to wait a single minute longer. She grabbed her computer and sat on the couch among the piles of torn wrapping paper and new presents, and started looking up moving companies to get her belongings from her apartment in New York to Leiper's Fork. Her legs were across Henry's lap while he bonded with Mr. Ferguson and Mateo, the three of them united in football banter, as she read through the different moving companies' offerings and reviews. Luckily, with all her travel, she hadn't collected a lot of personal items and didn't have a lot to pack, but she wanted to move her things home as soon as possible.

While she searched, a text from Amy pinged on her phone. She opened it.

It's unofficial, but I wanted to text you as soon as I heard. It looks like you'll only have to do two trips a year and the rest of the time, you're going to work virtually. We'd still love to see you in New York to accept the promotion. Merry Christmas! A.

Stella couldn't believe her eyes. She'd managed to keep her job after everything. Pop had been right: what was meant to be certainly would be. She believed that now. And what she knew without a doubt was that she could run, she could push away what was meant for her, but in the end, her true future would always find her. And she was pretty sure Pop could see it all.

Stella closed her computer and snuggled up next to her husband, ready to start their happy ending.

# Epilogue

## Two Years Later

Stella put the final touches on the turkey before the family arrived for Christmas dinner. Henry took her hand and twirled her on the rustic hardwoods of their kitchen in their newly remodeled farmhouse, then kissed her before heading into the living room.

"I'm just gonna prepare the last few things before everybody gets here."

Stella grinned at him. "By 'things' you mean the bowls of popcorn are set out, the football's on the big screen, and the beers are in the fridge?"

He stopped and looked at her. "Is there anything else you can think of?"

She laughed. "That's all we need, right?"

Henry had worked overtime with his crew to finish renovations on the house just in time for their two-year anniversary and the holidays. The wide Craftsman-style banisters that flanked the steps and mantles were all covered in fresh sprigs of evergreen with sweeping red ribbons and little bunches of berries, an enormous Christmas tree—the biggest on the lot—was in the corner of the living room, its angel on top hovering in the vaulted ceiling that Henry had installed to modernize the space. She'd even tied red ribbons around her old potter's wheel that Henry had restored for her. With the scent of nutmeg and sage in the air, and a fire in the stone fireplace, everything was perfect.

After spending a year landscaping, Henry had taken all his savings and invested in more employees, then transitioned his company to full home renovations and landscaping. His work was so good that he'd caught the eye of a few Nashville celebrities. After renovating their homes, his handiwork was displayed on the glossy pages of national magazines, the articles in frames in his office.

This past week, however, Stella was the one who had done the work. She'd been busy decorating Christmas trees, stringing garlands of holly, and hanging mistletoe above the doorway leading to the porch.

Stella set the serving dishes of stuffing, potatoes, and vegetable casseroles onto the large kitchen island. Then she started putting gravy and cranberry sauce into serving dishes. Mr. Ferguson's calico cat, Lucy, purred as it nuzzled Stella's leg. The old cat loved its new home and enjoyed warm days out in the pasture with the horses and long winter days in the sunny spot of the bay window that overlooked their old cabin where Mary Jo lived when she wasn't traveling. She'd organized the farmhands to work in her absence and she'd spent a few weeks each season seeing the world like she'd wanted to.

With so many rooms in the house and two on the ground floor, a few months after they'd moved in, they'd decided to have Mr. Ferguson live with them. The proximity had definitely helped when he needed to meet them at Christmas for the parade, since he'd continued to be Santa. To Mama's relief, Henry had taken over planning the parade each year and he was amazing at it—so much like Pop. Mama was just down the street from them and enjoyed taking Mr. Ferguson to the farmers market on weekends and to his church meet-ups on Wednesday nights.

"Mama," a little voice called from the other room. "Wook at dis!"

Stella turned to see Henry across the open room holding the little boy upside down on his lap as he and Mr. Ferguson sat together on the sofa. She laughed. "How was your nap, buddy?"

"Good!" he squealed as Henry wriggled him around.

Stella pulled out the boy's dinner—cubed pears and little spears of broccoli, along with perfectly sized meatballs.

"Dawson, is that comfortable?" Stella asked with a giggle.

"Of course it's comfortable," Henry said, answering for the little boy, tickling his adopted son's sides, and making him collapse in a fit of giggles.

It had taken about six months, but they'd finally been able to bring Dawson home, and after their time with him, Stella wasn't sure she'd ever loved anyone as much as she loved that little three-year-old.

"You make it look so easy," Lily said, coming into the kitchen and setting a chocolate pie on the counter. She rubbed her protruding belly. Right after they'd gotten married, she and Mateo had found a house nearby and were expecting their first child in three more months. Mateo waved hello and joined Henry and Dawson in the living room.

With Dawson's food ready, Stella stood at the kitchen counter plating the sweet bread she'd made yesterday with Dawson's help. "Make what look so easy?"

Lily gave her a loving smile. "Motherhood. It suits you."

"It does, doesn't it?" Mama said, coming straight in and washing her hands to help. She dried them on a towel and then got right to work, sprinkling powdered sugar over the bread.

Stella beamed. She'd been so busy with Dawson that she'd pulled back on her writing, but she continued to write part-time for *Brain Borders Magazine*. The decision had been easy. The minute Stella and Henry stepped foot in that empty farmhouse after Mary Jo's things had been moved out, she knew her life was bigger than her work. She spent mornings writing and then the rest of the day she helped Henry restore the house, getting it ready for their new little one, and spending time with her family.

"Hel-lo!" Mary Jo called, coming in with holiday gift bags hanging from one arm and local football hero Charlie Jenkins on the other. Apparently, he'd had his eye on Mary Jo throughout high school, so when he came back to town looking for investment properties and heard she was close by, he'd called her. They'd been dating seriously ever since.

Dawson wiggled down from his daddy's lap and waddled over to Mary Jo, then wrapped his arms around her legs.

Mary Jo set down her bags and scooped him up. "How's my favorite nephew?" She nuzzled his neck, making him laugh again, a sound Stella would never tire of.

Henry stood. "Who's ready for presents, dinner, and Christmas pie?"

Dawson let go of Mary Jo and ran to Henry, calling, "Me, me!"

As they all gathered around the sparkling tree, Stella touched the Christmas Diamond at her neck. She'd worn it each year as her way of letting Pop know she could feel him with them. Stella thought back to her life before and took a moment to revel in the happiness that filled her life now. She was truly living her dream, surrounded by the people she loved most in the world. They were all there together—one big happy family.

# A Letter from Jenny

Hi there!

Thank you so much for reading *Meet Me at Christmas*. I hope it made you feel all warm and fuzzy inside and put you in the holiday spirit.

If you'd like to know when my next book is out, you can **sign up for my monthly newsletter and new release alerts here:**

www.itsjennyhale.com/email-signup

I won't share your information with anyone else, and I'll only email you a quick message once a month with my newsletter and then whenever new books come out. It's the best way to keep tabs on what's going on with my books, and you'll get tons of surprises along the way like giveaways, signed copies, recipes, and more.

**If you did enjoy *Meet Me at Christmas*, I'd be very grateful if you'd write a review online on the retailer's site**. Getting feedback from readers helps to persuade others to pick up one of my books for the first time. It's one of the biggest gifts you could give me.

If you enjoyed this story, and would like a few more happy endings, check out my other novels at www.itsjennyhale.com and www.harpethroad.com.

Until next time,
Jenny xo

         7201437.Jenny_Hale

         jennyhaleauthor

         @jhaleauthor

         jhaleauthor

         www.itsjennyhale.com

# Acknowledgments

I am forever indebted to Oliver Rhodes for taking that big risk when I was a brand-new author who knew nothing about the business and shaping me into the author I am today. As I always say, he set the bar for my own publishing journey. His example has inspired every choice I've made along the way and continues to inspire me even now.

I owe a huge thank you to my amazing editors who worked tirelessly to get this done under a tight deadline: Jocelyn Bailey who showered me with praise, lifting me up every step of the way; the fabulous Jodi Hughes, who shaped this book right up; Lauren Finger, my copyeditor extraordinaire, whose touch is an absolute necessity for me—I want her hands in every book I write; and the most wonderful proofreader, Liz Hurst. I couldn't have had a better team to help me get this story ready than these women.

The amazingly talented Kristen Ingebretson, my cover designer, is the best of the best. Working with her on concepts is effortless and an utter blast. I'm so very thankful to have her for cover direction. There's no one better.

And to my husband, Justin, who is always by my side in this wildly unpredictable career I've chosen. He listens to my endless chatter about word choice, doesn't flinch when I nearly force him to give me his opinions about branding and design, and then go another direction entirely, and he roots for me in every single thing I do. He handles my crazy with ease and is always my biggest cheerleader.

Printed in Great Britain
by Amazon